I0589156

# Trapped by a Mouse
## and Other Stories

Bob Zumwalt

Ctrl-Z Press
Hallettsville, Texas

ISBN: 978-0692846339

Cover Designed by: Mary Palowski
Interior Designed by: Danielle H. Acee, The Authors' Assistant

Printed in the United States of America

*I dedicate this book to the memory of three persons who especially helped me spread my wings as I entered the real world: Victor Pavlu, who gave me my first job, in his hardware store; my Texas Aggie buddy, Roger Melton, who nudged me into trying unfamiliar things; and my mentor, Tom Herndon, who taught me an engineering career involves more than equations and numbers. And to the anonymous mouse whose death opened the door to meeting my wife.*

# Author's Note

This collection of mostly humorous short stories serves as a different kind of memoir. All stories are related to my personal experiences: either I am directly the actor; someone similar to me is the actor; it's a situation I've observed; or it's a fantasy story similar to what I had daydreamed or imagined. Some stories are pulled from my youth and used as a framework in the telling. Some come from writing group prompts or literary tradition, such as Romeo and Juliet. Others are inspired by news stories.

As a variation on first-person narration, I sometimes switch to third person and let another character stand in for me. For example, Paul Choans is a teenaged lad like I was; he appears in several stories. Billy Joe Cunningham (*Moving Target*) is a teenaged quarterback who could be my doppelganger. Bill Barnstable and Jennifer Daly (*Love Match*) are a tennis playing couple resembling my wife and me.

After reading the instructions for my first prescription of a certain medication, I created Jake Slocum and sent him on a calamitous adventure (*The Erector Set*). I even let my carry-on bag do the talking as it describes the ups and downs of business travel in *Frequent Flyer*. As a parody on bad business trips, *The Baa's Motel* describes the misadventures of four engineers as they cope with farm animals.

I include five fantasy stories, representing the not insignificant time I spent daydreaming up a big hackberry tree, hiding from my mom to avoid work. Invisibility and talking with animals were hot daydreaming topics. *Ingeneous Mouse* is partly inspired by my experience raising white mice.

Three stories are short on plot but long on vivid description of cherished places we enjoyed while living in different countries: *Love Match*, *Through the Lens and Beyond*, and *Queuing for Court*.

Hyperbole may be the bane of memoir purists, but it finds a useful place in many of these tales. *Herding Lizards* describes a real incident, grossly exaggerated in a different setting.

The stories cover growing up, dealing with girls, serving in the US Army, getting married, working in industry, and retirement. They should give the reader a good idea of who I am and what I have done and observed over my eighty-something years.

# Have Bowel—Won't Travel

"**M**ama, Mama," I screamed as I ran down the stairs and dashed into Aunt Ima's kitchen, where my mother and her three sisters sat talking and laughing. "I made ah-ah in my pants and it's running down my legs!"

This dramatic entrance is one of my earliest recollections from my childhood. My aunts mercilessly kidded me about this episode as I grew older. It was the first of several instances of bowel anxiety linked to travel—anxiety I learned to overcome as I grew up and went out into the world.

We were at Aunt Ima's house again a few weeks later, but this time, my problem was just the opposite; I tightened up and couldn't go. When I complained about the pain, the sisters decided I needed an enema. I was subjected to the indignity of this procedure in the presence of all my aunts.

Perhaps this case of anxiety was caused by something else: Aunt Ima's husband was a big rancher and Uncle Charlie always wanted to get me on a horse, in spite of my fears about the big animals. Whatever the cause, my young brain associated bowel problems with travel. My entrance into the grownup world slowly cured me, through the medium of necessity.

My first success in overcoming reluctance was on bivouac in the army, where the latrine was a trench with a 2x4 across it—nailed to two trees.

Many people don't like to use airplane bathrooms, for a variety of good reasons. On domestic flights I could wait it out without a problem. But when I started traveling overseas, I quickly learned to grin and not bear it.

I am happy to report to you that…well…maybe I don't need to report it. Instead, let's just enjoy the following amusing stories—some with a touch of pathos. Each story is either directly or somewhat tenuously related to my experiences: growing up, coping with girls, getting married, traveling to and living in far-away places, and retirement.

# Hidden Problem

*Experimentation with invisibility reminds one to*
*be careful about what he asks for.*

I t all started when I did something unusual…well unusual for me. In a fit of curiosity, I opened a piece of junk mail. Normally, I just toss the stuff. But this junk offering had an eye-catching message on the envelope: "Is there someone in your life you would like to make disappear? Then try **Disapirum**, an exciting new product from the cutting edge of scientific and metaphysical research."

For some reason, I couldn't toss this out. Maybe I wanted to see if I could resist a pseudo-scientific commercial appeal. Maybe I was just bored. I opened the envelope and read the well-crafted commercial message about the new product. Disapirum was a yellowish-brown powder that contained molecular fragments of DNA, several exotic minerals, vitamins, lots of herbal substances, and a few mysterious sounding "vapours." Purportedly, each of the vapours embodied one of the essences of life, whatever these were.

"Imagine, you could make someone invisible in just a few hours," the junk letter spieled. "For just $29.99 plus shipping you will receive a vacuum-sealed vial of Disapirum. Mix it with an unsuspecting person's food, and in a few hours, the molecular vibrations of the person's cells will be re-phased. Light interacts with the re-phased cells much differently—it passes straight through them without being reflected. The cells, and hence the person, are no longer visible in ordinary light. Disapirum affects only the light-reflecting properties of cells; it does not harm the subject in any way."

I still don't know why I didn't place a mental Outrageous stamp on this letter and toss it out. Instead, I sent in my money. Don't get me wrong, I get along well with my friends and relatives and don't want to make any person disappear. But a certain scamp of a monkey had made my life miserable for the last few months, and I could do without seeing him.

Erasmus is a rhesus monkey. He was rescued from the ranks of medical research subjects by my Uncle Leo.

I was very close to Uncle Leo and saw him several times a year. Uncle Leo was a kind soul with a soft spot for unfortunate animals, especially Erasmus. Rhesus monkeys normally don't make good pets, but Uncle Leo had the good touch with even the most reluctant species. He trained Erasmus to respect people houses, and the monkey had the run of his house without unfortunate incidents. Uncle Leo loved this rambunctious old monkey, and the two seemed to be close pals.

Uncle Leo knew his time on earth was getting short and he worried about what would happen to Erasmus when he was gone. On one of my visits, he approached me with his concern and asked if I would take over the care of Erasmus—for a substantial stipend, of course. I agreed as I thought it might be fun to have a monkey for a pet. Also, the annual stipend had an appealing ring. Uncle Leo's lawyer drew up a trust fund with me as beneficiary, payable annually as long as Erasmus was alive and I was caring for him.

Erasmus arrived at my house shortly after Uncle Leo's demise, and I soon realized I had done a deal with the devil. Erasmus was a very old animal in monkey years—crotchety, persnickety, and completely set in his ways. Somehow, he felt it was his duty to train me, as Uncle Leo had done with him many years ago. Since he wouldn't respect the cleanliness of my house, I kept him in a large cage in the utility room. I let him roam the house a few hours each evening, and kept my eyes and nose alert for any of his unclean leavings.

He chattered incessantly when in his cage, no doubt telling me what a lousy master I was. But he was friendly enough when he roamed the house. He often came up to me, wide-eyed with anticipation, wanting to play the game of toss the teddy bear. That poor battered teddy bear! I must admit, I enjoyed playing with old Erasmus, even when he overdid it. He liked to sneak up on me and give me a playful nip on the neck. It was not enough to break the skin, but certainly enough to cause a painful pinch. I would swat him, and he would dash off, chattering excitedly as if this were the most fun in the world.

After a few months, I grew weary of Erasmus and his uncivilized ways. I couldn't just palm him off to the local zoo, as this would break my pact with Uncle Leo. And then there was the trust annuity, which made a substantial dent in my mortgage payments.

That's when I read the junk mail and sent off the order for Disapirum. The trust didn't say anything about invisible!

A few weeks later, the postman delivered the Disapirum in a plain, unmarked package. He smiled at me knowingly as I signed for the package, no doubt thinking I had ordered some girlie pictures. With the anticipation of a kid unwrapping a new model airplane kit, I tore open the package and pulled out the vial of Disapirum. According to the instructions written in Chinese-derived English, I carefully measured out the number of fluid ounces of powder proportional to the monkey's weight. Too little would not cause the desired effect, and too much might be harmful.

I fooled the old primate by mixing the Disapirum with his favorite fruit salad. I watched him closely for a short time, although the instructions said the powder took about two hours to show the full effect. Since I had to go out for a meeting that evening, I put Erasmus back in his cage, in spite of his protests.

Late that evening, I returned home and immediately peeked into the utility room. I couldn't see Erasmus in his cage and thought he might have escaped again, for he was clever at unlatching the cage door. I looked around, couldn't find him, and then called, "Eras…mus, Eras…mus."

He quickly responded with a terse chatter. I couldn't see him and called again. This time his response seemed to come directly from his cage. Erasmus was invisible! The Disapirum powder actually worked!

I clapped my hands and jumped with joy. I was going to get my life straightened out and put this hoodlum of a monkey in his place—out of sight. I could earn my annuity and not be bothered by the unseen beast. What a misguided thought that turned out to be!

Things went well for a couple of days. I kept Erasmus in his cage and gave him his favorite foods. But I noticed his droppings were also invisible; apparently, the Disapirum worked its way into the cells of the excrement. I had to clean the cage by trial and error, guided by my senses of touch and smell.

But out of sight didn't mean out of mind. I felt guilty about poor Erasmus confined to his cage. Uncle Leo certainly would not have allowed this. In a moment of softness, I opened the cage and felt old Erasmus brush by me as he dashed into almost forgotten freedom. I could hear him as he checked by his favorite haunts in the house, but I could see neither hide nor hair of him.

Shortly after releasing him, I sat down to read the paper; that's when I saw this tattered, disembodied teddy bear approaching my chair. Erasmus wanted to play again. I tossed the bear to the far corner of the den, and it seemingly levitated and floated back to me. If a guest had walked into the den during this play, he would have thought he had entered the Twilight Zone. I confess, I was happy to play toss the teddy again.

The game ended and I resumed my séance with the sports page. All of a sudden, I felt this presence at my neck. Ouch! Erasmus had nipped me again. I swatted him and scolded him as usual; I could feel his hairy body, although I couldn't see it. But Erasmus came back to nip my neck time after time. This mischievous monk finally exhausted my patience—and I stood up to deliver one of my famous scolds. *How can you properly scold someone without looking at him?* I wondered. I didn't have the slightest idea where he was, so I just waved my arms and shouted my frustration at whomever might be watching. When I finished, I heard some muted chatter behind me. It sounded suspiciously like a snickering monkey.

This has been going on for several months now. I keep trying to catch that rascal, but he is always two or three steps ahead of me, and I never come close. He must think this is a game. To trick him, I put his food in the cage and carefully watched, waiting to see when the food started moving so I could rush over and slam the cage door shut. But Erasmus is too clever for this ruse; he simply waits for me to go to sleep before he eats.

By now, my neck is fairly peppered with monkey-nip welts. I'm at my wit's end with this wretched rhesus! I have stepped in invisible but pungent monkey leavings in every room in the house. I am forever running around with broom, mop, and disinfectant, guided by my overloaded olfactory organ.

I keep hoping there's a way to terminate the invisible effect of Disapirum. I tried calling the junk mail merchant's 800 number, but got only the computer-simulated voice: "This number has been disconnected."

Sorry, I have to stop this story now, for I hear the postman on the porch and I've got to check out today's mail. I now scrutinize the junk mail first. If the genius who thought up Disapirum is half as smart as I think he is, he will recognize the obvious market value of the antidote product Bringumbak. He will probably charge ten times the price for it, but I plan to be among the first to try it. I want to set my eyes on Erasmus again!

# Lost Soles

*An older guy gets into touch with his youth as he examines his feet.*

I toweled off after a hot shower and quickly dressed, eager to start the day's activities. As I started to pull on my socks I said to myself, "Wait a minute, look at those toenails! They're long enough for an anteater!" The neglected nails were so long that they threatened to slash holes through my socks. As one gets older, it's easier to postpone trimming the toenails because the nails on the big toes are so thick and tough. And if you're having lower back problems, it's a real pain to reach down and trim them.

Today, I was out of excuses. My back was fine, and I really didn't have to start on the yard work my wife had suggested at that very moment. Furthermore, the toenails were still somewhat softened by the hot water from my shower, so they would be a lot easier to trim. I rummaged through the top drawer of my dresser and grasped my favorite, very sharp, toenail clippers. I doubled over, reached for my left foot, and tried to coax my ankle and knee joints into positions difficult to achieve at my age. Next, I had to fumble with my bifocals to get my foot into the right position where I could see, or almost see, what I was doing. Trimming toenails is always sort of a hit or miss adventure!

I paused briefly before starting to hack away at the big toenail. I massaged the bottom of my foot and noticed the softness of the heel and ball. *They weren't always like that,* I reflected. Then I remembered:

"Bobby," my mother called out, "It's too cold today for you to go to school barefoot. Put on some shoes!"

"Nah," I answered. "It's not that bad. My feet are tough!" Never mind that a blue norther was howling and the temperature was plunging below freezing. I put on a heavy coat and a wool cap and walked out barefoot. What a sight I must have been as I trudged the two blocks to school! My feet were insulated from the cold by the toughness that comes from spending your childhood barefoot.

Now, my feet are soft and pliant. I still love to go barefoot in the house, and I remove my shoes at the first opportunity. But walking on carpets doesn't make for tough feet. I recalled that the bottom of my feet, the heels and balls, used to be so thick and tough that I could walk across hot pavement in the summer, negotiate wintry roads, and scamper over grass burrs without feeling a thing:

It was a late spring weekend and a school pal and I decided to see what was going on down by Reckaway branch. We hoped old Mr. Moore's alligator had gotten out again from his pen by the swimming pool. We walked through the pasture where Ridgecrest Road is now located and crawled through a couple of bob-wire (I only learned later how this is spelled) fences and dodged a few cow patties. At the branch, we were delighted to find swift running water, thanks to heavy spring rains.

I was barefoot, as usual, and my pal wore old tennis shoes (they weren't sneakers then). The grass burrs didn't bother me if I stayed out of the higher grass. They couldn't penetrate my feet's tough heels and balls. But the arches were certainly vulnerable, and I had to stop often to pull the stickers from them. My friend laughed at me, "Why don't you wear shoes in a place like this?" But I was proud to be a barefoot boy, and maybe just a little stubborn about it.

We enjoyed the freedom of doing boy things down by the branch. We competed to see who could make a rock skip on the water the most times. Both of us carried our trusty slingshots, fashioned from forked branches, old inner tubes, string, and old shoe leather. We had crammed the pockets of our blue jeans full of chinaberries—hard, round, and green—the perfect slingshot missile. As we strolled down the branch toward Moore's swimming pool, we peppered the resident birds and squirrels with chinaberries. The animals answered with excited chatter—probably laughing at our errant efforts!

We stopped suddenly as a pulse of fear surged through our bodies. A large cotton-mouth water moccasin, mean-looking and aggressive, dropped from a limb overhanging the creek and swam right for us. Instinctively, we did the heroic thing: turned and ran. Unfortunately, wild rose vines blocked our way from the branch. We ran right through them—my friend in his tennis shoes and me in my bare feet. I didn't feel a thing!

Trimming the big toenail is always the hardest part of a pedicure. You have to twist your foot to get just the right angle so the clippers will work okay. And then you have to twist the other way to smooth the jagged edges with the file. I could see part of the arch, and I noticed they were still there—the scars from my childhood:

It was shortly after dinner (noon-time back then) on a nice early summer day. While Mom was taking her nap, I sneaked quietly out the front door to walk around the neighborhood. Sandrock covered the unpaved streets, an often dusty but mud-resistant alternative to asphalt. I traipsed along watchfully because randomly spaced stones protruding from the sandrock were magnets for unsuspecting toes. How many times had I stubbed a big toe and mangled a toenail?

Drainage ditches lined each side of the street and culverts at the end of each driveway spanned them. I noticed the green, inviting tall grass at the bottom of the ditch. With an irresistible urge to enjoy its softness, I jumped from the culvert.

Crunch! My left foot landed directly on a discarded light bulb, concealed by the tall grass. Badly cut, I pulled as much glass from my foot as I could and limped home. Mom examined my foot and decided I needed to see the doctor. The nurse removed more glass fragments and the doctor stitched up the wound.

"Yikes," I said to myself as I ran my fingers over the scars. It still gives me the creeps when I hear a light bulb crunch! I continued with the pedicure and soon finished with the interior toes of the left foot. When I grasped the little toe, I noted its thickened and distorted toenail, caused by the pressure of unyielding shoe leather. My first experience with leather shoes started with Sunday school and church:

Mom was a faithful Methodist lady. She insisted I start Sunday school at an early age, forcing me to endure a more civilized lifestyle for at least two hours. I couldn't wear blue jeans or go barefoot—ugh! More comfortable tennis shoes wouldn't work, either; I had to wear brown leather shoes.

Mom went to church with her Methodist lady friends, and I walked, dressed neatly with slacks, sport coat, and tie. But people who saw me had a big laugh as I went down the street dapperly dressed for a Hallettsville kid—walking barefoot with my slacks rolled up and my church shoes tied together and slung across my shoulder! When I arrived, I sat down on the curb in front of the church and put on my shoes before entering (I found out later that Muslims also do this but in reverse order).

I finished working on the left foot. As I twisted and turned the right foot to get it into a good position, my hand brushed against the ugly reddish bunion that protruded from the knuckle of the big toe—a bunion caused by wearing shoes that were too tight. *My poor misshapen foot!* It started coming back to me, how the shoe period of my life began:

It was the first day of school, in middle September (school started late back then, so the farm kids could help get the crops harvested). I was starting eighth grade. I was cheerful and eager to return to school. Summers were fun, but I wanted to get back to the books. Mom made sure I had a freshly ironed shirt, and I made sure my hair was neatly combed (yes, I said hair). I walked down the street toward school, whistling a happy tune, barefoot as usual.

Miz Hope taught eighth grade (in those days, Miz meant Mrs. We called unmarried teachers Miss). Miz Hope, a refined and cultured person, took her job seriously: turning rough kids into more cultured adults. She greeted us warmly, but before starting classroom formalities, she took a long look at me and sternly said, "Bobby Zumwalt, you're old enough to wear shoes now. I want you to leave this classroom right now and not come back until you have shoes on!"

Stunned, I sat there a moment before rising to leave. Some classmates snickered as I went out the door. Luckily, I didn't have to face Mom at home, since she was a substitute teacher and had to be at school on the first day. I figured she'd probably put Miz Hope up to this anyway. I had a simple choice: my church shoes or my old tennis shoes. I never wore my church shoes long enough to properly break them in, so I returned to class in my tennis shoes and received cheers from my classmates.

Shoes are a bothersome pain: they cause bunions, they track dirt into the house, they can foster athlete's foot and foot odors. And they can interfere with first-aid procedures, as I recalled from another incident:

I was helping Pop with some carpentry chores around the house. Thanks to Miz Hope, I was a regular shoe wearer now. I still had only two pairs of shoes, and I wore the tennis shoes most of the time. I was helping hold something for Pop and stepped backward to keep my balance—right onto a board with an upright nail. This went through the tennis shoe and into my foot, effectively pinning me to the board. Pop had to pull the nail from the board before I could take off the shoe. We treated puncture wounds then by soaking the foot in kerosene. Afterward, I got a tetanus shot.

Of course, I realize that barefoot wouldn't have protected me from the nail either. Stepping on nails has been a horrific thought for me ever since. I cleared my mind by resuming the contemplation of my bunion. Bunions develop because of ill-fitting shoes, and they will turn into serious problems if this source of irritation is not relieved. For much of my adult life I had to make compromises when buying shoes: too long versus too narrow. I have always opted for too narrow. During my footloose and carefree childhood, my unconstrained feet grew wide—very wide—in fact, too wide to fit comfortably into the normal range of shoes. Only recently have I discovered comfortably wide shoes—EE and EEEE widths—that don't aggravate my bunions. They look clunky, but I don't care.

Decades of shoe wearing have thoroughly tenderized my feet. Now, I must wear shoes whenever I go outside—even treading on the slightest pebble hurts. The thick leathery bottoms of my feet are but a memory.

I had just finished trimming the rest of the toenails when my wife called from downstairs, "Bob, are you going to take all day? Come on down and let's get some work done before lunch." (After learning to wear shoes, I became an adult, went to work in the big city, and started taking dinner in the evening.)

"I'll be right down, dear," I answered, "let me get my shoes on."

A jolt of pain stabbed my left foot when I turned toward the closet. I muttered some choice expletives as I bent to pull a pin from the foot—a relic from one of Doris' quilting projects. In my youth, I would have hardly noticed this. Without a thick leathery bottom, natural or artificial, my feet are vulnerable!

# See Saw

*A young lad learns the importance of returning tools
to where they belong.*

My grandfather was a carpenter; he built many fine homes in Hallettsville, Texas, including the 120-year-old house we now live in. Papa Zumwalt was also an accomplished cabinetmaker. He kept his tools in a huge wooden toolbox with many compartments, which we found stashed under the old house.

My father was the only one of Papa Zumwalt's descendants who stayed in Hallettsville. The others moved to Houston to participate in the growing economy of that region. Some became engineers, and others were entrepreneurs. But all of them liked to come back to the old place as often as they could.

During the Great Depression, Pop, as I called my father, worked at various jobs in the area until he signed on with the Postal Service and became the town's letter carrier. In the meantime, he picked up the family trade—carpenter—by working odd jobs and helping his father. He and my grandfather built the house where I spent my first eleven years.

Pop often built parade floats for local organizations such as the garden club and reading club. He continually added improvements to our house, such as built-in cabinets and shelves. He stored his tools in a smaller, wooden toolbox; he also used some of Grandpa's tools.

When I was a boy of six or seven, I eagerly volunteered to "help" Pop. He kindly explained what he was doing and even let me hold boards when he was sawing or nailing them. In those days he worked with a handsaw.

I soon learned to hammer nails, pull nails, shape wood with a rasp, and saw boards. I was going to follow the family tradition and become a carpenter! Sawing boards was very difficult for me since I could barely manage the full-sized handsaw, which was almost as big as me.

Santa Claus had already brought me a small hammer and some real tools: a pair of pliers and a screwdriver. Pop wanted me to have a few tools so I could not only learn how to use them, but more importantly, learn how to take care of them. And, time and again, he impressed upon me the necessity of, "always putting up your tools when you finish the job."

"If you put them up," he explained, "you will always know where to find them when you need them again." That was a lesson I would learn and unlearn too many times, even in my supposedly more responsible adulthood.

I had often mentioned to my parents how much I wanted a smaller saw so I could cut boards and fallen tree branches more easily. On my birthday, I was delighted when I unwrapped a shiny new saw with a wooden handle. It looked just like my father's saw (except it was about three-fourths the size). This wasn't a wimpy play saw—it had teeth that were sharp and really cut wood. I don't know for sure, but I guess the teeth were pitched at #10, instead of the #8 saw Pop used. That made it a lot easier to start the cut.

The saw was my only birthday present, but I'm sure I would have ignored any others I might have received. You can't imagine how proud I was of my new tool! I learned to make cuts with it, although the cuts only approximated right angles. Pop tried to explain the intricacies of sawing out the pencil line or leaving the line. That was a bit too much for me at the time, but I mastered that technique years later when I became a daddy and had a house to fix up.

I helped Pop whenever I could. I mainly held boards while Pop made the cut. He could saw through a board so fast it made the sawdust fly. He must have had Popeye-level upper arm strength, because sawing always made my muscles go into spasm, even as an adult. Perhaps once each session, when the cut wasn't critical to the success of the project, Pop would let me make a real cut on a smaller board for his project. Pop coached me and encouraged me when I became disconsolate over my slow progress.

Pop threw pieces of scrap lumber on a pile in our backyard. Mom also placed fallen tree limbs on the pile. That scrap pile was a fantastic resource for a kid with a saw and an urge to cut up!

I made two stacks of bricks, to serve as a sawing platform. I placed the board on the bricks, held it in place with my foot or knee, and used my left hand—first to guide the saw during the start of the cut and then to further hold the board steady as I completed the cut. I sawed and sawed, and made the average length of board and tree limb in that pile a fraction of what it was. I proudly felt the bulge of muscle in my right arm as my strength increased.

I sawed almost every day after school, as well as on weekends. I carefully cleared off the sawdust and oiled the saw after each use—to keep it shiny like new. Then, I put it in its special place in the hall closet. When I complained about the saw not cutting well, Pop used a special file to sharpen it a little. "That's not as good as a professional saw-sharpener could do," he said, "but it will be good enough for a while!"

One day after school, I went to the closet for my saw; I wanted to show my friend Johnny how well I could saw boards. He was eager to try it, and I was going to coach him, just like my Pop did for me. I reached in to grasp it, but it wasn't there!

I crawled into the closet, figuring the saw had slid to the floor. There was no saw. I looked all over the house, opening all closet doors. By now, my heart was racing and panic was about to set in. I wasn't far from tears.

"Mom, what have you done with my saw?" I called out.

Mom was in the kitchen, fixing supper, and in no mood to be distracted. "I haven't touched your saw," she replied, "it's probably in the place you last left it!"

"But I looked all over the house," I whimpered. "I can't find it anywhere."

"Maybe you left it outside. Have you looked for it there?"

The back screen door slammed shut as my friend and I headed for the backyard. We looked everywhere—front yard and backyard. Nothing. I started crying. My friend touched my arm consolingly, then announced he had to go home.

I was a real sad sack the rest of the day. I could hardly eat my supper. I picked up my cat, Dusty, to seek the comfort of her soft fur and sweet disposition. But she sensed my distress and squirmed out of my grasp. My saw—the tool that had made me so proud when I completed a good cut—was gone. This saw was going to make me a good carpenter, just like Pop and my grandfather.

By the next day, I started acting like a normal kid again, but I couldn't get that saw off my mind. *What had become of it? Where did I leave it?* Day after day, these questions cycled through my mind during idle moments and when I lie in bed before going to sleep.

One night, I had a vivid dream—you know, the Technicolor dream people often talk about:

I could see myself sawing a nice board, and I was making a great cut. My friend walked up and shouted, "Hey Bobby, there are some tadpoles in the ditch by our house! Want to come help me catch some?"

I dropped the saw on the scrap pile and took off with Johnny. We caught a bunch of tadpoles with his mom's kitchen strainer and dumped them into a big pickle jar full of water. We were going to have the best frogs in school!

Johnny's mom called him for supper, and I figured I better get home right away before my mom got mad.

That's where the dream ended.

Sometimes, you can remember the details of a dream; most of the time you can't. When I awoke the next morning, my brain replayed the dream, just as in the newsreels. I ran down the stairs, barely pulling on my cut-off blue-jean shorts as I descended. "Mom," I shouted, "I dreamed where the saw is! I'm going to go out and get it!"

I dashed straight out to the scrap pile, where my heart sank to the bottom of my stomach. The scrap pile wasn't there! It was just a heap of ashes! I grabbed a stick and frantically poked through the ashes until the stick hit something solid. I cleared away the cinders and there was my saw, handle burned off, saw blade warped by the fire's heat, and the shiny surface reduced to a burnt rust.

"Mom, Mom!" I shouted as I ran into the house, "I found my saw, and it's ruined. It's burned up!"

Poor Mom was left with the task of consoling a thoroughly heartbroken youngster. This was a Saturday, and Pop had already left for the Post Office. She hugged me and caressed my face; she wiped away my tears. She did what moms know how to do.

I was afraid Pop might give me a hard time when he learned of my misfortune. But he knew I was grieving the loss of my favorite possession. He gently reprimanded, "Good tools are very important to people. You must always take care of them and put them where they belong. I'm especially sorry about your saw, since I was the one who set fire to the scrap pile. I didn't see the saw."

Many years later, I have lots of nice tools, and I usually take pretty good care of them. That's important to me, especially as I try to fix this balky door lock.

"Doris, what have you done with my little red screwdriver?"

# The Clean Window Policy

*The jolt of a sudden impact ends an exciting pursuit and ambush.*

I'd just managed to spot his head as he sneaked up behind the big salt-cedar bush. He had been stalking me for the last ten minutes, and I was getting a bit antsy. I thought I might have a clear shot soon, so I could put an end to this sorry scenario. But I had to be certain of this, for I was getting low on ammo.

He pushed down a limb of the salt-cedar, hopeful he might catch a glimpse of where I was hiding. He knew I was near, for his attack dog was yapping at my heels as I crouched behind the holly bush. I peered through an aperture in the holly and saw his round face, framed by two clusters of red berries and smiling in anticipation of victory as he searched in vain for my exact position.

An inspired idea suddenly gave me some hope I might get him this time. I picked up a small piece of wood, which was the partly rotted remnant of a dead limb from the overhanging oak tree, and looked toward the dog. He had ceased barking and just sat there alert, snarling, and looking at me menacingly; he dared me to hit him with that puny stick.

That damned mutt! He always messed up my stalking and hiding. *Why couldn't he just leave me alone?* With stick in hand, I drew back my arm. The dog tensed with anticipation. I gave that sorry excuse for a tree limb a mighty heave and the dog inanely took off after it, yapping with the glee only the canine species can muster.

I had created my diversion and instilled a feeling of premature confidence in my stealthy opponent. He now knew where I was hiding and he had actually spotted the movement as I threw the stick. He raised his head to get a better view for his terminal shot, as I had hoped. I moved to the other side of the holly bush and extended my arm for the ambush shot that should have finished off this hunt. I squeezed the trigger, but nothing happened. I squeezed again, instinctively harder, and still, nothing happened. Damn! Out of ammunition at such a critical point!

My adrenaline glands kicked into overdrive. This was a fight or flight situation and my muscles and enzymes were prepared for either. My instant analysis of the situation opted for flight, and I took off around the back porch steps. Unfortunately, my stealthy stalker turned into a fleet-footed pursuer. He had anticipated this, and he ran around the bushes and over the smooth grass, where he confronted me.

I was trapped in the corner between the porch steps and the main part of the house, thoroughly exposed without any nearby bushes in which to hide. I crouched in the corner and looked up at him. He glared at me triumphantly, then raised his arm, and carefully aimed his pistol.

"Don't shoot!" I implored, "We can still be buddies, just like always. It doesn't have to be like this!"

He ignored my helpless pleadings and solemnly squeezed the trigger. Instinctively, I ducked to my right, just before his shot went "Splat!" against the wall. My left shoulder had just been there.

I lay there on the ground, uninjured but immensely frightened. I looked up at him, totally helpless. I expected him to charge in to finish me off. Instead, he dashed off around the corner, toward the front of the house. Perhaps, he was also out of ammo.

I rose and dusted myself off, thinking about what I could do to counter this rapidly evolving combat situation. I looked at my dripping, but now empty, water pistol and tossed it on the lawn. This would be of no further use as there was not enough time to crank up the hose and reload. The dog ran up and dropped his stick at my feet, then started sniffing and fooling around with my impotent weapon.

I heard doors slamming. That rascal was going into the house! This called for an entirely different set of tactics, so I opened the door into the enclosed back porch and stealthily crept up to the window. Before the porch was enclosed, this had been an outside window, but I guess they kept it as a window to let in light and circulate air better during the hot Texas weather. We had one like this at home.

I peered through the window into the dining room in an attempt to find out what old Tommy was doing. Tommy Holmes and I were boyhood pals, and my mother was good friends with Mrs. Holmes. Tommy's mother was a refined and educated lady, a music teacher, who had many beautiful things in her house. The house always seemed very neat and clean, but you can't necessarily depend on the discriminating eyes of a twelve-year-old boy in this regard.

Tommy and I played together often at the end of the school day, sometimes at my house and sometimes at his. Mrs. Holmes was always very nice to me, and she gave us lemonade and cookies after we played.

I spied him under the dining room table, looking toward the front of the house as if he expected me to follow him. Now was my chance to win this battle. He was just a few feet away, looking the wrong way. It would have to be hand-to-hand combat—Mrs. Holmes would kill us if we squirted water pistols in the house. I tensed as I prepared myself to spring through the open window and pounce upon the unwary Tommy.

*Crash!* I landed on the dining room floor amid a shower of glass shards.

That damn window wasn't open after all! This was an old-style, full-frame window pane, kept squeaky clean by the meticulous housekeeper, Mrs. Holmes. In the heat of battle, I failed to notice any slight glimmers or reflections the window might have offered as warning. Many birds have made the same mistake and paid heavily for it.

Mrs. Holmes rushed into the dining room in response to the clatter of broken glass, probably expecting to see some of her beautiful china and pottery reduced to rubble.

"Oh Bobby!" she exclaimed, "Are you hurt?"

I lay there on the floor, in a mild state of shock, my face racked with anguish. The impact of that window on my head initially surprised me, and then I realized I had messed up big time. Broken glass lay everywhere, even on top of me. The window frame was jagged with razor-sharp vitreous daggers.

But it wasn't my close call with serious injury that pained me—it was the thought of what Mom was gonna do when she learned how much I had messed up Mrs. Holmes' beautiful house. She might even wallop me on the back with a frying pan again!

Tommy's mom removed the glass on top of me and helped me to my feet. That kind lady was genuinely concerned about me and not mad that I broke her dining room window. She anxiously looked me over to see about any cuts or punctures. Miraculously, she found none—not even a scratch! My state of anguish and stupefaction ended in a cascade of tears. I bawled like a baby.

Mrs. Holmes consoled me and then brought us some cookies and lemonade. I apologized as sincerely as only a truly errant lad could do. Again, the nice lady soothed my anguish, "Don't you worry about that, Bobby! We can easily fix that window. I'm so glad we don't have to stitch you up!"

When I got home, Mom already knew about what had happened; I guess Mrs. Holmes must have called her. Instead of giving me a walloping, she hugged me and looked me over again to be sure I wasn't injured. Later, Pop paid for repairing the broken window, with hardly a grumble.

At the time, I didn't realize how lucky I was. After all, kids *are* indestructible! But since then, I have often thought about how close I came to serious injury. Many people have been badly cut, crippled, deformed, and even fatally injured when they crashed into big glass windows or doors.

I've thought about this a lot since then, and I am convinced there should be a new policy: People who have large windows should not keep them so clean!

# Famous Fox

*The word for a modern technical concept emerged from a*
*random pastoral event.*

The fox family joyfully gamboled in the pasture, staying close to the sheltering woods in case the farmer's dogs showed up. On this beautiful spring day, the bright sun melted away the memory of last week's frigid days. A slight breeze rippled the tall grass, the expansive pasture resembled a sea with waves—occasionally dotted with schooner-like dairy cows. Mama fox occasionally glanced at the farmhouse across the vast pasture, ever alert for danger.

This was a happy, fun-filled family—Mama fox and three cute, boisterous pups. Mama caught small animals to nurture the pups and teach them about hunting. She licked them affectionately and encouraged them to play vigorously—a big part of becoming adult foxes.

"Vicki" was the cutest pup, slight of build with long, tapered ears. Her flowing tail was almost the same color as her body—bright reddish brown. From a distance, she looked almost red. She was playful and friendly; everyone liked her, including some of the neighboring boy foxes.

"Micki," with short, grayish brown fur, was the biggest pup—a bit overweight and not as mentally sharp as the others. An awkward pup, he often stumbled when running or jumping. But he played very hard, almost too hard for his mates.

And then there was "Quirti," a handsome lad of a fox if ever there was one. Quirti was strong and looked it. His rich, brown fur shone, with just a few red hairs on his ears that sparkled in the sunlight. He could jump higher than most young foxes—almost as high as Mama could. His name might seem funny to you and me, but it's really a famous fox name that goes back to the old days.

The pups alternately played and rested, lying down in the soft grass to relax the tensions of rough jousting and to enjoy the sun's warmth. Mama decided to lie down for a while, after checking out the farmhouse to make sure all was clear. She nuzzled her nose into the tall grass, drowsily savoring the sun-warmed aroma of spring grass.

In the distance, Michael Choans[1], a well-known dairy and poultry farmer, shouted to his teenaged son, "Hey Paul. Look over toward the woods. Isn't that a bunch of foxes over there?"

Paul put down his comic book and peered in that direction. "Yup," he answered, "that's sure 'nuff a buncha foxes!"

Now you might think Paul was a country bumpkin from the way he talked, but he was on track to become valedictorian at the high school in town. And his comic book was about Dilbert.

Mr. Choans suggested, "Why don't you get the dogs and chase those guys?"

So Paul roused the dogs from their slumber on the porch, and the three-some walked across the pasture toward the woods. The dogs were an undisciplined and excitable duo, both of questionable ancestry. This was not exactly a stealth operation and a normally alert fox family should have had no difficulty detecting their approach. Paul knew this but did nothing to quiet their march. Actually, he liked the fox family and often admired them through his binoculars.

But Paul knew the realities of dairy farming. Just last week, a newborn calf was killed, perhaps by foxes, bobcats, or marauding neighborhood dogs. Nobody knew for sure, so he reluctantly went about his duty, hoping the foxes would get the scent and move on.

Vicki picked up the excited yapping of the dogs. "Mama!" she shouted in fox language, which was simular to dog language, "*Iay inkthay Iay earhay ogsday!*" Vicki then roused Micki and Quirti from their naps. Mama fox sat up tall to survey the scene before taking flight. But it was too late. The dogs spotted Mama and

---

1    The unusual surname Choans has a colorful history. When my wife Doris was a child, her German father read to her from a popular book, *Farmer Jones*. He could not pronounce the English "J" sound and Doris remembers the book as *Farmer Choans*.

ran toward her. The four foxes headed for the fence and the safety of the woods, where they would find sheltering brambles to thwart the dogs.

Mama easily jumped the fence and turned to encourage her pups, hoping they could wriggle through the hole used to enter the pasture. But Vicki panicked and dashed to and fro, seeking the hole. Quirti guided her to safety as the wildly barking dogs stormed toward the fence. Poor Micki, hindered by his pudginess, couldn't get through the hole. Quirti pushed him through. But poor Quirti couldn't escape, for the dogs were right on his tail. The deft young fox dashed from the fence and circled back to the pasture, hoping to find a way to safety.

Amazingly, the two dogs just stood in front of the fence, doing nothing, peering at the hole. Maybe they were tired from the long run; maybe they were satisfied to have chased the foxes; maybe they wouldn't have known what to do with a fox had they caught one.

Quirti assessed his predicament and desperately sought a means of escape. After a running start, he made a mighty leap and sailed right over the dogs' heads. He cleared the fence with room to spare and scampered into the brambles. He found his mama and nuzzled her nose, and then flopped and snuggled against Micki and Vicki, happy to be with his family again. Quirti, the fox hero, was safe!

Paul walked toward the fence, not wanting to keep up with the dogs by running. He arrived in time to see the fox's desperate jump, imprinting his mind with this verbal image of Quirti sailing over the dogs and the fence: "The quick brown fox jumps over the lazy dogs."

Paul vividly remembered this event for the rest of his long life. He attended college and then became a prominent teacher. He wrote a famous book, which included the fox jumping image—a sentence copied by legions of typing teachers after him. Everyone who types knows this sentence; now you know its origin!

For the first few summers after college, Paul returned to the farm to visit his father. He saw Quirti many times; the agile but aging fox was slowing down a bit, but he could still jump!

You can see how Paul became famous as a typing teacher. But how did Quirti the fox become famous? He gave his name to the modern typewriter keyboard! Unfortunately, they misspelled his name.

# The Day I Shot My Brother

*A younger brother taunts his older sibling and learns the limits of excessive force.*

I remember my excitement of a special Christmas. For weeks, I had been thinking of a certain gift item. I looked at catalog offerings and newspaper ads; I inspected various models in the stores. At the age of twelve, I was now old enough to qualify for this type of gift, and I made sure my parents knew exactly which model I preferred.

The three boys of our family awoke with varying degrees of expectation on this bright and warm Christmas morning. My older brother, Joe—a high-school junior past the magic of Santa Claus—was nonchalant about the whole thing. He expected the usual unexciting assortment of shirts, jackets, and trousers. My younger brother, John, a mere toddler of four, was goggle-eyed with anticipation of more kiddy toys.

Without a doubt, I was the most excited member of the family. Our parents had arisen early to be near the Christmas tree when we straggled in from the bathroom. We knew we had to wash our faces after arising, to get rid of the "sleepy man" in our eyes—otherwise Mom would give us the dickens.

I believe our parents were just as excited as we were. Their eyes focused on me as I gazed at the long, narrow, neatly gift-wrapped box. I knew in an instant what it was, and I excitedly ran straight toward it. I tore off the wrapping paper and pulled my long-anticipated gift from its box: a shiny blue-black lever-action Daisy BB gun with a wooden stock. I started to cock the gun, but Pop shouted, "No, not in the house! Wait till after breakfast and I will show you how to use it safely."

First, Pop made me read the instruction booklet, something hard to do given my level of excitement. Maybe it explains why to this day I still take the time to read the instructions before using a new gadget, something my more intuitive wife, Doris, now makes fun of.

In the backyard, Pop instructed me in safe shooting. I still remember his first lesson: "Never, ever, point this gun at another person. It can still hurt people, even if it's a BB gun!"

He demonstrated safe shooting techniques by setting a tin can in front of a big hackberry tree. He plinked the can a couple of times, showed me how to aim, and asked me to try. My first shot missed the entire tree—no satisfying plink or thud. We were shooting toward the old gully, now the site of North Market street, and nothing but empty field lay beyond. After a few more lessons in aiming, I was rewarded by a metallic plink after almost every shot. That tin can really got dimpled by BB pellets!

Pop emphasized safe shooting and explained: "Aim only at safe targets, be aware of what might lie beyond, and handle the gun carefully. Before putting the gun up, make sure the gun is not cocked when you store it in the house since somebody might accidentally pull the trigger."

He showed me how to oil the gun after each use to keep it from rusting. Afterward, I placed the gun in a back corner of the old black cabinet in our "family room"—a closed-in back porch where we ate our meals and listened to our Philco radio.

I had so much joy over the next few months, shooting at tin cans, match boxes, pecans, or whatever imaginative target I could find. I never shot at bottles or jars, since Pop told me I would have to pick up every splinter of glass with my bare hands if I ever did that.

Because of the boy in me, I wanted to shoot at birds. Pop said this was okay, but only if I bagged sparrows. He also instructed me to aim upward, and not at an angle, to keep the BBs from going into the neighbors' yards. I was thoroughly drilled in safely shooting a BB gun in town (it's questionable if this can actually be done). In addition to sparrows, I confess to plinking more than one mockingbird, dove, and blue jay, as well as one unfortunate pecan-stealing squirrel.

I must have been a laughable sight: a shirtless, barefoot, skinny school kid, wearing drooping cut-off blue jean shorts, carrying a lever-action Daisy air rifle, and acting like an urban Daniel Boone.

I treasured that BB gun and proudly showed it off to all my buddies. I had learned to shoot very accurately, and I could usually beat my friends when we were target shooting in the backyard. That BB gun was a joyful part of my life, as I played out the last of my innocent preteen years.

One warm spring day, all of this changed dramatically, and the ensuing events affected me the rest of my life.

Like most younger brothers, I loved and adored my older brother, and stood in awe of his many achievements. Joe and I played sports, dominoes, and card games almost every day. Of course, I tried to tag along when Joe was enjoying activities with high school kids his own age. Joe was my mentor in many things in life, and I emulated a lot of his actions and attitudes. He paved the way by going to Texas A&M and studying chemical engineering. I easily followed in his path, encountering professors who asked, "Are you Joe's brother?"

But Joe had a domineering streak, typical of older brothers. When he decided I was stupid enough on some inane issue, or I was interfering in his play with friends, he resorted to extreme corporal punishment. With closed fist, he pounded me on the shoulder so hard it raised welts and left bruise marks. I complained often to Mom, but this simply ended with a scolding for both of us. Secretly, I felt Mom was just as happy to let Joe mete out justice.

One Friday morning, there was no school because of a teachers' meeting. Pop was walking his mail route and Mom was judging a flower show in a nearby town; we three boys remained at home. Mom designated Joe to be in charge.

John was outside playing with his friend, Danny, and Joe was outside throwing a baseball with his friend, Charley. I grew tired of reading my current book, so I grabbed my baseball mitt and went outside to join Joe and Charley's game.

"Get outta here, you little squirt!" Joe snarled. "You've only played softball. We're playing with a real baseball—hard ball. We're practicing for the high school team."

"I can, too, play hard ball," I confidently responded. "I can throw the ball into the air and catch it just fine. I'm good at it!"

I chased after a ball Joe had thrown wide of Charley and tossed it back to Charley. "See, I can play," I puckishly shouted to Joe.

"You stupid little runt," Joe berated me, "we don't need you here and we don't want you here. Go back in the house." Then, he delivered a teeth-rattling punch to my shoulder, which really hurt. I can almost feel it now. I wanted to cry because of the pain, but I couldn't do that in front of Charley.

I stayed out of the way and watched until another wayward toss came rolling my way.

"Throw it back to me," Joe yelled.

"No!" I yelled back, and impulsively grabbed the ball and ran toward the house.

I was running as fast as I could, but Joe, with his longer legs, was gaining on me. I knew that I was in big-time trouble and that he was going to pound much more than my shoulder this time. I dashed up the back steps, slammed the screen door, and locked it.

Joe, embarrassed in front of his friend, stood at the bottom of the steps and glared at me. "You stupid idiot, you are really in trouble this time. I'm gonna walk up the steps and push the door in. Give me that ball or else you are really gonna get it!"

By this time, my heart was pounding, and I was totally panicked. I dropped the ball and reached into the black cabinet for my Daisy air rifle. I cocked the lever, carefully aimed at Joe's belt buckle, and fired through the screen. The BB bounced harmlessly off Joe's belt buckle, but the shot sure got his attention! He retreated down the steps and shouted, "Pop's gonna kill you when he finds out what you did!"

I placed the air rifle on the table and sat down, thoroughly disconsolate. I started crying. My body was involuntarily shaking because of the fear of Pop's wrath and the realization of what I had done. I had aimed my BB gun at my brother and shot him. That was awful!

Pop soon came home for lunch. He stopped by the back steps as Joe briefed him on my dreadful act. I sat in my chair, looking down at the two, completely frozen with fear about what would soon be happening to me.

I unlocked the door as Pop walked up the steps with a serious scowl on his face. I knew my moment of retribution had arrived.

"Bobby," he gently but seriously scolded, "you didn't do what I told you. You should never point a gun at a person, even playfully. To think you deliberately did this to your brother, and then actually shot him, tells me you are too young to have a gun."

Mom always doled out the physical punishment, and Pop gave me the serious verbal lashes. The pain of her strokes quickly dissipated, but Pop's words, few but effective, lingered on.

"Where's the box this gun came in?" Pop demanded.

I fetched it, and Pop placed the gun inside and taped up the box. "I know some poor people on my mail route who could never buy such a fine gift as this," he lectured. "I'm going to give it to a family who can use it and who will use it responsibly."

We ate lunch, some cold leftover fried chicken, and Pop took my cherished Daisy back to work. I was devastated, not so much because of losing the air rifle, but because I had failed my father. I was not old enough to have a BB gun, and I knew it.

I've often thought, in the years that followed, *Suppose that gun had been a .22 caliber rifle, or something bigger? In my youthful panic, would I have still fired it?*

I shudder when I think of what might have happened. How many youthful tragedies have we read about that followed a similar scenario?

# Cold Turkey

*A young lad discovers the secret of communicating with wild turkeys,*
*which reveals to him some amazing acts of compassion.*

"Gobble, gobble! Gobble, gobble, gobble. Grlck, grlck. Gobble, gobble, grlck."

This might sound like gobbledygook to you. It did to Paul, too, until last year. Until then it sounded like the noise turkeys make. But it's more than noise: those funny looking birds are actually talking to each other. Even if you've got only one turkey, it will talk to you that way. That bird is actually telling you something, such as: "Give me some more food, you jerk! I'm too cold in this pen at night. My water is all dirty and needs changing." The bird can't help it if you are so stupid you can't understand.

Paul Choans is the teenaged son of Michael Choans, a prominent farmer in South Central Texas. Last year during summer vacation, he found a very special place in the woods, far enough away that he couldn't hear his mom calling him to do some work. Lots of oak and maple trees surrounded the clearing, which was shaded by the trees and shielded by berry-laden yaupon bushes.

One day, a flock of wild turkeys came into the clearing, gobbling away among themselves. Paul surreptitiously watched them eating yaupon berries. The leader of the flock was a huge turkey gobbler, with a bright red crest and wattle. He seemed to be a very proud fellow. But he was also a very stern leader. If a couple of hen turkeys started squabbling over a scrumptious berry bush, the chief turkey came over and quickly straightened them out.

The next day, Paul filled his pockets with corn and returned to the little clearing. He laid a string of kernels in a little trail that led up to his sitting place; he then put several in front of him. Sure enough, that flock of turkeys showed up again. They didn't seem to mind him because he sat very still and kept quiet. He anxiously waited to see what would happen.

Turkeys love corn. They started eating the outer kernels and showed no concern about Paul. They were happily eating and chattering to each other with all sorts of gobbles and grlcks. Chickens make clucking sounds when they are happy; turkeys make grlcking sounds. When the outer kernels were all gone, the hens looked longingly at the trail of corn, but they didn't dare move toward the golden kernels. They were gobbling nervously to each other. One brave hen stepped up to the trail and took the first kernel, then hesitated. She looked toward the chief turkey and said, "*Gobble, gobble?*" Then she stepped back among the other hens.

The main job of the chief turkey was to protect the flock. All sorts of nasty critters in the woods like to eat turkey, so he kept pretty busy. He strutted confidently up to the corn trail as if this were no big deal. He looked at Paul, daring him to do something threatening, and made sure Paul could see his big sharp spurs. Paul sat still and quietly watched this big bird.

The chief turkey ate a couple of kernels, looked over at Paul, and said, "*Gobble, gobble!*"

Paul looked him straight in the eye and replied with his best impression of what turkeys say, "*Gobble!*" Paul figured one gobble was the safest way to go, since he had no idea what he was saying. Also, his pronunciation of turkey talk must have been awful, which might have changed the meaning of *gobble*. For all Paul knew, he might have been calling the chief a chicken turkey.

The turkey returned Paul's stare, then answered with an emphatic and distinct "*Gobble,*" as if he were correcting Paul's poor pronunciation. Then he lowered his head, ate a few kernels, turned to the hens, and said, "*Gobble, gobble, grlck!*"

The big gobbler stepped aside and let the hens eat. They ate their way up the trail, stood directly in front of Paul and chattered a bit, and then ate the rest of the corn.

Paul noticed one of the hens looked a bit different from the rest of the flock. Also, there was one other male turkey, who didn't come anywhere close to looking like a chief. Paul learned later these two had a real interesting story to tell.

Paul kept coming back, day after day, bringing just enough corn to keep the turkeys' interest without spoiling them. He listened very closely to their gobbles, noting the inflections of voice, the accenting of syllables, the tone of voice, the volume of the sound, and the number of gobbles. When Paul first came, a gobble sounded just like one word; now, he realized many meanings could be wrapped around that simple sound.

Paul recorded these sounds on his portable tape recorder and listened to them carefully in his bedroom at night, trying to understand the slight differences in the sounds. He especially listened to his own feeble attempts at gobbling, and to the turkeys' responses to his utterances.

One night, his mom heard these strange sounds coming from the bedroom and inquired about what Paul was doing. He assured her, "Just practicing my turkey calls, in case Pop decides to go wild turkey hunting!"

"Fat chance that will happen!" she laughed. "With all the fine turkeys we have around here, why should he go wild turkey hunting?"

That was true. Choans Turkey Farm supplied all the big grocery stores with turkeys for the Thanksgiving and Christmas holidays. So Paul turned down the tape recorder's volume and listened to it under the covers. This stuff was beginning to make sense; he could actually pick up a pattern to those seemingly random gobbles and grlcks.

With summer vacation ended, Paul saw his wild turkey friends only on weekends. While working with the caged turkeys, he listened carefully to their gobbles; although their accents were different, Paul heard some of the same patterns the wild turkeys used. For sure, the caged turkeys' sounds were not as free and animated as those of the wild turkeys—more gobbles than grlcks.

Paul labored at making sense of the turkey sounds, inspired by the archaeologists who had deciphered the hieroglyphics of the ancient Egyptians. Throughout the fall and into the winter, Paul often returned to the little spot in the woods, eagerly greeted by the black-feathered flock.

Unbelievably, by the time winter ended, Paul was talking turkey with those big wild birds! He could actually carry on conversations with them, ultimately making friends with the two strange-looking turkeys: Terry and Henny.

Paul is probably the only person in the world who can talk turkey. He had considered writing the language down—in the form of tape recordings and explanations—and turning the research over to some professors. Although he might have become famous for this, Paul dropped the idea, figuring it would only be bad for the turkeys.

Incredibly, Terry and Henny told Paul a bizarre, mind-boggling tale. Paul spent more time with these odd birds because they looked a lot like the turkeys raised on the Choans farm. But something was different, and he couldn't figure what it was.

Here is the turkeys' story, as they told it to Paul, who translated their tale and wrote it in his diary while keeping his fingers crossed that he'd understood them correctly:

Terry Turkey started talking first, describing conditions in the Choans' turkey houses. Crowded into tight quarters, the turkeys ate as much as they could. In fact, Farmer Choans kept the lights on at night so the turkeys would sleep less and eat more. The food was good, so Terry and the rest of the turkeys "pigged" out.

When they weren't eating, the turkeys gobbled with each other—gossiping. One suspicious turkey kept talking about something he had overheard a new bird just brought in from a nearby turkey house say: "Farmer Choans wants us fat for market. People have a holiday, called Thanksgiving, where they eat turkeys!"

A wave of gobbling reverberated throughout the turkey house. Most of the turkeys were shouting, "They're going to eat us! They're going to eat us!"

To get attention, the chief turkey jumped up on a feeder and flapped his wings. In a calm, steady voice he said, "Calm down, calm down. Farmer Choans is fattening us up because winter is coming. We have to be ready for the cold. They're not going to eat us!"

The murmur of gobbles changed slowly into a stream of hesitant grlcks, as the turkeys calmed down. But Terry was not calm at all; he was worried sick that people were going to eat him. Terry was a pretty smart bird, and he thought, *Maybe they won't eat me if I don't get good and fat!*

That's when he made his decision to just stop eating, cold people.

Terry was faithful to his zero-calorie diet. After his resolution, he didn't eat a further bite of the Choans' turkey food. But he did wet his craw with water. Sure enough, Terry started shrinking, compared to his fellow turkeys.

About the middle of October, Farmer Choans walked through his turkey houses, looking for turkey culls. He didn't want to send any sick or puny-looking birds to market. He quickly spotted skinny Terry, whose fluffed up feathers couldn't quite cover his protruding bones. Mr. Choans grabbed the undernourished fowl and thrust him into a small cage. He found two other turkeys, both sick with some sort of turkey malady, and pushed them into the cage with Terry.

Safely in the cage, Terry thought he had dodged a Thanksgiving bullet. Mr. Choans was going to take him somewhere to regain his health. Imagine his surprise when he was unceremoniously dumped in the woods!

Instinctively, Terry sought shelter and ran for a dense green shrub with red berries. The other two birds were too sick to follow and slumped onto the ground.

Terry was hungry and looked around for some turkey food. He didn't see any, since he never had a momma to teach him that berries were good to eat. It was getting dark, and Terry wondered why somebody didn't turn on the lights. The confused and hungry turkey hunkered down for the night under a yaupon bush, his feathers fluffed out to keep warm.

A frosty October morning greeted him when he awakened. Hungry, he emerged from the yaupon bush but could see no food. He shivered in the cold air and wrapped his wings around his body as much as possible to conserve heat. He cried out in desperation, "*Grlc-grlc, grlc-grlc!*" just as a frightened chick might have done when he couldn't find his mommy.

Much to his surprise, Terry heard a soft "*Grlck, grlck*" in response. He thought he must be dreaming, when he saw a turkey hen resembling those at Farmer Choans' place.

The two turkeys introduced themselves. "My name is Henny," said the kind hen who had appeared from nowhere. Actually, she had come to the yaupon bush to grab a few berries for breakfast.

Terry said his name and explained how he became isolated deep in the woods.

Henny exclaimed, "You came from the same place I did! I was dumped into the woods last year because I had not gained enough weight. I was almost dead when a kind wild turkey hen showed me how to find food. She also helped me join the wild turkey flock and convinced the chief turkey not to run me off. I've become fully accepted; maybe we can do the same for you."

"Great," Terry replied, "but I'm starving. Can you show me what to eat?"

"It's right in front of your face," she answered and started pecking at the red berries.

Terry took the cue. Those berries tasted funny, but they did make his craw feel better.

"Okay, that's just a good starter," Henny said, "let's look for some really good stuff."

She scratched around some leaves and found several grub worms. She ate one of the wiggly white worms, because she was pretty hungry too after the cold night. She offered one to Terry, who looked at it disgustingly.

"You don't expect me to eat that repulsive thing, do you?" he inquired of his gracious hostess.

"Terry, you must eat these—all of them. They are good turkey food and they will certainly help put some fat back on your miserable bag of bones!"

The apprehensive fowl tentatively picked up a wriggling worm and forced it down in one gulp. *That wasn't too bad,* he thought, and happily ate the rest of the grubs.

Henny also taught him to find insects and warned him about stink bugs— she pointed out one of the obnoxious smelling insects. Her next lesson was berries. She explained which berries were good to eat and which were bad for turkeys. She told him about seeds, which were plentiful in the clearings. "But turkeys must be careful in the clearings," she explained, "because of hungry foxes or hawks."

Fortified with food, Terry was ready for the next event in his forest education—joining a wild turkey flock. Henny explained wild turkey culture. "Normally, the dominant male, chief turkey, chases a wayward male turkey from the flock. The unattached male has to form his own flock by stealing hens from other flocks—a tough problem for the uninitiated."

Terry doubted he could steal any hens.

"Go hide in the yaupon bush," Henny commanded, "and I mean don't budge. Don't even move a feather! I'll talk to the chief turkey and try to make a special case for you. I'll get you when it's okay."

Henny sought out the chief, who was briefly snoozing after his breakfast. "Oh, Chief Turkey," she implored, "I need your help. The turkey farm has dumped a nice male turkey. He doesn't know anything about living in the forest; he's just like I was last year. You know I turned out okay, and I think he will, too. Please help us!"

The chief stretched, yawned, and replied, "I'm the chief turkey around here. We don't need any more male turkeys. Let the young lad find his own way!"

Henny gently went over to the chief, schmoozed him a little, and cooed, "You know, I've been a real good turkey hen!"

The chief reluctantly said, "Okay, we'll let him stay awhile. Bring him right to me so I can explain a few things to him."

Terry arrived in front of the chief, anxiously deferential to the established pecking order. The chief carefully explained how things worked in the turkey world, told him about the Chief Turkey system, and made it clear that Terry could stay only if he didn't try to become the chief. "Otherwise, I'll run you straight out of the woods."

Amazingly, things worked out very well. The other turkeys welcomed Terry and he did more than his share of gathering food for the flock.

Unseen by the turkeys, a storm was brewing in the direction of the Choans farm. Farmer Choans relaxed a few days before Thanksgiving, since all turkeys had been delivered to market. This year, he wanted to hunt wild turkey. Paul said he was sick and didn't want to go. (He was sick at the thought of harming his turkey friends.) Armed with his .410 shotgun, Mr. Choans and Paul's older brother, Joe, set out for the woods, joined by their good-for-nothing mutt, Rip.

The turkey flock moved to the little clearing on this cold and sunny day, full of berries, but now hungry for seeds. The chief bravely walked out into the clearing to check for predators before the hens came out. He strutted around, his chest thrust forward, the orange and red wattle on his throat puffed out to its fullest, his deadly spurs pointed upward. He looked like a one-man army marching on the parade ground.

Some distance away, Pop squinted through his binoculars, watching this amazing display. "Okay," he said softly to his son, "that guy's strutting his stuff for the ladies. We're going to have us some wild turkey gobbler for Thanksgiving this year!"

Terry was watching the chief as well. He was much more forest-wise now, so he also scanned the horizon for trouble. And found it. He saw the glint of sunlight on Mr. Choans' shotgun, as he was raising it to fire. Terry ran out into the clearing, flapping his wings, and making strange gobbling noises—sounding the alarm. The chief mistakenly thought the farm bird was staging a poultry *coup d'etat*, and turned to fight him. But Terry threw himself into the air and knocked the chief away, just as Mr. Choans pulled the trigger. The loud boom that followed panicked the turkeys into a desperate race for the safety of the woods.

Everyone was present when the flock gathered again—none of them was injured. One pellet knocked out a few tail feathers of the brave bird Terry. There were plenty of worried gobbles before the tormented turkeys could find their *grlck* tongues again.

Terry came right up to the ruffled but untouched chief and squatted before him in deference; he wanted the leader to know he had no ambitions. The chief stood tall, emitted a few unintelligible gobbles to warm up his vocal chords, and then announced, "Hail to the brave Terry. He is now an official member of the flock! What do you say about that, Terry?"

Terry said humbly, "I am honored to be a member of such a well-led flock." Then he proposed the flock should gather up berries, seeds, and grubs for its own Thanksgiving dinner. "Let us give thanks for surviving the shooting. And let us honor those turkeys at the farm, who gave the ultimate sacrifice for people's Thanksgiving."

Thus started a tradition lasting for many a turkey year.

In Paul's own words, "Well, that's about it from the turkey farm. *Gobble, gobble, grlcky?*"

Translation: You don't really believe this, do you?

# Strained Measurement

*A hardware store clerk deals with a Czech lady's*
*reluctance to speak English.*

During my high school years, I spent Saturdays and summer vacations working at the Vanek Hardware Store. The store, situated just off Hallettsville's courthouse square, attracted a lot of walk-by visitors and walk-in customers. At that time, the square was a much more bustling commercial district than it is now. Alois Vanek, the owner, was an affable, stocky fellow of Czech ancestry, whose slightly rounded face flashed a big warm grin at the slightest opportunity.

This was a Norman Rockwell type of hardware store. We sold nails by the pound out of large wooden kegs. Rolls of fencing and chicken wire framed the plate glass show windows, partly hiding their amateurishly arranged displays. We stacked items in the windows according to the season, and I dusted it on Saturdays.

Shipping boxes were stacked haphazardly throughout the store. Sometimes, the merchandise within corresponded to the label on the box, but often, the contents were randomly chosen. If we needed to put something away, and it fit in a convenient box, then that's where it went. Some of the regular customers amused themselves by challenging Al to find a certain item. Al would assure the customer he had the item in stock, and then smile victoriously after going unerringly to a battered box in the corner and pulling out the merchandise. After a couple of years, I could do that, too, but the customers thought it was more fun to challenge Al.

My duties were to sweep out the relatively small box-free area of the store's concrete floor, sweep the sidewalk and entrance areas, and help customers. I cut and threaded water pipes, loaded barbed-wire and heavy-duty fencing, unloaded shipments from the hardware wholesalers, and waited on customers—those customers who would allow me to serve them.

Although Al's first language was Czech, he spoke English very well, with the slightly clipped Czech accent so typical of many Lavaca County residents of that time. Of course, many of the store's clients were of Czech heritage and still spoke the language. Lots of Czech got spoken in the Vanek Hardware Store! There were even some Anglos who knew a few words and enjoyed bamboozling me with a request. I never got much beyond *jak se mas* (how are you) and a few numbers.

A cadre of hard-core Czech speakers insisted that only Al should serve them. They just brushed past me when I came over to help them. Instead, they went straight to Al, even if he was busy with another customer. He would turn with a big smile, say something reassuring to them in Czech, and continue with the customer in front of him.

I felt so helpless and inadequate about this, until I finally understood what was going on. I came to realize they probably just wanted something simple, like a few lag screws or stove pipe joints, and they could have related their needs to me in English. This was not the quick-turnaround commerce of today; these customers wanted more for their hard-won dollars than some pieces of hardware. They wanted to share a few pleasantries, talk about the weather, and engage in a little human discourse to break the isolation of living on the farm and dealing with farm animals. And they could do this most easily in their mother tongue.

I remember one little old lady who often rebuffed my attempts to serve her. She was short and small-framed, wore narrow metal-rimmed eyeglasses, and had some streaks of gray in her sternly coiffed brown hair. Once, the indomitable lady came in during Al's noon-time dinner break. She looked all around the store before realizing that this time, she had to deal with me.

I approached her and politely inquired in my best retail style, "May I help you, ma'am?"

She stared at me suspiciously, and then stated in perfectly understandable English, "I need chicken wire. Three feet high."

After reflecting on her good use of English, I asked her to clarify what she needed, "Do you want two-inch mesh or one-inch mesh?"

She pondered my question awhile, and then wisely said, "Show me!"

I grabbed a pair of wire snips from behind the counter and escorted the lady outside, where the chicken wire rolls stood against the show windows. I showed her the difference between the two mesh sizes.

She pointed to the one-inch mesh and said, "That's what I want!"

When I asked her how much she wanted, she replied, "I need 30 feet!"

I placed the free end of the roll carefully at the edge of the sidewalk in front of the store and set a couple of bricks on the wire to keep it from rolling up behind me. Then I unrolled the wire for the entire length of our sidewalk, which was exactly 25 feet and two inches, and extended the wire onto the next merchant's sidewalk for an estimated five feet more. I added an extra two feet for lagniappe. I placed two more bricks on the rolled-out wire, reached for my snips, and cut the wire.

"Wait!" the lady called, "You didn't even measure that. Where's your yardstick?"

I carefully explained how I measured the wire, relative to the length of the sidewalk. But she was completely unsatisfied with my explanation and demanded, "I need exactly 30 feet. Get a yardstick and measure it!"

Exasperated, I retrieved the yardstick from within the store and painstakingly measured the unrolled chicken wire, making sure she could see what I was doing. When the yardstick came to the 30 feet demanded, I cut off about 20 inches of excess wire. I thought I had added 24 inches, but that's what lagniappe is all about.

The lady was wordless about what I had done, but she knew she was getting the exact amount of wire for which she paid.

About two weeks later, she came in when Al had gone to the bank. Again, she said to me, "I need some more chicken wire. This time, 60 feet."

I went through my usual wire measuring routine and rolled out her 60 feet, according to the sidewalk. I added another two feet of lagniappe and cut the wire.

She didn't say a word. When we completed the transaction, she smiled and said, "Thanks!"

She knew she was getting something extra, and that was important to her.

Both of us had learned to respect each other. I had gained more of an understanding about the way she was thinking, and she had learned she could trust me. This little lady came into the store many times after that. She would walk over to Al when he was not busy, but she readily let me serve her when he was.

Amazingly, I even succeeded in making a little small talk with her, although that was not my strong suit! She was happy to talk with me—after I inquired about her chickens.

# Improbable Love

*Two strange lovebirds help retell one of the world's oldest stories, in
a way to mist your eyes.*

The farmstead almost smiled with productivity under powder puff clouds and bright blue skies. Golden grain heads undulated in the fields, gently caressed by a southerly breeze. Ripening tomatoes were blushing, flattered by the solar limelight. The second crop of butter beans was bursting its pods, building up to the late-summer completion of a great growing season.

Even the cows seemed contented on this glorious bright day, calmly chewing their cuds as they rested under the welcome shade of a group of maple trees in the pasture. Their bellies were just beginning to bulge with the anticipation of spring calving season.

Farmer Choans stood on the back porch, surveying his agricultural fiefdom and admiring the promising yield of his labor and investment. He sipped from his after-lunch coffee, turned toward his wife and said, "What a wonderful year we've had! It seems like every crop we planted was successful. We didn't have any long dry spells, and the summer temperatures were mercifully mild. We're probably going to make good money this year!"

Mrs. Choans agreed with their current good fortune, then demurred, "But we've got to find a way to earn even more. Paul is off to college in three years, and tuition and costs keep rising, even at State University." She took time to enjoy a sip of her coffee, and then continued, "Have you thought any more about that poultry change we discussed? Which way do you think we should go?"

He paused for a long time, as if he were still struggling with the pros and cons of the pending decision. Finally, he answered, "No, but I'm getting close. I've been talking with some of the other farmers."

All the barnyard mammals seemed content on this lazy sunny day. Old Rip, the farm's mongrel pooch, was stretched out in disgusting comfort at the other end of the porch. He got his name because of his propensity for spaced-out sleep.

But it was an entirely different matter for the feathered inhabitants of the barnyard. An undercurrent of angst pulsed through the two barnyard flocks: the chickens and turkeys. For many years, Farmer Choans raised both types of fowl: Rhode Island reds and domestic black turkeys. He liked working with both types of birds and had learned to interact with the flighty creatures fairly well. This was a small-scale operation that produced both eggs and fowl for the market.

Farmer Choans had built a strongly fenced enclosure and let the birds wander freely, so they could graze on grass and weeds, scratch for grubs, and forage for insects. He clipped their wings so they couldn't fly over the fence. The chickens and turkeys somewhat amicably shared the same space but kept to their own flocks. Of course, he fed them proper chicken and turkey rations, but he felt that free-range birds were likely to be happier and more productive. The respective flocks had their own houses within the enclosure.

Old Rip spent nights in the enclosure, where he had his own shelter. He was gentle and protective with the birds; no snake, fox, skunk, raccoon, or possum was going to ravage his flock. The docile sleeping dog of the day turned into a caring werewolf of the night.

So why should there be worry and discontent among the chickens and turkeys? A few weeks ago, several new hens arrived in the flock. Farmer Choans had bought them from a neighboring chicken farm to provide a little genetic diversity.

At first, the new hens huddled together, afraid of the discrimination and harsh treatment meted out by the established leaders of the flock. To ease their fear, they talked of the differences between their new barnyard and their old chicken house. One of them asked, "What's with all these turkeys? Why do we have to live with them?"

A brash young hen clucked loudly in response, "We can't live with those ugly birds. Farmer Brown raised only chickens and kept us all in one big house. I bet this new guy is going to choose between us chickens and those stupid turkeys. I hope he chooses chickens!"

Some of the surrounding chickens overheard this idle chatter, and started clucking among themselves. Just as in the human world, rumors among chickens can get distorted. Pretty soon, some chickens were clucking loudly and confidently to their cousins, "Farmer Choans is going to get rid of chickens and only keep turkeys!"

By the opposite fence, another group of chickens were also clucking to each other, confidently. "Farmer Choans is going to get rid of turkeys and only keep chickens!"

Little did they know that Farmer Choans was indeed about to make such a move.

Good rumors don't die quietly, and soon the turkeys had picked up on the ominous news. The turkeys became agitated that Farmer Choans could even think of getting rid of them, and they plotted to do something about this.

In a few days, a type of gang warfare had broken out: the Reds against the Blacks. The chickens invaded the turkey feeding area and scratched the feed out of the troughs. The turkeys came over to the chicken area and defecated into the watering troughs. This went on for a few days until both sides agreed to an uneasy truce. There would be no more hostile activity, but the days of friendly coexistence were gone. Each group looked down coldly at the other group, internally seething with the desire to see the other group exiled. There would be no further gossipy confabs between the handful of bilingual chickens and turkeys.

Chelsea Chicken was a bright spot in the disconsolate array of chickens in the Choans' flock. She was a lovely young pullet, with graceful brown legs, whose feathers were a gorgeous brownish red. She enhanced her physical assets with a delightfully friendly, perhaps too innocent, disposition. She stood by the fence, looked out at the world beyond the enclosure, and thought dreamily about the previous evening. She couldn't stand to huddle with the rest of the hens that were so down in the beak with gloom and doom. *And that nasty old rooster—yuck!*

That pompous old bird! He thought he was God's gift to henhood, as he fluffed his feathers and proudly plumped out his chest. He seemed the fool as he spread his tail feathers like a paltry peacock. His feet were encrusted with days-old poultry excrement. *Doesn't he know anything about personal hygiene?* she wondered. Chelsea almost gagged as she recalled the moment he came over and tried to nuzzle her neck. *Ugh, he had the breath of a swamp alligator.* When she flinched from his advance, the rooster strutted confidently away, giving her a "you'll-do-just-fine" glance.

Chelsea thought fondly of her clandestine meeting with Truman last night. Truman Turkey was a dashing young turkey tom—strong, muscular, and nice to a fault. His feathers were always neatly preened—and his feet were clean! Of course, Truman had to be careful how he acted among the turkeys, for he was a long way from being top turkey. Truman kept his natural aggression in check and either acquiesced to the demands of the turkey hierarchy or went off to be by himself. Mostly, he chose the latter, and that's how he had noticed Chelsea, who was standing by herself.

Truman thought she was the loveliest female he had ever seen, and didn't care that she wasn't a turkey. He was besot by her beauty and dreamed of making her acquaintance. Finally, he summoned enough courage to walk over to her and make small talk. He hoped she was bilingual, as he was. He tried in vain to compose an opening line, but just blurted out in fairly fluent chicken, "What would you say if I told you I'm a bashful turkey tom?"

Chelsea was silent as she appraised the interloper. *What a gorgeous hunk!* she thought to herself, shuddering as she recalled her encounter with the rooster.

She responded in flawless turkey, "I'm a little bashful, myself. I'm so pleased you were not too bashful to ask!"

With the ice broken on the poultry social scene, the two young birds chatted happily about many ideas they shared, switching often between chicken and turkey. They also talked about the regrettable feelings currently alienating the turkey and chicken flocks. They glanced furtively back toward their respective flocks, and each noticed a few stares of disapproval from their peers.

Before parting, Chelsea suggested impishly, "Why don't we sneak out of the houses tonight and meet here again, by the fence?"

"Great idea," agreed Truman, "I'll find a way to sneak out."

They met clandestinely for several nights, and their conversations progressed from casual to personal to intimate. One night, Truman intertwined one of his wings with hers and started nuzzling her neck, muttering how much he loved her. Chelsea responded warmly to his advances, knowing in her heart how much she loved this sensitive and bashful fellow. She responded breathlessly, "I love you, too, Truman!"

Old Rip had been watching the two from a distance, during each of their nocturnal meetings. His job was to guard the poultry houses against dangerous intruders, and he wanted to be sure nothing bad happened when these birds were outside their houses at night—although they shouldn't be outside. Usually, they didn't meet for long and quickly returned to their houses. Rip was concerned but relieved that he didn't have to act.

But this particular night, Rip was worried that things were getting out of hand. The two birds had morphed into one as they embraced. If poultry had sweat glands, they would be dripping wet by now. So Rip loped over toward the fence, making himself abundantly evident, and then casually lifted a leg against the fence post. The young lovers looked over at him, embarrassed, and started rearranging their feathers. Rip calmly ushered them toward their houses.

Rip was not the only one watching the clandestine meetings. Even in the poultry world, there is always a "big sister," keeping an eye on wrongdoers, listening to furtive words. The earlier meetings caused twittering in both houses about the scandal unfolding beneath their beaks. In each house, there was the same refrain: "This is not right. Chickens cannot love turkeys. We've got to stop this before both our houses are put to shame!"

Chelsea was almost floating on a cloud as she entered the chicken house. "I'm in love!" she happily sang out for all to hear. "I love Truman, and I want to marry him. I want to spend the rest of my life with him. I don't care if he's a turkey!"

The hens gathered around the truant young chicken; they shook their heads in dismay and cluck-clucked at the radical suggestion professed by the starry-eyed pullet. The distraught hens chanted in unison: "No, no, never! Chickens and turkeys cannot marry, ever! No, no, never!"

The top hen looked over at the rooster, who simply shook his head in disgust. She huddled with some of her top lieutenants to discuss what to do. One ambitious hothead shouted, "We must kill the traitor! Peck her, peck her!"

But calmer heads prevailed, and the senior hens decided the errant pullet must be watched throughout the night. They organized a monitoring roster and then informed Chelsea of her fate. "You will not marry Truman Turkey," the top hen notified her, "that is impossible. We forbid you to see him anymore. We are going to watch you carefully. You will not leave this hen house at night. Do you understand me?"

Chelsea just stood there, dumbfounded and broken-hearted by their stern decision. Her enthusiasm and joy of life leaked from her as if a gaping hole had been blown in her spirit. Never again would her spirits soar. Her wonder of the miracle of life, and her aspirations to be lifted above the humdrum existence of the chicken pen were dashed. She stood there, deflated, speechless. Her silence was *de facto* acknowledgement of the sentence served upon her.

Meanwhile, in the turkey house, the same sad story was unfolding. "How could you do such a thing?" the turkey hens asked poor Truman, "Turkey toms must love turkey hens. You've shamed all of us! How do you think a self-respecting turkey hen could ever respond to you now that you have shamed our entire flock by commingling with a common chicken?"

Truman, too, was at a loss for words. He slumped dejectedly in front of the flock, waiting for more abuse to be heaped upon him. He knew he should protest and pronounce his love for Chelsea to all of them, but he also knew this would be hopeless.

The turkey hens stepped aside as the top tom strode purposefully up to the hapless Truman. He stretched to his maximum height, fluffed his feathers to look as big and mean as possible, and then stuck his beak in Truman's face. "You shameful turkey; you're a disgrace to our flock!"

Then he slashed at the disgraced young swain with his spurs, purposefully not wielding mortal blows, but singularly tearing enough feathers to leave a clear message. The top tom snarled, "This thrashing is only a warning of what will happen if you continue to see that chicken hussy. You are now at the bottom of the pecking order, and you might not get any higher. If you as much as talk to that chicken again, I'll tear your heart out instead of your feathers!"

A veneer of calm covered up the anxiety in the enclosure for the next few days, but a palpable tension pervaded its inhabitants. Neither Chelsea nor Truman tried to leave their houses at night, but they could not have done so even if they tried. Both young lovers moped through the days, idly pecking at things, although they had no appetite. They were dejected. Defeated.

Occasionally, one would cast a glance at the opposite flock, spot its forbidden love, and lock eyes with its paramour. In those moments, their spirits soared, but then flagged again when they noticed the other birds giving them the evil eye.

Suddenly, a shadow swooshed in a great arc across the ground in the enclosure. Instinct sent the birds scurrying for the shelter of their respective houses. They knew a ravenous raptor was in the vicinity and an attack was imminent. If Farmer Choans had looked up, he would have spotted the big hawk as it circled above the poultry enclosure—a big red-tailed hawk. But Farmer Choans was out in one of the pastures, cutting hay. Old Rip was on the porch, cutting Zs.

All the birds ran pell-mell for shelter, except one. Truman just stood there, looking forlornly over at the chicken house. The turkeys peered through the openings of their house, amazed at the stupidity of this turkey who wouldn't run, open-beaked, but speechless at what was about to happen.

The chickens looked out of their house, equally amazed at the scene before them. Chelsea ran to the door opening and screamed in clear turkey at the top of her chicken voice, "Run Truman! Run for your life! Get away from the hawk!" She tried to run out the door to help him, but the hens held her back.

Frightened birds looked on with saucer eyes as the big hawk swooped silently out of the sky, sunk its sharp talons into the forsaken bird, and flapped its wings mightily to lift its heavy prey slowly, but surely, heavenward. Chelsea looked upward, and her keen young eyes spotted what she longed to know: Truman had no fear on his face as he looked back toward the chicken house and Chelsea—there was only relief.

Truly, Truman had had no life to run for. And Chelsea now knew that she, too, had none.

Old Rip came running and barking as soon as he heard the commotion in the poultry enclosure. He knew he was too late when he saw the turkey being carried away. So he sat awhile by the fence, looking in, hoping his presence would give some comfort to the birds. The chickens and turkeys filtered slowly back onto the enclosure ground. One by one, they started pecking and scratching at things and began normal feeding activities. Nature, in its benign way, began to heal over the pain of life.

Chelsea was the last to leave the chicken house. She remained behind, thinking of the glorious times she had shared with Truman and of what could have been. She choked up a bit with the little moans and grunts that pass for sobs in the chicken world. Then she cleared her mind and went out the door with a determined stride.

She headed straight for the fence and started scratching at the dirt beneath it. The other hens were unmindful of what she was doing, either out of the numbness of fear or of the joy of eating. The rooster saw what she was doing, but he didn't care.

Old Rip had resumed his nap on the porch.

It didn't take long for Chelsea to dig out enough dirt. She wriggled through the small opening and stretched her wings with her new-found freedom. She set out through the front pasture, avoiding the cows, and especially the cow piles. She ignored some tempting bugs; she had no need for that now.

Soon, she arrived at the road and waited patiently by the side. When she heard a car approach, she waited for the right moment and dashed onto the road. She ignored the blaring horn and screeching brakes, inwardly smiling at the prospect of rejoining her lover.

The unfortunate driver frantically braked and swerved, doing everything he could to avoid disaster. But he was rewarded only with a sickening thud.

And now, dear reader, I implore you to consider: The next time you see a chicken by the road, it might have a good reason for crossing over to the other side.

# Shucking Pecans

*A teenaged lad finds something weird while cracking pecans and
comes to grips with what it means.*

"**H**ere's another one!" the teenaged boy declared. "Just like the one I found yesterday." The lad brushed fibrous material away from the object and held it up between his forefinger and thumb to inspect it more closely.

A blackish powder stubbornly clung to the almost spherical object. Working in stages, he cleaned the object with a paper towel. Slowly, the features of the spheroid emerged: jet-black portions contrasted with bright white, interlaced by small daggers of multi-shaded gray. When he turned it in the sunlight, the thing sparkled vividly. *Just like yesterday,* he thought.

Paul Choans paused to admire his scintillating new bauble, which shimmered in the sunlight with its iridescent variations on black and white. Its diameter was not quite a quarter inch. Paul squeezed the object tightly between the tips of his fingernails and found it rock hard.

Puzzled, Paul wondered, *What's this doing in a pecan?* He shrugged and placed the curio in his jacket pocket to join the mysterious object he had found yesterday. He zipped the jacket pocket shut to keep his little treasures secure. They would become very dear to him, like the agates he occasionally found for his marble collection. But something tugged at his inner being, *I wonder if these lustrous curios might be valuable?*

The tall, skinny high school junior was a serious-minded student, a football and baseball player, and a genuinely nice kid; he was well-liked at school and in the community. He reliably accomplished his chores around the farm.

Paul bent over to resume cracking pecans; he had a lot more to crack, since the trees were loaded this year. Five huge pecan trees, bearing different nut varieties, grew in the fenced-in yard of the Choans' farmhouse. The pecans in Paul's bucket were from the "special" tree—the smallest of the five. Its bark looked more like an oak than a pecan.

Strangely, the special tree's pecans this year were different—abnormal. The nuts were irregular in size, and the shells were much thicker and harder. The feed store's machine cracker did not handle irregular nuts well, so Paul had to crack them manually with an antique lever-operated cracker.

Paul could sense when a nut was bad: the crunching sound was different, and the cracker's lever jumped forward much too quickly. Paul checked the cracked nut pan when he suspected a bad nut. He gingerly picked up any moldy, black pieces and threw them away.

On his first discovery of these strange objects, Paul had almost tossed out the bad nut before he noticed something different: instead of an oblong mass, this one was round. Also, he had seen a glint from the object. Curious, he cleared off some of the black material with a stick, revealing the dust-covered sphere. Paul had seen many variations in the contents of a nut. But this round, black mass was way beyond anything he had ever seen in his short life.

Paul was almost finished with his bucket of pecans when his mom called for lunch. At the table, she asked, "You seemed very preoccupied with something when I looked out the window. You kept holding it up, like examining it. Did you see the face of the Virgin Mary on a pecan or something?"

Paul wanted to keep his discoveries a secret for now, so he simply replied, "Nah, just a bad pecan. But it was perfectly shaped and glossy black. Strangely beautiful."

After lunch, Paul refilled his bucket with the same type of pecans and cracked them with renewed fervor. Sharp-pointed shell fragments flew in all directions as pecans exploded under the cracker's impact. Some bounded off Paul's face, leaving faint pinpricks of pain. He encountered dozens of bad pecans and thoroughly examined each one. All were oblong and worthy only for the trash pile. Discouraged, Paul began to feel his earlier finds had been nothing more than flukes.

As November progressed, successive waves of blue northers and cold fronts roared down from Canada. Gusty winds buffeted the Choans' farmstead and brought down a hail of pecans, along with pieces of the pecan trees: brackets of leaves, twigs, and small limbs. When the wind abated, Paul concentrated on picking up the nuts from his special tree. This exasperated his mom.

"Pick up the pecans from the other trees so we can get them machine cracked," she yelled.

Paul worked hard after school and on weekends, cracking these special nuts. He lucked out on his first bucket and found another pretty bauble, which encouraged him to work even more intensely. By the Thanksgiving holiday, he had accumulated six little treasures. He kept them in a small cloth sack, closed by a drawstring, stashed safely in his jacket pocket.

When his older brother, Joe, came home for the holiday, Paul showed him the contents of the bag and explained how he found them.

"Wow! Terrific! I never saw anything so pretty," Joe exclaimed.

"Wonder what these are?" Paul queried.

"Could be some kinda pearl," Joe surmised, "but from a pecan tree?"

"I thought pearls came from oysters."

After consulting the Internet, both were confused; indeed, pearls—natural and cultured—were produced only by oysters. "Pearls are formed from the mother of pearl lining of the oyster shell, so how could a pecan tree do that from the brown, craggy interior of its shell?" Joe wondered out loud.

The brothers cracked the remainder of the special pecans during the holiday weekend. Eleven of the little black objects rested in the bag.

Joe suggested, "Why don't you take these to the Herzog jewelry store. Maybe they will know what these are."

Paul added, "While I'm there, I think I'll ask if they can make a nice necklace. These are so pretty and would make a great Christmas gift for Mom. Wanna share the cost?"

"Deal!"

Paul stood hesitantly by the door of Herzog Jewelry, looking at the wondrous items on display within and wondering how he should handle this transaction. He entered the store and immediately recognized David Herzog, the father of one of his football teammates.

"Hey, Paul," David greeted. "Are you ready to do a little early Christmas shopping?"

"Kinda."

Paul pulled the bag of treasures from his jacket and haltingly continued, "I, uh, don't know how to start. I've got these pretty little stones, which oughta make a nice necklace for my mom. Can y'all make one here?"

David glimpsed into the proffered bag and drew back in amazement. He had never seen anything like these lustrous pearl-like stones.

"That's not part of my current expertise," he responded, "I took over the store, but my father keeps an office and workshop in the back. He handles special projects like this. Come on." He ushered Paul into his father's office.

Abe Herzog sat at his desk with some gems and jewelry parts spread out before him. Paul thought his tousled gray hair made him look a little like Einstein.

"Father, this is Paul Choans, a friend and teammate of David Jr. He has some very interesting gemstones and hopes you can make a necklace for his mother." The younger Herzog withdrew from the office.

The elder Herzog rose and extended his hand. The slightly stooped man spoke first, "Glad to meet you, young man. Let's see what you have in that bag."

Mr. Herzog cleared his desk and Paul carefully laid out the black and white objects.

Mr. Herzog sat to examine the objects more thoroughly. He pulled over a jeweler's microscope, peered at each of the stones, and then rubbed two of them together to feel any sensations caused by their surfaces.

He rose and almost shouted, "These are the most wonderful, beautiful, lustrous black pearls I have ever seen! These are real pearls—not imitation. Where did you get them?"

Paul squirmed a bit, not knowing how to answer this unexpected curve ball. But the confirmation that these were indeed pearls gave him a clue.

Obviously nervous, Paul shuffled his feet and stammered, "I…I found them in…oysters…we…collected in Matagorda Bay."

Mr. Herzog reflected on this for a long time. He knew the boy was hiding something—not telling the truth. The facts conflicted with the young lad's tale. He went through a mental checklist: *natural pearls are extremely rare, black pearls even rarer, black pearls don't occur in Texas waters, one has to dive or dredge to get oysters…did the boy steal these pearls?*

Finally, Mr. Herzog told Paul, "I need some time to plan your mother's necklace. Can you leave them here? I will call you when I have a plan and we can discuss it."

"That's fine. I hope it works out great!" Paul responded, and left the office.

Mr. Herzog returned the pearls to the cloth bag, attached a label, and placed the bag in his office safe. Then he picked up the phone.

The black-and-white pulled into the high school visitors' lot. Sgt. Connors walked to the principal's office, a trip he had made many times. "Howdy, Sam," he greeted as he strode into the office.

"What brings you here?" the principal asked.

"I need to interview Paul Choans about something; can you call him to the office?"

A few minutes later, the principal ushered Paul into the private cubbyhole reserved for such occasions. "Hi, Paul," the sergeant greeted, "Sorry to bother you, but I've got a few questions."

Paul froze a moment, then tentatively relaxed. He knew he had lied to Mr. Herzog about the pearls and feared he might have to reveal the almost magical power of his special pecan tree.

"Did you show Abe Herzog a bag of eleven black pearls?"

Paul nodded affirmatively.

"Did you steal these pearls?"

Paul emphatically shouted, "No!"

"Then you've got a lot of explaining to do!"

Paul took a deep breath, and then another to steady his nerves. He knew the jig was up. Paul described the special pecan tree—how different it was from the others. He told of his first discovery, and how he went on to find more—and more.

Dumbfounded, Sgt. Connors said, "This is totally unbelievable. The only way for me, or anyone else, to believe you is to see such a discovery in person! Why don't you and I go out to your farm so you can show me this in person?"

Mrs. Choans was worried sick when she saw the police car pull up with Paul in tow. Sgt. Connors explained the situation, but the mother was of little help; she was as much in the dark as the officer.

She angrily complained to the sergeant, "Why didn't Mr. Herzog call me instead of the police?"

Chagrined that he had misled his mother, Paul blurted, "It's okay, Mom. I shoulda told you about the pearls, but Joe and I wanted to make a necklace for you as a surprise gift."

Fortunately, Paul had some special pecans for his demonstration. A howling blue norther had blown in last night and dislodged a horde of pecans—hangers-on that had finally relaxed their grip after stubbornly resisting the forces of nature. Mrs. Choans had already picked up a grocery bag full for Paul to crack after school.

Thinking of his defense, Paul said to Sgt. Connors, "For my sake, it's important that you take pictures of anything I find!"

Paul started cracking and soon encountered a bad pecan—a black, oblong mass. He explained why he was tossing the black nut into the trash. He found many more bad pecans as he worked his way through the grocery bag—all duds. He kept working until only a few pecans remained. Beads of sweat formed on his brow, even on this chilly day, exposing his anxiety about going to jail.

The unusual crunch of the next nut elevated Paul's spirits. Indeed, when he retrieved the black mass he knew things were going to be okay—it was round.

"Bingo!" Paul exclaimed, holding up the round mass.

"That's no pearl," Sgt. Connors muttered, "that's just a black, moldy pieca junk!"

"Set your camera for video," Paul instructed, "and you and the rest of the world will see that what I said about the black pearls is the truth."

In utter amazement, Sgt. Connors recorded the unveiling of a black pearl.

"Mrs. Choans," he said, "you and Paul and I will take this video of the new pearl and show it to Abe Herzog."

Mr. Herzog was thunderstruck when he viewed the video and said excitedly, "Incredible! Did you actually witness this?" he asked Sgt. Connors. "I can't imagine how this could happen!"

"I saw the whole event, just like in the video. The boy cracked what looked to be a normal pecan and found a round, black thing inside. When he cleaned it off, there was a black pearl."

Sensing an opportunity, the old jeweler turned to Mrs. Choans and offered, "I never believed in magic, but this special tree of yours could be a big bonanza. Maybe we can cut a deal?"

"We will make no business deals," Mrs. Choans interjected, "but maybe we can cut a little side deal. Would you accept this new black pearl as payment for the necklace Joe and Paul want for me?"

"That's a deal!"

The deal makers shook hands and Sgt. Connors quietly left the room, thankful he didn't have to get into any nasty business with this good kid.

Mrs. Choans proudly wore her beautiful new necklace at the extended-family Christmas dinner. The kinfolk oohed and aahed about her spectacular neckpiece. Some asked in amazement how she could afford such beautiful pearls.

Mrs. Choans, wanting to keep the real source a secret, had a ready answer. "The necklace was a gift from Joe and Paul. Mr. Herzog gave the boys a special discount."

All the pecan trees leafed out in early April—and the trees were soon covered with blossoms. Having fulfilled their pollination mission, multitudinous limp tassels eventually fell, filling the gutters of nearby buildings. Every member of the Choans family was on tenterhooks, hoping the special tree would once again produce its miraculous bounty.

The trees produced tiny nutlets, most of which fell off shortly after their formation. Squirrels and crows devoured the few which survived, well before they had ripened. With pecans, a good production year is often followed by a bad one. There were no pecans to be gathered on the Choans' farm this year, and the family would have to wait until next year to see if the special tree would again bear the precious gems.

The next crop couldn't come fast enough for the Choans family. The following November, limbs on all the pecan trees were hanging low, laden by a heavy crop of pecans. Paul, in college now, scheduled a weekend at home early in the month, eager to test the new pecans from the special tree.

As he picked them up, he noticed the special tree's nuts resembled those from years ago—they were back to the normal, regular size. When he cracked the nuts, he found the shells were also back to normal—no longer thick and hard. He began to fear the special tree might not be so special now.

Paul cracked several buckets of pecans that weekend. As usual, he found many bad pecans, but all had the normal oblong, blackened mass inside.

Disappointed, the family decided on a better way to search for pearls. The parents separated the special tree's pecans from the others and had them machine cracked without air cleaning. The cracked pecans—good and bad—fell into the same bin.

The parents painstakingly examined each of the bad nuts among the cracked pecans. Each one was oblong shaped; none were round. The miracle had fizzled. There would be no riches harvested from the special tree.

Accepting reality, Mrs. Choans summed up their situation, "We are disappointed our special pecan tree didn't produce more pearls. We did nothing to cause this miracle, and we have no idea how or why it happened. But my beautiful necklace is reward enough!"

Afterward, the special pecan tree has had good and bad years, along with its four companions, although it continued to look a little different from the others.

Whenever Mrs. Choans wore her beautiful necklace, she would think about the mystery that surrounded that tree. *What caused it to produce a pearl instead of a pecan? Was this just a quirk of nature or was it a gift from the Creator? Will it happen again?*

Her questions were never answered.

*I must have hand-cracked a zillion pecans and discarded a barrel full of bad nuts. These were of multitudinous shapes, but I never encountered a round, mysterious one. But I still keep looking — and hoping!*

# Moving Target

*A TV ad gives a bashful young quarterback some much-needed help in making successful passes.*

Loud cheering was interspersed with Texas-style hooting and hollering on this pleasant, October Friday night. The hometown team had just made a first down, near the opponent's 20-yard line. A comeback was in the making; the local team had scored a touchdown on their last possession, and they were now driving forcefully toward the winning score. The Centerton High School Peacocks were only four points behind, and a win tonight would improve their season's record to fifty percent. But only 30 seconds remained on the clock.

"Go Peacocks!" the cheerleaders chanted as they fanned their faded and tattered feathers, "Go Peacocks!"

The quarterback deftly faked a handoff, completely fooling the hard-charging defense, and stepped back quickly with the ball. He looked to the left to confuse the pass defenders and then looked downfield toward the right, where he figured old Curly might be open. Curly Jones was a tall and strongly built senior with long straight hair that dangled beneath the edges of his shiny helmet. His glue-like hands could pull in all but the most errant of passes.

Curly had made a good move, and there was no defender within five yards. *Just get me the ball, and we've got this game won!* he silently implored of his quarterback.

Billy Joe Cunningham, the sophomore quarterback, spotted the wide open receiver and launched a beautiful spiral toward him. He knew that if Curly could catch this in stride, the game was won.

But the throw was behind Curly, and he had to stop and backtrack slightly. He vacuumed up the ball from the ether and pulled it to his side, as reliably as ever. However, the slight delay allowed the defensive back to catch up to Curly and tackle him hard, well short of the goal line.

Billy Joe rallied his team and moved the ball closer to the end zone, but time ran out before the Peacocks could score the winning touchdown.

The loss silenced the hometown crowd. Cheerleaders forlornly folded their fans and band members packed their instruments into their cases. The much smaller group on the visitor's side of the field chanted victoriously as they filed out of the stands.

Billy Joe bounced his helmet on the turf, totally dejected. They had played a good game tonight. He had played a good game, with one not-so-minor exception: he hadn't hit a running receiver all night. He had been perfect on those plays where the receiver went to or came back to a prearranged spot, but he hadn't hit a single moving target. And this failure had just cost them the game!

Coach Ernie Thompson came over to console the disappointed young warrior. He tousled the short stubble on Billy Joe's head and said, "You played a good game, Billy Joe! It's a shame you couldn't have the satisfaction of finishin' the comeback. But that's part of life's ups and downs—and what football is all about. Ah like the grit and determination you showed throughout the game."

Coach Thompson was a brute of a fellow, over six feet tall and well over 240 pounds. His massive body showed bulges where football players are supposed to have them, and a few where they shouldn't. Some of the muscle on his forty-five-year-old frame was turning to flab. His remaining hair showed hints of gray, and his suntanned scalp complemented his rounded face.

It wasn't always like this for Ernie Thompson. He had been a star defensive tackle for TCU, where he was known for his aggressive pass rushing. He had played at a very muscular 220 pounds, which was formidable in those days before massive "refrigerators" and "busses" started playing the game. His dense brown hair, combined with his angular face and good ol' boy smile, made him a very attractive fellow to the ladies. He was an East Texas boy straight out of the Piney

Woods country. He concentrated his academic career on football, majoring in physical education. Tutoring kept him academically eligible.

Coach Thompson ran the football program and taught Phys. Ed. in this small Central Texas rural town. He single-mindedly believed football was a strong factor in the development of young boys. He took pride in mentoring a group of unfocused and often scrawny kids, and poking, prodding, and otherwise propelling them toward manhood. Centerton High School was small enough that the coach had to compromise on the athletic skills of the boys chosen for the team. In fact, the team barely had enough players for a full scrimmage at practice sessions.

Billy Joe was not the coach's first choice for quarterback; he was the only choice. One other boy, Pete Besecny, took a few snaps at the position during each week's practice, in case Billy Joe was taken down hard. Pete was a very skilled defensive corner back; he was chosen as the backup quarterback mainly because he was smart enough to learn the plays rapidly.

Billy Joe was a lad of about five feet ten inches with a slight build. His sandy blonde hair would have been attractive had it not been cut short enough to satisfy a Marine drill sergeant. Alert blue eyes glistened with anticipation of whatever came next in the day's sequence of events. He might weigh in at 155 pounds on a good day at the gym; however, knobby knees, protruding elbows, and wiry muscles emphasized the inherent skinniness of his frame. A thin coating of peach fuzz on his chin and above his upper lip softened the angularity of his face. He was now having to shave a couple of times a week!

The disappointed young quarterback arrived morosely at the breakfast table Saturday morning, but his spirits turned upward as he chatted with his parents. His dad put in long hours at the local bank, and mom taught in elementary school, so they made sure weekend meals were family affairs. Because they strongly supported the intellectual development of their only child, along with his diverse outside activities, he was encouraged to express himself at the dinner table.

He and his dad worked all day in the yard on fall cleanup chores. Their conversation ranged from movies to football to his prospects for entering a good university.

Billy Joe was primarily a serious student, but athletics came in a strong second. In addition to football, he played on the baseball team, and ran track. At Centerton High School, one could participate in a variety of sports if he had just a modicum of hand-eye coordination. Billy Joe loved math and science, especially chemistry, and spent most of his spare time reading. He was pretty sure his career would involve medicine, especially medical research. First, he had to be accepted to a university with a good pre-med program; then he faced many years of hard work at med school and as an intern. He readied himself by hitting the books hard and keeping his eyes firmly on the goal.

The young lad was what the old folks called a "late bloomer." In fact, he had not yet blossomed at all. Billy Bob was not yet into girls, despite signs of emerging manhood: a rich, deep voice and nascent whiskers accompanied by a few pimples. Most of his classmates were dating now, and a few were even going steady. Instead, he focused on his books and his athletics.

Billy Joe was friendly with almost everyone, but he had no really close friends. He was good friends with some of the bright girls, but he was not even aware of them as girls. Billy Joe had not received the "call" yet; in fact, he probably wouldn't know what to say if the phone rang.

On Sunday morning, Billy Joe spiffed himself up and accompanied his parents to Sunday school and church. Centerton was one of those Bible-toting towns where everyone was expected to attend church.

During Sunday school, Billy Joe's attention wandered from the day's lesson—some nonsense about the problems plaguing the relationships between teenaged boys and girls. He didn't really understand what they were talking about. And he didn't want to say anything stupid, for fear the other kids might laugh at him again. Instead, his mind drifted back to Friday night's game, and how he kept missing those throws when the receivers were running fast routes. *Why couldn't I hit a moving target? Why couldn't I lead the receiver correctly, so the guy could catch the ball without breaking stride? There must be a better way to aim those passes!*

After Sunday dinner, the family retired to the den to watch the Dallas Cowboys. They cheered as the "Boys" made a big comeback in the second half.

Billy Joe's attention was riveted to a commercial that appeared twice during the game. He watched, engrossed, as an older guy, who looked like he could have been a quarterback at one time, threw a football through a tire swinging back and forth from a tree. That guy was hitting the moving target, time after time! The ad implied that initially, the man couldn't hit the side of a barn, but after he took those advertised pills, he couldn't miss the target.

The desperate young quarterback made a quick connection with his own problem and started to mention something to his parents. But he noticed they seemed to be a little embarrassed about this commercial—he didn't have a clue why, so he didn't say anything. But he did memorize the name of the pills.

Most TV viewers understood the graphic symbolism of this commercial, and how it referred to an embarrassing problem suffered by quite a few middle-aged and older men. Those who didn't get it were either clueless or innocent; the naïve young quarterback surely fell into the latter category. The lad had picked up the ABCs of the birds and bees pretty well but had not yet mastered the Ps and Qs.

Since Billy Joe had finished his homework on Saturday, he had Sunday evening free to search the Internet. He typed the pills' name into his favorite search engine and got pages of hits. Not knowing where to start, he simply clicked the first, which led him to an online pharmacy. He didn't realize it, but this site was listed first only because it had paid a hefty sum to the search engine site.

He avidly read the description of this drug and all its wonderful properties. This confused him, so he read it again. There was plenty of stuff about sexual problems and a suitcase full of potential side effects. The website clearly stated that the best performance would be achieved with two pills a day. He wondered why there was nothing about hitting moving targets. But there was a lot about improved performance.

He was about to flush the site and forget the whole thing when the image of that last botched pass Friday night flashed through his mind, followed quickly by the image of the old dude throwing the football through the swinging tire.

"I surely need improved performance," he muttered to himself. "Maybe I can take only one pill a day to avoid side effects." Then he started clicking through the pages for buying the stuff and filled out the simple form:

| | |
|---|---|
| Age: | 42 |
| Symptoms: | Can't perform |
| Credit Card No.: | 8888 9999 7777 6666 |
| Delivery: | Overnight |

He felt guilty for lying about his age and using the credit card his parents had given him, since he was home alone so often. He figured they probably wouldn't sell this stuff to a kid, so he had no choice about lying if he were ever going to get some help. Before he hit the "Buy" button, he heard his mother's voice in his head: "Don't use this card except in an emergency. If your allowance won't cover it, you don't need it!" He needed this.

It cost $30 extra for overnight delivery. Otherwise he must wait two weeks. Billy Joe figured this was part of the emergency, since the big game with their arch rivals, Dinwiddy, was next Friday night. He clicked the "Buy" button and anxiously awaited his performance-enhancing elixir.

Coach was pleased with how well Billy Joe threw the ball during practice as they got ready for the big game. He thought about opening up the game plan and going for some big plays. Billy Joe did have a strong arm, but he'd also had a season filled with missed throws—all susceptible to interception. Finally, he opted for a conservative game plan: relying on their defense.

The much anticipated Friday night finally arrived, and the Dinwiddy Dragons roared into town. A large complement of their boosters followed them and filled the visitor's stands. The local crowd was excited, and the larger hometown stands buzzed with animated chatter. There was a lot at stake tonight—primarily community pride. Although it had been a losing season, beating Dinwiddy would be enough to crown it a success.

The local cheerleaders yelled, "Demolish the Dragons! Demolish the Dragons!" as the local team ran onto the field, led by their captain, Curly Jones. The local crowd roared with anticipation. The visiting throng jeered, "Stomp Centerton! Stomp Centerton!"

Centerton's conservative game plan unfolded slowly, yard by begrudging yard, and produced one touchdown in the first half. Billy Joe threw mostly short spot passes, good for first downs. He also tossed two short passes in the flat to Curly, who ran at top speed and gained about twenty yards on each.

Unfortunately, their defensive game plan didn't follow suit, and Dinwiddy held a three touchdown lead at halftime. Coach Thompson built a fire under his defensive unit, and then he addressed the offense.

"We're changin' the game plan. We gotta get our offense goin', big time. We're gonna pass that ball all over the place! Are you ready, Billy Joe? You ready, Curly?"

The two players affirmed their readiness, and the rest of the team chimed in.

"Okay," Coach Thompson exhorted, "let's git out there and kick butt!"

The hometown crowd cheered as Centerton took the opening kickoff and started a long touchdown drive. Billy Joe threw three long passes, the last a thirty-yarder to Curly, which set up the score. The defense lived up to their promise and stopped the Dragons after three downs. Curly was also the kick return guy. He took the Dragons' punt, got some good blocking, faked a couple of Dragons almost out of their shoes, and ran it all the way for the second score. Centerton now needed one more touchdown to tie the game.

After the blitzkrieg by Centerton, the Dragons' defense dug in tenaciously. Neither offense could move the ball well. Centerton tried a long pass, but Billy Joe got sacked. They tried other long passes, but the receivers were covered, and Billy Joe had to scramble. The teams drove back and forth, with neither threatening to score, and there were only a few minutes left in the game.

The Dragons' punt ended up at Centerton's thirty-yard line. The Peacocks had to march seventy yards to tie the game. A running play gained five yards. Then, Billy Joe hit Curly on a running pattern for fifteen yards. Billy Joe passed with surgical precision on their march down the field, immensely pleasing his coach and the hometown crowd.

Finally, with only ten seconds on the game clock, Coach called another pass play: a post pattern. Curly streaked for the goalpost, with the defensive back right on his trailing shoulder and another back racing from the other side. The scenario was clear: if Billy Joe throws the football too far ahead or behind, it gets intercepted. If he throws it just a little behind, Curly will catch it but won't score and time will run out. Billy Joe saw that ball go through the tire as he carefully aimed the pigskin. It had to be absolutely right on, and by golly, that's how Billy Joe threw it. Curly fell forward across the goal line for the tying touchdown.

Coach Thompson had to make a decision: the game would be tied only if they successfully kicked the extra point. *What if we went for the two-point conversion and the win?* Coach Thompson mulled this question, and then signaled Curly to call a timeout. He beckoned his troops toward the sideline.

"Let's go for the two-pointer and not risk an overtime battle. We win if we succeed, lose if we fail. We'll use the special two-point play we practiced during the week. Think you can grab one, Curly?"

"You bet, Coach!" the team captain confidently responded.

Billy Joe faked the handoff and rolled to his right, waiting for Curly to clear the linebacker. A defensive back picked him up as he headed to the side of the end zone. A Dragon tackle had broken free of blockers and was heading straight for Billy Joe. The quarterback's brain automatically calculated how to lead Curly correctly, loft the ball over the defensive back, and still have room for the big receiver to catch it inbounds.

Billy Joe spiraled the ball goalward, just ahead of the charging tackle's grasp. He thought he saw the ball going straight through that tire, and he knew from the huge cheer in the hometown stands that Curly had pulled it in. Centerton had beaten the Dragons, 29 to 28, and their season was a success!

The two senior cheerleaders, both very pretty young ladies, ran to the game's hero, Curly, embraced him and kissed his sweaty cheeks. The proud young gladiator thoroughly savored his moment of adulation.

The two very cute sophomore cheerleaders came over to Billy Joe, smiling enticingly, and each grasped one of his arms to escort him off the field. The blushing quarterback almost flinched, fearing they might try to kiss him, too. Billy Joe didn't hear it, but his phone had just rung.

Coach Thompson watched all this and just shook his head in amazement.

At practice the next Monday, Coach beckoned Billy Joe for a private discussion. "Ah cain't believe how well you threw the ball last week! You been takin' some of those stee-roid pills or somethin'?"

Billy Joe's face belied his guilt, and he admitted, "Yes, but it's those pills that let you hit the swinging tire—you know, like you see on the TV ads."

The Coach slapped his thighs in disgust, "It sure worked good for you. Ah been takin' that stuff for three months, and Ah still cain't hit that damned tahre!"

# Ingeneous Mouse

*A laboratory mouse finds himself almost as smart as humans.*

I am going to tell you a story about one of the smartest little critters I ever knew. Mind you, I never saw him, but I really feel like I know him. We met on the Internet and quickly became cyber pals. His name is Soori, his fur is thick and pure white (so he tells me), and he says he is a "retired" laboratory mouse who works in his old research building on his own behalf. By now, you probably think I've been drinking too much Shiner beer, so let me tell you the full story.

You may recall a press announcement about the completion of a huge research project for mapping the human genome. A government contractor, Genformatics, Inc., worked over seven years and spent almost a billion dollars. Hundreds of scientists and research technicians labored mightily amid much doubt that anything useful would ever come of it.

Let's imagine we were at the Genformatics wrap-up meeting at their head-quarters in a Washington, D.C. suburb before the research results were released to the press. It is there that the assembled scientists, managers, and Department of Health officials have carefully crafted some appealing paragraphs about the direct benefits of the project. These benefits include isolation of rare diseases and development of their cures, prevention of birth defects, and development of safer and more effective vaccines. The laboratory director, anxious for a catchy news release to spark the public's imagination about the project might have said, "We found over thirty thousand genes, fewer than originally expected; maybe humans aren't so complex after all. Let's grab the public's attention—get them thinking, or even chuckling!"

"I've got it!" shouted a senior scientist. "Let's use the mouse analogy. Our parallel studies of laboratory mice identified just a few less genes for mice. In fact, humans have only 350 more genes than the lowly mouse."

The group liked this attention grabber. And sure enough, after the public announcement, the news media obliged with sensational coverage of this almost trivial point.

A few days after the press release, another group of concerned scientists gathered to assess the impact of the genome project's press release on their own research projects, but this group is in a run-down building in an industrial area near the Chicago stockyards.

ImaGenes Corporation's prospectus stated their ostensible goal: develop methods and equipment for making three-dimensional pictures of DNA strands via electron microscopy. However, the corporation's undisclosed goal was to add certain genes to specific places in the DNA, with the intent of cloning humans with much-improved intelligence. "Just think what some people would pay to propagate themselves with super-smart kids!" the ImaGenes president had said.

The ImaGenes investors had no compunctions about risky genetic research work on humans. Their key scientists wanted to take maximum advantage of the genome project's results, hoping the genome maps would lead them to their goal faster.

Fascinated with the side-story about humans having only 350 more genes than mice, their scientists compared the mouse connection with their own re-search—genetic experimentation on laboratory white mice. The scientists inserted genes thought to be related to intelligence into the mouse DNA and rigorously tested the mice with cleverly designed intelligence tests—the mouse equivalent of the college entrance exams. They bred and re-bred the animals, producing multitudinous generations of smarter and smarter mice.

"It's a shame that smart little fella escaped," the chief researcher lamented, "he might have been the answer we were looking for." Mouse specimen A13442Z had indeed gone missing. He continued, "After lots of gene splicing and breeding, we managed to give him 100 of those 350 genes—specifically, genes related to intelligence. He solved the toughest problems we could devise for a mouse; no other mouse came close to his skills. I sure wish we could catch him again!"

Someone said, "Hopefully he will mate with some of the native mice around the lab, and then we can work with his smart offspring; we are always trapping the local mice."

The lab supervisor laughed and bellowed, "Not a chance! We neutered that guy good; if he joins a mouse choir, he'll sing soprano! The smart mouse, A13442Z, had been a very assertive fellow, often challenging other precocious males. We intervened to protect our brainy rodents. Overactive hormones shouldn't risk the important research tasks slated for these mice."

Specimen A13442Z, known to himself as Soori, was much smarter than the ImaGenes' staff thought. In fact, had they an inkling of how bright the mouse was, they would have been very close to achieving their unspoken goal—and certainly wouldn't have neutered him. Unknown to the scientists, Soori had more than the extra 100 intelligence-related genes added by ImaGenes.

Mutations caused by intensive breeding had added, by pure chance, twenty more genes that promoted higher-order intelligence. Soori's brain was literally pulsing with high-order mental activity, which included language, logic, emotions, and concern about others. Soori's extra genes were all about intelligence and were not of the stand-up-and-walk-around type. If you saw him, you would never mistake him for a human, but a human mind scampered around in his mouse body.

Before his escape, the lab technicians had been discussing the coming demise of mouse A13442Z. "It's really a shame we have to put him to sleep," one technician said.

"Yeah," her colleague answered, "I sure like that mouse, so playful and friendly. Sometimes I think he's communicating with me. Since he can't breed, the scientists want tissue samples for cloning. Also, they want to examine his brain under the microscope."

Soori was indeed communicating with them, at least in one direction. Soori didn't have the genes for human speech, but he could listen to and understand the technicians' conversation. When the scientists were setting up the intelligence tests for A13442Z, they verbalized the testing instructions, much as if they were carefully explaining a task for their own small children. They repeated the instructions over and over, as if they thought the mouse would soon get the drift of it. And sure enough, Soori would complete the task very quickly. He listened carefully as the scientists discussed his performance.

Soori learned human language (specifically English) as babies do, by repetition and association. The higher-order language center in his gene-augmented brain processed the spoken sounds and placed them into mental bins where he could recall and associate them with what he had seen and done. Babies take a long time to develop language skills, due to the longer time span of humans. But the mouse life span is short, and Soori learned very fast.

The mentally adept mouse soon learned to read, also by association. He saw the technicians as they read the testing instructions from a lab notebook. When they left the notebook lying around during a test, Soori took every opportunity to glance at it and try to memorize the strange symbols on the paper. In time, he began to associate spoken sounds, tasks, and written groups of symbols. Soori was learning to read!

That night, after hearing the technicians' somber chatter, he knew he had to get out of there. When one of the night staff opened the cage for cleaning, he bolted under the frantic hands of the worker and raced to safety behind a file cabinet. The worker immediately sounded the alarm and others came to hunt down the footloose mouse. They even employed a ferocious looking cat, who reached his big paw with its saber-like claws behind the file cabinet. Luckily, Soori found a slight opening in the wall for computer wires. He wriggled through the tiny space and disappeared into the woodwork, never to be seen again by laboratory staff.

But Soori saw them, every day and every night, from his hideaway in the laboratory attic. He made small but strategically placed holes in the ceiling tiles, so he could view what was happening in the lab and listen to the workers' conversations. He watched the workers when they sat down at the computer, and he quickly noted they always did the same thing at first. He figured that initial task must be important, so he watched more closely from a few feet above. Soori soon deduced they were entering some sort of key to get into the computer, and after a while, he learned their passwords.

Around 2:00 AM, when most of the night staff were more somnolent than alert, Soori scampered down to the computer in the office and logged onto the Internet. This must have been a sight! Some of us humans can touch type very efficiently, and others have to hunt and peck one key at a time with a single finger. But that poor mouse had to scurry over the keyboard, position himself with three legs so he didn't inadvertently hit a wrong key, and then press the desired key with his free forepaw.

Manipulating the computer device that most humans call a *mouse* was a formidable task. He knew what *they* called it, but he wondered, *How can anybody call that clunky looking thing a mouse?*

He used it only when absolutely necessary, usually when he couldn't find a menu or keyboard operation that would do the needed function. He would position himself behind the device and push mightily while glancing up at the computer screen to see if the cursor moved to where he wanted it. Often, he overshot the mark and had to backtrack with much effort.

To click the mouse, he had to position himself to apply sudden downward pressure with both forepaws, without moving the device. Double clicking was extremely difficult, and he could not do this reliably. Soori understood the value of drag and drop operations, but a mouse body simply couldn't do this. He mouse chuckled to himself as he thought, *I oughta sue ImaGenes for not supplying me with a mouse-compliant computer mouse!*

Soori sent me a desperate message over the Internet; his notes were always very terse, because of the difficulty in typing: bob. must help me. need links on cloning. they want to clone me. can i do it myself.

Several weeks earlier, Soori had accidentally clicked my email address. I couldn't believe his first email! A few questions and answers convinced me he really was a mouse—a very intelligent mouse. I never talked to anyone else about our nocturnal chat sessions for fear I might be nudged toward a nursing home.

When asked how he got his name, he replied: thats what the lab lady kept calling me, cute little soori, smart little soori.

He said her speech sounded a little funny. Then it came to me. I typed the message: You misspelled your name. It should be souris; that's French for mouse and the last "s" is silent.

Soori quickly responded: you think a smart mouse should know french too. it sounded like soori and I spell it that way.

I quickly learned that Soori was not only smart, but the mouse had a sense of humor.

Soori was interested in cloning, because that's what ImaGenes had planned for him. He wondered which of his parts ImaGenes would want, or if they wanted to make tissue-bank pâté out of all his parts.

I researched the Internet, asked a few colleagues "what if" questions, and compiled a substantial list of promising web links for cloning technology.

Soori sent a quick note, thanking me as soon as he saw the list. He also told me that he was going to do a little research himself. He would use ImaGenes' own research facilities and camouflage his research apparatus so it looked like normal work at the lab. Soori knew he was a special kind of mouse, and it was important to him to pass on his good fortune to some heirs. But since he was sterile, he would have to rely on cloning. He didn't trust ImaGenes personnel to do the right thing, so he would do it himself. He wanted passionately to see a few cute little *souris* at his knee!

I checked our message board every night. After he started his research, Soori sent me a short note from time to time, but he said he was too busy to communicate very much. I left many notes for him, which he ignored. It's been several months now, and I haven't heard a squeak from my little mouse friend. I'm really worried about poor Soori: *Had the rogue scientists at ImaGenes finally caught him? Did that bad cat get him? Or, did he complete his research work, clone himself, and escape from the lab with his progeny?*

My advice: Pay attention the next time you see a cute little mouse peering at you from behind a piece of furniture. Note the slight quivering of his whiskers, the knowing, sniffing motions, the appealing look of his black, watery eyes. Is he trying to communicate with you? Think twice about scotching that mouse; you might be dealing with one of Soori's offspring!

# Rites of Passage

*A timorous teenager compounds the difficulty of learning something most people take for granted.*

"**B**ob, could you please run down to the store and pick up another half-pint of whipping cream?" implored my wife, as she was preparing another gourmet meal for a small dinner party. "The one I thought I had in the fridge turned out to be bad!"

Although I was playing a vigorous game of hide-and-seek with the cat, Laci, I didn't mind being interrupted by such a mundane task. When Doris gets into the mood to host a meal, I want to ensure she doesn't have to make any compromises. Mind you, we eat very well at Doris' table, even for just the two of us. But when company comes, her cuisine becomes the *crème-de-la-crème*. Therefore, we'd better have fresh cream!

So I grabbed a shirt, pulled on my sneakers, and headed for the garage. I poked the garage door OPEN button, jumped in the car, and, without thinking about it, routinely checked to make sure it was all clear before backing out.

Mission accomplished! I delivered the needed item to the chef and then endeavored to keep out of the way. The cat became bored during my absence, and as Doris was ignoring her, she sought out an empty box in the utility room to hide and sleep. Exhausted by my heavy labor, I pulled a beer from the icebox and headed for the chair on the back porch.

Thoughts of idleness turned to idle thoughts as I sat on the porch of the old family home and sipped my Shiner Bock. Over fifty years ago, when Mom requested a similar errand, I walked to the store—always barefoot and often shirtless. What a wonderful invention—the automobile! And how easily and routinely we use it!

Have you ever thought much about the delicate hand-eye coordination required for driving a car? Have you ever questioned your ability to guide two tons of rolling steel along busy city streets, without injuring yourself or someone else? You may have considered it if you sprained an ankle, or the eye doctor just dilated your eyes, or your arm is in a sling! As long as you're not physically or mentally incapacitated, driving a car is about as second-nature to most people as walking or talking.

But it doesn't necessarily start that way! For some, learning to drive is simply a speed bump in the rites of passage; for others, it's a fearsome challenge. And for a disheartened few, it's a lifelong mental block. If you can't drive, you are confined to a few nearby activities and excluded from pleasures most people take for granted. And you must rely upon the good nature of friends and relatives to ferry you to places otherwise out of your reach.

Wannabe toddlers take many a tumble before they master the intricacies of bipedal locomotion. Greenhorn cyclists suffer ignominy among their peers and painful abrasions to their knees and elbows until they learn to avoid wipeouts. One of our sons refused to touch a bicycle for years because of a psychologically disastrous crash. Some novice swimmers take to the water like a porpoise, while others make strange flapping motions and gurgling sounds before they can keep their head above water.

Why should it be any different for learning to drive?

My mother never drove in her entire life, including almost forty years of widowhood. I sometimes wondered if she tried to learn, but had calamitous results. She never confessed to any embarrassing mishaps. Let's just say, I've got bad learning-to-drive genes.

Some people make a smooth transition between walking and driving. Doris, for example, learned to drive down on the farm in Delaware—in a truck, and at a ridiculously young age! The only mishap she confessed was a police stop where the officer believed she might be too short to reach the pedals. If a subject can be mastered via intuition, Doris will accomplish it seamlessly. Fortunately, our sons inherited her good learning-to-drive genes, which helped to counter my bad ones.

Aromatic cooking smells permeated the kitchen and spilled out to the back porch, deliciously interrupting my ruminations. *That's surely gonna be a great dinner tonight!* I chased the wonderful smell with a sip of beer and imagined how the real thing would taste with a chilled Chardonnay. Then my thoughts swung back to that time, long ago, when I first tried learning to drive.

Most youngsters pester their parents incessantly about learning to drive. Not me, for I was a teenager of a different stripe. I did things I liked to do and put off things that might publicly embarrass me. I was big on books and athletics, and very shy on almost everything else, including girls. My inherent lack of self-confidence at that time turned simple tasks such as learning to drive or learning to dance into monstrous challenges. Much later, it took two things to turn me into the assertive and outgoing fellow I now am: marriage and a job.

My mom suggested to Pop, "Bobby's over 14 now, and I think it's time he learned to drive a car. Why don't you take him out and teach him?"

So that's what Pop did. The next Saturday morning, he put me behind the wheel of our 1936 Buick. The old Buick was a classic four-door sedan, with a wonderfully curved V-shaped chrome grille. It had been a deep blue for its previous owner but now was faded by years under the hot Texas sun. The headlights were set in their own streamlined nacelles, atop each front fender. The almost vertical trunk sloped sharply to the rear bumper. The massive front and back fenders were connected by a black rubber-lined running board. I've seen such cars in old Humphrey Bogart movies, and they are indeed classics. How I would like to own one of these now!

Pop pointed out the gear shift stick ahead of the front bench seat. This was the classic "four on the floor" (three forward speeds and one reverse) configuration of later years, except that term hadn't been invented yet. He carefully explained the clutch, brake, and gas pedals and instructed me how and when to shift gears. This was actually the contents of a Driver's Ed course spewed out in about ten minutes. I nodded my head when Pop asked if I understood, too sheepish to acknowledge my thorough confusion about the whole business.

When Pop sat down on the passenger side, he asked me to push in the clutch and start the car. The engine responded with the vroom of V-eight vitality. I let out the clutch and the car lurched forward, then the engine sputtered and died. Pop explained again about the need for smoothly letting out the clutch while simultaneously increasing the throttle. Alas, that requires coordination, which was never my strong suit.

After a couple of attempts, I finally managed to keep the engine running long enough to roll a few yards down the road. We were on North Market Street, which was not very heavily traveled (the connection with Page Street wouldn't come until many years later). The street at that time was even narrower than it is now.

Once the car was moving, I was confronted with yet another coordination problem: steering the vehicle. There were no fancy toy cars or simulators available then—you learned to steer a car by trial and error, which meant discovering which steering-wheel moves kept you from running into something.

I was fascinated by the fact I was driving a car and, at the same time, terrorized by the realization I didn't know what the heck I was doing. I gripped the steering wheel firmly with both hands, probably with white knuckles, and frantically made tentative steering motions.

Suddenly, a huge live oak tree swerved into my path. I pulled the wheel to the left to avoid the collision, but the right front fender crashed into the tree with a horrible crump. I could hear the tinkle of the smashed headlight as glass shards scattered over the fender. The engine had died, and I sat limply behind the wheel, ashen-faced and ashamed at the miserable mess I had made of our family's fine car.

Pop managed to kick out part of the dent in the fender, although the metal in those old cars was much thicker than now. Mom greeted us as Pop drove into the driveway, "Looks like things didn't go too well!"

Pop never berated me for this costly episode. I think he felt as bad about it as I did. He probably realized that he'd pushed me too hard to get behind the wheel. He hired a mechanic to hammer out the fender and replace the headlight. He kept driving the old Buick for several months with the wrinkled fender serving as a badge of poor driving instruction. I never drove that car again.

Less than a year later, when I turned 15, Mom again suggested to Pop that he better teach me to drive, before it was too late and I got some kind of hang-up. Little did she realize I already had one!

We now had a black 1941 Buick. This car had avant-garde, swept-back styling, which would be the dominant look for the post-war 1940s cars. The Buick was a big four-door sedan, which rode very comfortably. It had another innovation: a four-speed gearshift lever mounted on the steering column.

This time around, I knew the theory of driving very well. Also, Pop knew he'd better make sure that I got some carefully constrained practice before exposing the road to the hazards of my driving again.

He took me out to Aunt Lelia's place in the country and let me practice driving up and down her long lane. There were no trees in sight—just a few cows that eyed me with justifiable wariness. Pop made sure I could steer the car properly and could brake quickly on demand. He made me turn around on the narrow lane time after time, and he forced me to practice backing up over the *entire* lane. After about two hours of hard practice, Pop pronounced me "ready for the road," and we joined Mom who was visiting with Aunt Lelia.

For the next several days, Pop took me out for short practice spins all over town. Finally, I was ready for the "big one" (the driver's license exam). The day before the scheduled exam, Pop took me out for a final practice. I could do the parallel parking and all the other moves the examiner was likely to ask of me.

On the way home, I had turned off Highway 77 and was cruising confidently along LaGrange Street, just off the square. Suddenly, some old fellow parallel parked, but not too close to the curb, and, without looking, opened the driver's door directly in front of me. I couldn't swerve because of on-coming traffic, so I jammed the brake. But it was too late, and my right front fender crunched his open door.

Pop and I jumped out to see if anyone was hurt. The other guy was not injured, and his car door was only slightly dinged. There was a cosmetic crease in my fender. The other driver apologized profusely for opening his door into traffic without looking. We agreed to take care of our own damages.

My muscles turned to Jell-O, and my spirits sank into the toilet. Pop drove home, talking all the way as he tried to rev up my depressed feelings.

Mom shook her head, hugged me, and muttered, "Poor Bobby!" when she learned of my misfortune.

I reckon most teenaged boys would have shaken off this incident and gone on about the business of driving. But it devastated me. There was no driving exam the next day. I didn't drive again for several years. I wouldn't even talk about driving. I was too embarrassed to admit I didn't have a driver's license; I simply avoided all situations that might involve driving. I was in serious danger of becoming just like my Mom—an established non-driver. I could drive okay, but I didn't. In college, I drove only a few times, when some of my classmates were too impaired.

Pop died a few months before I graduated from Texas A&M, and the old '41 Buick sat in the driveway, unused and gathering dust. Finally, I received two important pieces of paper: my degree in Chemical Engineering and a commission as a second lieutenant in the army. I realized I desperately needed yet another piece of paper—a driver's license.

I knew I could drive properly, but I wasn't sure I could shed the mental block. There was a great job with a big chemical company waiting for me. *I damned well better get over that block!* I scolded myself. The day after graduation, I passed my driving exam. And the next day, I drove the old '41 Buick to the company town to start a new phase of my life, which included independence and liberation from begging others for a ride.

When I grew up to be a daddy, I made sure our sons had proper tutelage before they were placed behind the wheel. They both steered the car, off-road and with me behind the wheel, before I allowed them to drive on the road. They started with the automatic transmission car and graduated to the manual shift Pinto. I'm not sure my tutelage actually contributed to their smooth transition to driving since both were gifted athletically and much better coordinated than their clumsy old dad.

I still wasn't finished with driving exams. Many years later, we moved to England, and I had to learn how to drive on the left side of the road. The English required all foreigners residing in the country more than a year to pass their driving exam, which was much tougher than the Texas exam. My employer paid for five hour-long driving lessons, and those were really needed! I flunked the first time, when the examiner got me into a tricky road layout and I ended up on the wrong side of the road. I passed easily the second time. That license just expired when I turned 70.

I never saw Doris' driving intuition in England. She decided to pull a "Bobby stunt" and not drive for the five years we were there. No driving on the wrong side of the road for her!

I finished my beer, got up, stretched, and opened the screen door into the kitchen. The cat followed me in. Doris was busily involved at the stove, amid mouth-watering gustatory smells. I walked up to her, schmoozed her a little, and tried to cadge a taste.

"Get outta here!" she rebuffed. "Go take your shower!"

I watched from the dining room door as Laci padded over to Doris and went through the same routine, but with a lot more success. Cats can do that!

As I entered the shower, my mind switched back to my reflections on learning to drive. I recalled my engineering colleague, John, who had learned to fly at age forty. He often talked of the exhilaration of soaring through the air, above the houses, roads, and trees. Several times, John urged me to take flying lessons so I could experience the joys and convenience of private air travel. Each time, I had a simple but compelling reply, "No, John, I had a heck of a time learning to drive a car, and learning to swim wasn't a piece of cake, either. Flying isn't a good choice for coordination-challenged people!"

# Ranch Chickens

*Two college students learn something about themselves when they try to pass one of life's way stations.*

The large two-story white farmhouse stood in all its Victorian splendor within the pleasant confines of a white picket fence. The surrounding lush green lawn was neatly clipped, and no doubt nourished by the composted droppings of the plump dairy cattle that grazed in the adjoining pastures. A black and white cat sat passively on the gleaming white banister of the front porch, front paws tucked under her torso, seemingly asleep, but undoubtedly alert to the slightest deviation from normal.

A swing ebbed welcomingly to and fro on the curved front porch, nudged by the capricious but warming breeze on this gorgeous spring afternoon. The swing was paired with an old-fashioned wooden rocking chair. Three similar chairs adorned the side portion of the wrap-around porch. They were jostled slightly by the evanescent breeze, and eerily rocked in syncopated rhythm to the random air currents. All were painted green, to match the shutters on the old house's tall windows. The porch floor seemed newly painted, with the glossy "porch gray" so popular with older houses in the region.

Several hanging pots of bright red flowers dangled gracefully from the rim of the porch, overseeing the ornate woodwork of the banisters below. Carefully tended flower beds ringed the old house. A variety of flowers grew from these beds, their multicolored faces smiling on those who approached. To the drive-up visitor, there was a simple warm message: "Y'all come!"

A large TV aerial loomed high over the gabled roof, a rarity in Central Texas in the early 1950s, where fringe-area reception guaranteed you would see mostly snow. Clearly, the people who lived in this farmhouse were extremely proud of their beautiful dwelling, and they surely must have been prosperous.

Forty miles to the north, a trio of sophomore Aggies sat at a small table in the modern Memorial Student Center, sipping fountain Cokes and talking about worldly matters. In contrast to the bucolic homes of the surrounding countryside, Texas A&M College's new MSC was a modern brick building of box-like architecture, erected in honor of the hundreds of former students who perished in America's wars. The MSC was the focal point of campus social life, a welcome relief from the austerity of the military dormitories that reigned on this ROTC campus.

At that time, Texas A&M was an all-male institution of higher learning; the only women in class were married—wives of students or faculty. For the first two years, students were required to be in the Corps of Cadets. We wore military uniforms and acceded to round-the-clock military discipline. Each dormitory housed two military companies of cadets, where we were subject to 10 p.m. bed checks. However, we could stay out until midnight on Saturdays.

About half the sophomores who didn't flunk out elected to sign an ROTC contract for the next two years. This provided us with subsistence money each month, a six-week summer camp at the end of our junior year, and a second lieutenant's commission upon graduation.

We three close friends at the table in the MSC were engineering students, which meant we had to take Saturday morning classes as there was no other way to achieve the required semester hours. With classes finished, we had marched to Duncan Hall for a midday meal of chicken-fried steaks. Afterward, we bolted for the MSC. We sat there, full of idle chatter, enduring the enforced ennui of a weekend on campus. Actually, we were rather experienced at this!

Barney was a petroleum engineering student, who always amused us with humorous chatter and astute observations. He was a little under six feet tall, and a little over the ideal weight for his height (but nowhere near the bulk of today's goliaths). The extra pounds further softened his cherubic face, making him appear younger than his biological age.

Mike was even shorter, and his slight frame belied his mental and physical toughness. The serious mien of his heavily bearded face made you think twice about crossing verbal swords with him. Yet, we liked to be with him because of his worldly experience and his frequent droll comments. Both Mike and I were serious students of chemical engineering.

Most students left the campus at the first opportunity in search of girl-friends. The few who remained, some of whom shared with us the empty expanse of the fountain room in the MSC, either had no girlfriends or were too far behind in their studies to leave for the weekend.

The three of us, all "A" or "B" students, apparently had no reason to study this weekend. So, we focused our conversation on what was lacking in our thoroughly deprived lives.

"Guess what?" Barney blurted.

"You finally got a girlfriend, but you can't leave campus because of too many demerits," I wisecracked.

"Yeah, that's right," quipped Mike, "Your room is always a mess. And I haven't ever seen you with your tie properly straightened!"

"Nah, you guys got it all wrong. Today's my birthday—I'm twenty years old today," Barney proudly explained.

"You cain't be twenty!" Mike almost shouted. "You don't even look like you're shaving yet. I cain't see any evidence of stubble on your chin. But I guess peach fuzz doesn't make stubble!"

"I do too shave," assured Barney, "and I shaved extra close this morning, because this is a very special day."

"Today's my twentieth birthday," Barney repeated, "and I'm going to get laid!"

"Hell, you cain't do that," I protested. "You don't even have a girlfriend! Have you ever had a girlfriend?"

"Well, not a regular girlfriend," Barney sidestepped, "but I did take a very cute girl to our high-school senior prom. And I had a date for the Rice University game on the Houston Corps trip!"

"Did that lead to anything? Did you get to first base with either of the girls?" I prodded.

Barney hesitated, then explained, "Not exactly, but I did get a goodnight kiss from both of them!"

Mike just sat there; he said nothing, but his eyes were dancing. Mike had a real girlfriend, a really cute girl he had been dating since high school. We talked with her a couple of times when she came to campus for football games. Actually, she did most of the talking, since Barney and I were usually tongue-tied in the presence of pretty girls. Mike didn't leave campus too often, since she was a student in a college near Dallas.

There was something else distinctive about Mike, which undoubtedly factored heavily in Barney's plans for the afternoon. Mike was one of the few students who had a car. Most students could not afford the expense, and on-campus parking was at a premium.

Barney signaled for us to huddle closer to the table, then addressed us in muted voice, "I was talkin' with Joe Barnes this morning, and he clued me in about how to get laid."

"What were you doing talkin' with a senior on something like that?" I asked.

"He called me up to his room before breakfast formation today, to give me my birthday licks," Barney explained.

At Texas A&M, the old tradition called for upper-classmen to beat the rear ends of 'deserving' freshmen and sophomores. The instrument in this assault on human dignity was a shaved-down baseball bat. On your birthday, you got your age in licks.

Beatings by then were officially forbidden at A&M, but that didn't mean they no longer existed. Most students, including me and Mike, refused to submit on the legitimate grounds we could be kicked out of college if a random ass inspection detected bruised buttocks. A few, like Barney, thought it was fun to take risks for the old traditions.

"When he was finished," Barney continued, "Joe shook my hand and asked if I had ever been laid. When I said 'no,' he told me about a place that could take care of my problem, just like it did for him. He called it the Chicken Ranch, and said they have lots of good-lookin' women. It's in the country, between Brenham and La Grange. He gave me detailed instructions on how to find the place."

"Why don't we all go out to the Chicken Ranch this afternoon?" implored Barney. "They've got lots of girls, and I bet we could all have some fun there. What do y'all think?"

I shrugged my shoulders, squirmed a little, and then said without a lot of commitment, "Sounds okay to me. Why don't we give it a try?"

Mike sat impassively, then wryly commented, "I've had a steady girlfriend for the last three years. I don't think it would be right for me to do that."

"Hell, Mike, you probably been gettin' plenty all along," Barney shot back.

Mike glared at him like he had just plopped the proverbial turd in the punchbowl, then sternly announced, "Barney, you take care of your sex life, and I'll take care of mine. But I'm damned sure keepin' mine private!"

Mike softened a bit and said in a more conciliatory tone of voice, "If y'all want to go out to the Chicken Ranch, I'll be happy to drive. But I'll be sittin' in the car. It'll be interesting to see what that place looks like. Besides, that might be a good story I can tell my kids sometime!"

"Let's go!" Barney urged.

We set out on the country roads south of College Station, with adventure in mind, in search of every teenaged lad's unholy grail. Mike drove, with his usual grim determination. Barney sat in the front seat and navigated, and I sat in the back enjoying the pretty wildflowers that often color the spring landscape in that part of Central Texas.

Mike followed Barney's directions and turned into an unlikely looking drive. Mike stopped the car and we again consulted the directions. "This has to be the place," Barney said. So we drove farther down the driveway.

My heart was racing with trepidation about what I had offhandedly agreed to do. I had never been so close to doing something like this. I knew so little of these matters that nervous apprehension was beginning to overwhelm my senses. I was having much more than second thoughts about the wisdom of this ambitious enterprise. In fact, my brain was churning in a desperate attempt to find a face-saving way out of this jam.

Soon, we arrived at a picture-pretty white farmhouse; a big one, with two stories and a wrap-around porch. There were lots of flowers and a white picket fence. It looked like the house of a rich dairy farmer—probably a big supplier for the dairy in Brenham.

"Hell, this don't look like no cathouse!" I exclaimed; my tone full of hope. "It's just a plain old farm house."

"Who knows? Maybe it is," corrected Mike, "There's a black and white cat sitting on the porch banister!"

When Mike parked the car in front of the picket gate, Barney reached back, grasped my shoulder, and urged, "Come on, Bob, let's go!"

I shuffled my butt on the seat and finally stammered, "I … I don't think I can go in there. I'm gonna stay in the car with Mike. You go and celebrate your birthday, Barney!"

"Ha, you're turnin' chicken on me," Barney commented, "but I'm gonna go in there and lose my virginity right now. You don't turn twenty but once!"

Barney climbed the porch steps and disappeared into the doorway of the welcoming old house, while the two of us remained in the car admiring the pretty place.

"How long do you think we will have to wait for Barney to do his thing?" I asked.

Mike thought about this a long time, then replied, "The truth is…I don't know. Probably a half hour."

Before we finished our speculation, the farmhouse door flung open, and Barney hastened out. He walked quickly toward us and pulled open the car door. He didn't look like he had lost anything.

"What happened?" we demanded in unison.

Barney was breathing in rapid, shallow bursts; he was totally stressed out. When he regained his composure, he related what happened inside:

"A nice lookin' lady met me when I entered the door; she was a little older, but still very pretty—prob'ly the Madam. She knew I was an Aggie, because of my uniform. She brought me into the parlor and introduced me to two very nice lookin' young women sitting on the sofa. Gosh, I never saw such flimsy clothes on a girl—you could almost see their boobs! Somethin' happened to me then. I totally panicked. All of my muscles tightened up, except the ones that counted. I needed air; I had to get outta there. I explained this to the nice lady, and she patted me on the cheek. 'That's all right, sonny,' she said, 'you come back when you start shaving!' I got the hell outta there."

The Chicken Ranch got its name because generations of cash-starved but love-hungry country boys sometimes brought chickens to barter for a little companionship. Generations of Aggies also visited the place, to disencumber themselves of their virginity. But I'm sure that more than a few Aggies, like the two in Mike's car, turned chicken at the Chicken Ranch.

# Sky-High Torment

*A chance encounter leads a pair of vacationing comrades on an exciting adventure they will cherish for a lifetime.*

We were two dry-throated, road-weary Texans in search of some ice-cold Coors. We settled ourselves onto bar stools at the Silver Dollar Bar in Jackson, and after some friendly back and forth with the bartender, reprised highlights of our long drive from Laramie to Jackson.

Suddenly, the gray-haired fellow next to us, hunched on his elbows over the bar, sprang to life, and interjected with an impish grin, "You guys sound like Texans. I hate Texans!"

My Texas Aggie buddy and travel companion, Reggie Miller, quickly returned the insult, "I would get real mad at that, if you didn't have such a funny sounding accent!"

After trading more jocular insults with the guy, Reggie and I took a liking to this lively chap. The stranger introduced himself as Kurt (for the life of me, I can't remember his last name). Kurt was probably middle-aged, but to us two young engineers, he seemed old. We were intellectually compatible: Reggie loved the theater and often acted in plays; I was a classical music lover; Kurt was an English professor at the University of Minnesota.

Kurt was taking a very relaxed approach to his summer vacation, as evidenced by the gray stubble on his chin. We quit the bar in favor of a more comfortable table and ordered more Coors. Kurt was a little short of six feet, our height. He was of medium build and seemed very muscular, with no perceptible flab (pretty impressive for an older guy). His firm handshake didn't feel very "English teacher-ish."

Reggie turned to Kurt and remarked, "You have a strange accent. I can't place it. I've learned a few accents in my stage appearances, but yours is different."

"Ah, that's just my Swedish heritage squeaking through," Kurt muttered. "But my accent pales in comparison with your raw Texas twang. Doesn't sound like it's gone through any generational filter!"

Kurt continued, "What brings you to this hole-in-the-wall town?"

Keep in mind that in the summer of 1956, Jackson (often mistakenly called Jackson Hole, which is properly the Snake River valley) was not the popular destination of modern times. There were no luxury hotels, upscale motels, fancy restaurants, art galleries, or chic shops. This town was primarily a destination for the *cognoscenti:* hikers, campers, climbers, skiers, and the like. Instead of modern accommodations, the town boasted tourist courts and campgrounds. The spectacular Teton Mountains, which almost surrounded the town, were just as imposing, if not a little more pristine, than now.

Our new friend volunteered, "I come to Jackson each year for my summer vacation, where I relax, read, write, hike, and climb. Why did you come?"

We explained we had earned our first paid vacation after years of going to school and working to pay for it. Reggie had completed a year of chemical engineering at his company; I had done the same as a process designer with another company. We were cramming a massive auto trip to the Great American West into two weeks.

"You guys can't have experienced much of the true West with that grinding travel pace," Kurt countered. That's when he propositioned us, "How would you like to climb one of these magnificent, mountains?"

Reggie looked at me quizzically and stated emphatically, "Let's give it a try!"

I was a little apprehensive about the whole idea, but went ahead and nodded my head in assent.

"Where are you guys staying?"

"We just rolled into town. We hope we can find a room in a tourist court," Reggie answered.

"That'll never work; those places are jammed this time of year." Kurt suggested, "Why don't you stay with us? My sister and I have a big cabin on a large camp space that we lease every summer. This year my niece and nephew are also joining us. There's plenty of room to sleep on the floor."

Reggie and I gratefully accepted his kind offer.

Kurt explained what he had in mind, "I've always wondered if I could train some neophyte mountain climbers and successfully lead them up and down a significant peak. You flat-land Texans are ideal candidates. Would you like to be guinea pigs?"

By now Reggie and I were undeterred, "Let's keep the ball rollin'."

"Good!" Kurt exclaimed. "My sister and I are experienced climbers in the Tetons, but my younger relatives are beginners, just like you. That should make a good class."

Reggie and I picked up Kurt's substantial bar bill and followed him to the campground. It got cool on summer nights at that altitude, and thankfully, our hosts had a couple of spare sleeping bags. We settled in with our meager belongings. We were a compatible, talkative group. Kurt's sister, Clara, taught history at the University of Minnesota. His nephew, Carl, and niece, Sophie, were students at the university. Clara fixed a camp meal for all of us. Reggie and I chipped in some dollars to keep the larder stocked.

After the meal, Kurt briefed us on the climbing plan, "First, we must get you conditioned to the altitude. It's about 7,000 feet at the campground. We'll be climbing to about 12,000 feet. That's a heckuva lot thinner air than you coastal Texans have ever breathed! Why don't we start now and take advantage of these long, early July days?"

In addition to Scandinavian genes, we believe Kurt packed a full load of drill sergeant genes. He gave us spare backpacks and loaded them with heavy items. Kurt announced, "Strap these on and let's start moving. We will march until your tongues are hanging out and you are gasping for breath. We'll rest a bit, but I will lecture you about the many climbing techniques you will need when we ascend the mountain. During the conditioning hikes, I will bark at you and force you to extend yourself beyond what you thought you could do. I'll insist you pay close attention. Later, there will only be 'on-the-job-training' high on the mountain. We only have a couple of days for this, so we have to work hard."

Under Kurt's watchful eye, we four beginners spent the remainder of the day and the next two days walking farther and higher, to 8,000 feet and continuing above 9,000. The packs grew heavier, and we were truly sucking air. But our fitness improved as well.

Kurt's first lecture: "We will occasionally be traversing rock-filled slopes called *scree*. These are obviously dangerous because of loose rock. But you can dislodge a rock almost anywhere on the mountain. If you slip a bit and cause a rock to head downslope, yell 'Rock!' at the top of your voice. And if somebody else yells 'Rock!' hit the dirt—make yourself as flat as possible—a hurtling rock can kill you or force a tragic fall."

We continued our training hike on an upslope trail, picking our way over tree roots and large, half-buried rocks. Suddenly, Kurt tested us by yelling, "Rock!" Reggie and the other two trainees hit the deck. I hesitated and remained upright, thinking there was no current danger of loose rocks. Kurt observed this and chewed my butt royally—more severely than any I had encountered in the U.S. Army Officers Basic Course.

"You must do this instinctively," Kurt bellowed. "Don't think, hit the deck. Your life might be at stake." The other trainees observed and listened attentively.

The next lecture covered traversing a glacier, which would be necessary for this climb. Kurt explained how to use ice axes to help stop a slide downslope. He showed us how to strap *crampons* over our boots. These were necessary for slip-free climbing; crampons added fierce-looking, dagger-like cleats to the soles of our boots. A golfer would never dare to wear such fearsome cleats on a golf green! Finally, Kurt explained we would be roped together when climbing the glacier.

I foolishly asked, "What good would that do? Wouldn't that make us all slide down the glacier together?"

Kurt laughed, "That's why you have an ice axe. Dig it in and hold on! Besides, there are crevasses in the glacier; these are covered with snow, and you can't see them. If someone breaks through the snow and falls into a crevasse, he will remain frozen in time unless a rope stops his fall."

Our final lecture concerned *rappelling*, a technique for descending a steep rock face too dangerous for traditional climbing. With this technique, a rope is attached to something solid, such as a tree or boulder. The climber wraps the rope around his body in such a way that allows him to control the speed of descent. Kurt briefly described the technique and then more or less dismissed it, "We don't anticipate running into this situation, but Clara and I are prepared for it."

Mountain-climbing day finally arrived. Before dawn, Kurt and Clara supervised the packing of our backpacks, made sure we had ample food and water, and inspected the collection of gear each would have to carry up the mountain. We drove out to the mountain. Kurt told us the mountain's name, but fifty years later it's tightly nestled in a far corner of my brain and won't come out. Kurt suggested we leave one car at another parking place for an alternative ascent—just in case we had to change plans on the way down. We piled into the remaining car and drove to the main access point at the base of the mountain. We strapped on our backpacks and climbing gear and headed up the trail; our leaders carried the ropes.

At first, the climb was much like the training jaunts, except it kept getting steeper. More half-buried rocks and more tree roots, until the trees gave way to the rocks. We had passed the tree line. We looked up and ahead and saw nothing but rocks; a scree slope was our next barrier to the summit. We cautiously placed our feet flatly against the rocks, hoping not to slide; even a little slip could disturb a rock. As we grew more confident, our tempo up the slope gradually increased. And this led to the first cry of "Rock!" Our feet loosed a couple more errant rocks, but we completed the scree climb without injury—our training worked.

However, the glacier loomed ahead of us. Our leaders reviewed the training we had received earlier, supervised strapping on the crampons, and tethered us together with the ropes. We carefully trudged up the glacier, anxiously wondering if our next step would break through the snow and dump us into a crevasse. Walking on the snowy ice was very difficult and provoked a torrent of sweat in the glaring sunlight.

I remarked to Kurt when we had crossed the glacier, "That was easier than I thought. I was afraid we might run into serious trouble here."

"Being well equipped and well trained is the answer to serious potential problems," Kurt harrumphed. "Although it never seems to rain when you carry an umbrella, it's always best to bring one when there is a risk."

The remaining climb was across minor scree fields and rocky escarpments. As we neared the summit, we encountered rock faces, which we ascended via traditional rock climbing techniques. We observed Clara as she picked her way up the rock face and mimicked her choice of foot holds and hand holds. Kurt monitored our ascent, ready to advise in case we ran into trouble.

Before we knew it, we were at the summit—a fairly uniform stretch of massive rock outcroppings. As we sat a mile above the valley, we saw neighboring peaks—some higher, some lower. Look in any direction and it was down. Directly below us, the sinuous curves of the Snake River cascaded toward its ultimate destination, the Pacific Ocean. The town of Jackson lay to our right, shrunken by distance from its already small dimensions. Across the river lay the huge pastures where elk gathered each winter. Only a few clouds cluttered the bright blue sky, and the sun shone brightly over the glorious valley below.

How peaceful it was on the mountain top! How glorious were God's creations around and below us! I'm sure I was not the only one to have a very spiritual feeling while sitting on the summit. Even the least religious of us must have experienced it. Not a sound could be heard, no animal noises or bird songs, only the soft but excited murmurings of the climbers.

After a few moments of this alpine high, we realized we were tired—dog-tired. And we were hungry; the exertions of the climb consumed a huge amount of calories. We unstrapped our backpacks and gear, and dug into our rations. I had just begun unwrapping a sandwich when it arrived—a creature that shouldn't be here, at least by my reckoning—a common housefly!

This pesky fly dive bombed my sandwich, cavorted around the moist edges of my eyes, wallowed in the sweat on my forehead, and brushed against my lips as I tried to eat. I protectively cupped my hands around my food as I tried to keep the fly at bay. His wings beat rapidly to gain lift in the thin air. He buzzed around my face and I fanned the air in vain, trying to swat him. I managed to consume the sandwich and started peeling an orange. The pungent, sweet smell of the orange is what attracted him, and not to the orange itself, but to my sticky fingers.

And then he was gone. Thankfully, I could see no sign of that irksome insect. I asked if others had been bothered by him—none had. I ate a candy bar without problems. *Surely that would have attracted him*, I thought. *Where did the fly come from? Did he live up here?* Surely not, the cold alpine nights would have frozen his butt. *Did he get wrapped up in my lunch bag?* That made the most sense. *And where did he go? Did he fall to the ground with altitude sickness?* The answer hit me square in the face. In the fly's frantic forays near my mouth, I might have eaten him. *Oh well, a little extra protein won't hurt you at this altitude!*

My mind cleared with the disappearance of the fly, and I resumed my alpine reverie. The gorgeous scenery enveloped me, and as I nodded drowsily, the dreaded, far-from-home problems jolted my consciousness. You know the thoughts. Did I lock the back door? Did I close the upstairs bathroom window? Did I turn the oven off?

For me it was, "Did I calculate the heat exchanger right?" I had feverishly worked on the design of a key heat exchanger before leaving on vacation. As I peered over the luscious scenery below, I saw not the grandiose work of nature, but the ratio of two heat exchange coefficients—critical to the exchanger's design. The ratio was reversed!

I am a natural-born worry wart, and the possible effect of such a mistake dogged me for the rest of the vacation.

Our leaders had been conferring out of earshot from us rookies. Kurt turned to us and announced, "The good news is that we had a great climb up the glacier and to the summit. The bad news: we can't go down that way. It's after noon, the day is warm, and the sun is shining brightly. I don't think we should risk the glacier under these conditions—it could be too slippery. We're going to take another route down, away from the glacier. Let's saddle up and start down."

We clambered down rock faces and encountered similarities to our ascent. Sometimes we stretched mightily to go from one toe hold or foot hold to another. Other times, Clara and Kurt helped the youngsters down tough places. There was little ice, but we quickly ran into steep scree slopes. Going down the scree was even tougher than going up—you had to keep your balance while carefully placing your feet. Suddenly. I dislodged a four or five-inch diameter rock, and I immediately screamed, "Rock!" All climbers flattened themselves. I watched the rock as it bounded downhill, seemingly in slow motion. Reggie was the second person downslope from me. I watched with dismay as that rock sailed right through the space formerly occupied by Reggie's head. Thanks, Kurt, for chewing me out!

We cleared the scree field and negotiated a few more rocks before encountering some sparse vegetation. Kurt had been leading us down, but he stopped and told us to take a break and stay put. He and Clara seemed to be scouting the path down, first to the right and then to the left. His face was grim when the two returned, which stirred a little inquietude into at least one of us.

Kurt informed us, "Earlier, I said we probably wouldn't have to rappel on this climb. Well, I lied. There is a steep rock face just ahead, and it's very high. We looked on both sides, and there is no easier path down. Clara and I could probably climb down this rock face, but I think it would be too dangerous for beginners to try."

With a slightly tremulous voice, Reggie asked, "And you don't think rappelling by beginners is dangerous?"

"Nah, that's a piece of cake," Kurt answered. "Come over to the cliff, and I will show you how easy it is—you might even get to like it."

We peered over the cliff. Kurt said it was about thirty feet high, but to Reggie and me it was at least a hundred. Kurt secured one end of a rope to a tree and tossed the other end over the cliff. He showed us how to straddle the rope around one thigh and wrap the rope around our back and over the opposite shoulder. He grabbed the rope above his head and jumped into space, keeping his feet against the rock face as he leaned almost perpendicular to the face. He eased his way down the cliff by kicking against the cliff and letting the friction of the rope against his body slow his descent.

"Okay, that was easy," he shouted up to us, "Who's going to be next?"

Carl volunteered. Clara helped him place the rope around his body; he easily made his way down the face.

I stepped up next. My heart was pounding as my excitement grew. I felt trapped by a kind of Hobson's choice: risk jumping into the void or stay on the mountain. Amazingly, I took the leap and rappelled down that cliff, experiencing the exhilarating thrill of danger combined with recently acquired knowledge of how to overcome it. As I dangled from the cliff—thankful I hadn't fallen to my death—I grew more confident as I kicked my way down. A powerful feeling of *savoir faire* coursed through me as my feet touched ground.

Sophie was next, followed by Reggie, and Clara was the last. All climbers were down the cliff, but the rope still hung from the tree.

Reggie asked, "Are you going to leave that rope hanging down the cliff?"

"Yes. Even though there are techniques for bringing the rope down, I didn't want to try it with you guys. Besides, that rope was getting old."

Kurt's last statement didn't exactly reassure us. The rest of the descent was easy, but it was a long walk to reach our pre-positioned car. The Texans in the climbing party were exceedingly relieved to climb into the vehicle.

Back in camp, we showered under cold water and then got dressed. We went to town for dinner, where we drank lots of Coors and talked excitedly about our experiences of the day. We heaped thanks on Kurt for the unexpected thrill of experiencing the real West via a mountain climb. Kurt seemed a bit smug as he accepted our felicitations. Actually, I don't think he was feeling proud about teaching a bunch of beginners how to climb a mountain; it was most likely the relief he felt from getting all of us down safely!

At early light the next day, Reggie and I packed our belongings into my 1956 Chevy and headed south, back to work after a vacation never to be paralleled in our lifetimes. We no longer had the time to stop and visit the local attractions along the way; we just kept on our course to Texas.

When I drove into town late on a Sunday afternoon, I threw my belongings into my rented room, freshened myself, and hurried to the Engineering Building at the plant. That problem still worried me. I frantically dug into my project files and found the suspect heat exchanger calculations. Sure enough, I had reversed the ratio of coefficients, just as I had seen it on top of the mountain. I whipped out my slide rule and recalculated the heat exchanger's size. My error amounted to just a tiny addition to the size, much less than the safety factor the company normally applies to exchanger sizes. Thankfully, I drew a deep breath, went out for a big steak dinner, and slept soundly.

At work the next day, my engineering colleagues asked about my vacation. Boy, did I have a story!

# Missed by a Hare

*Three young men returning from a sun-filled weekend at the beach
learn about the danger of distracted driving.*

Three young lieutenants sped at a jackrabbit pace down a bunny tail highway in southern Alabama, trading insults and babbling excitedly about their visit to the beach at Panama City, Florida. It was our first weekend pass after two weeks of intensive training at Fort McClellan, Alabama.

As I drove back to post, my attention repeatedly switched between our banter and the traffic on this narrow, hilly rural highway. The 150 horsepower engine of my 1956 Chevrolet was fully engaged going up steep hills and accelerating through tight curves as this was well before the era of Interstate highways and cruise-controlled travel.

The radio blared country western and Kentucky blue-grass music. Rick Samuels, opposite me on the front bench seat, served as navigator and radio operator. The eco-friendly air conditioning system blasted away, meaning both front windows were rolled all the way down.

"Hey, you guys," Jimmy Adams shouted from the backseat, "You're poundin' me with hot Alabama air. Close those windows a little!"

"Come on, Jimmy," Rick chided, "just lie down on the backseat, close your eyes, and imagine you're still on the hot beach. Think about all the neat chicks we saw! If that's too hard, you can come up here, where it's really hot."

Rick and Jimmy were good ol' boys from North Carolina. I enjoyed listening to their tales of exploits and conquests, although I didn't believe half of what they claimed. I was a much less experienced small-town boy from Texas.

Allegedly, the three of us had been transformed into officers and gentlemen by the ROTC programs at our universities.

Two years after graduation, we had been called to active duty and were attending the three-month Chemical Officer's Basic Course (COBC). Successful completion of this course would show we were indeed sound officer material so we could be assigned to positions of responsibility in the U.S. Army Chemical Corps.

The COBC was the officer's equivalent of basic training or boot camp: marching, drills, inspections, firing ranges, bivouacs, class lectures, 14-mile marches—the works. We were grunts with lieutenant's bars on our collars. Some of our most capable instructors were Master Sergeants, grizzled veterans with decades of military experience and impressive combat duty. They chewed us out for our transgressions just as they would the ordinary draftee. They finished their tirades with a very polite and parenthetical "Sir!"

I had another insult ready to heap upon poor Jimmy, but I had to squelch it when I noticed a slow-moving, battered and muddy pickup ahead of us. I followed closely behind it as we climbed a steep hill, waiting for the traffic to clear in the opposite lane. When we crested the hill, the road was empty ahead of and behind us, so I gunned the powerful engine and passed the pickup handily. We waved to the old fellow who was driving and to the woman who might have been his wife.

"Who farted?" complained Jimmy from the backseat.

"It musta been a bunch of chickens what did that," answered Rick. "It looked like he had a load of chicken manure in the back of his pickup. Anyway, that's what it smells like."

"Well, a farm hick like you oughta know," retorted Jimmy. He added, "It stinks like shit in here. Roll down the windows some more!"

"Phewee, that's an awful smell!" exclaimed Rick, "We shoulda brung our gas masks."

"Hell, those things will stop nerve gas, but I betcha this crap would go right through them," opined Jimmy.

With the road clear ahead, I figured I could participate again in the conversation. But the subject matter definitely needed upgrading. I turned my head and asked, "What did y'all think of that gorgeous blonde on the blanket next to ours, with that big dude who looked like he could be a football player? You know, the one with the long hair, nice boobs, blue eyes, and matchin' blue bikini?"

"Yeah, what about that bikini?" exulted Jimmy, "That was the first one I ever saw on a real girl!"

"Hah! Showcase mannequins are just about your speed, you naïve little pipsqueak," jousted Rick.

Rick then turned to me, and observed, "She sure was displayin' a helluva lot of skin—skin I never thought you could show in public. Reckon she has to shave a little bit there, Bob?"

"Beats hell outa me," I deadpanned, "that's not my territory!"

In my rearview mirror, I noticed a car rapidly gaining on us. We were on a flat stretch of road, and the car passed us like we were on a motor scooter. Three sunburned young guys in a gleaming red Ford convertible zipped past us.

"Those guys must be goin' 80!" I exclaimed. "I'm cruisin' at 65, even though the road is marked at 55. I sure hope they make it back okay!"

We had spotted the red Fort McClellan sticker on their rear bumper—enlisted guys who had probably also been to the Florida beach. The two guys not driving turned, flashed big grins, and flipped us a couple of very obvious birds.

"Hey, those guys just gave us the finger!" shouted Rick. "They are enlisted personnel from Fort McClellan. They musta seen our blue officer's sticker; they showed us willful disrespect! Speed up and let's get their license number. We can report them when we get back to post. That'll teach their sorry asses."

"Relax, Rick," I urged in an attempt to calm the agitated lieutenant. "They've probably been wantin' to do that for a long time. What better time than in the boonies of southern Alabama?"

"Besides," I added, "Haven't you always wanted to do somethin' like that to Major Priestly?"

Major Priestly was finishing out his career in the army by teaching raw second lieutenants the military trade. He was looking forward to retirement, selling insurance, and playing golf.

The major was an excellent teacher, hard taskmaster, and world-class nitpicker. We couldn't go a day without a stern reprimand for the teeniest of infractions. The three of us had been confined to base last weekend because we didn't achieve a sufficient sheen on our combat boots.

I turned to Rick and asked, teasingly, "How many times have you called Major Priestly, behind his back of course, Major ChoirBoy?"

"You got a point," Rick demurred.

My heart jumped into my throat when I turned my eyes back to the road. We had just crested a hill and, for the first time, I spotted a slow-moving farm tractor ahead of us; it was pulling a load of hay. Gravity was accelerating our mass of 2,000 pounds of steel, rubber, and plastic, along with 500 pounds of flesh and bone. But the g's weren't working on the tractor; it was at the bottom of the hill.

I jammed and pumped the brakes as hard as I could, playing maximum braking against the danger of skidding. Although we steadily slowed, we were closing at a heart-pounding rate on the agricultural vehicle as it putt-putted along. In the opposite lane, a huge eighteen-wheeler raced down the hill ahead.

I envisioned plunging into that load of hay, then looked hopefully to the shoulder. It seemed clear to me, so I veered to the right, holding the steering wheel firmly with both hands and praying I wouldn't lose control. We came within inches of the tractor as we flew past its right side, just as the eighteen-wheeler roared past on its left.

Rick shouted, as he relaxed his bracing grip on the dashboard, "That old farmer's face turned just as white as his hair! Almost as white as your face, Bob. I bet he soiled his underwear on that one."

I didn't reply, as I had no intention of commenting on the state of my underwear. I further slowed the car, and then carefully eased it back onto the main roadway. I brought the car up to a safe cruising speed of 55 mph and tried to calm myself. When my breathing and heart rate returned to normal, I started reflecting on our good fortune: no sudden drop off at pavement's edge, no culvert at the bottom of the hill, and a wide and firm shoulder.

Rick and Jimmy prattled in subdued banter for the rest of the journey; I remained thoughtfully, and thankfully, quiet. We arrived safely at Fort McClellan before dark. Apparently, the happy-go-lucky enlisted men made it, too, since we saw no wreckage along the way.

While at the wheel, young men too often feel invincible, drive faster than conditions warrant, and let themselves be distracted. If you don't believe it, just read your local paper each day for a month. Fortunately, God looks over most of us and, in advance, sweeps up the messes we almost leave. Around our mid- to late-twenties, the rest of our brains finally develops, and we start exercising sound judgment.

Those of you who have ridden with me might wonder why I never talk much while I'm driving. Now you know!

# Army Shorts

*Overall, serving in the military is a serious business contributing directly to the national well-being. The hard work is sometimes accompanied by routine and boredom. Humor and spontaneous mischief naturally arise as soldiers express their individuality.*

The Hallettsville Writing Group proposed a challenging exercise: Write a story in exactly 76 words. I had always wanted to write a story about some of the humorous things I experienced during my two-year stint in the U.S. Army. But a full-fledged story would require an artificial infrastructure for suspending unrelated anecdotal snippets. The 76-word format was the answer to my army story!

### * * * **Routine** * * *

Lt. Walters loudly commanded, "Bat-tal-i-on, Ten-shun!" Three companies of scientific personnel snapped to attention. Duty Officer Walters ended the early morning ritual, "Unit commanders, take charge of your troops and dismiss them."

The next time, Walters changed the routine, "…take charge of your troops and *do something* with them!" The troops howled with laughter.

Afterward, his captain told the colonel, "I'm sorry Lt. Walters did that."

Walters' punishment: Duty Officer every day for a month.

### * * * **Contingency** * * *

Lt. Walters, Officer of the Day, stopped by the post's orderly room for a shotgun shell to simulate firing the howitzer. The sergeant handed him two shells.

"Why two?"

"If the first doesn't fire, use the second."

As the bugler sounded, the flag detail lowered the flag. Walters pulled the howitzer's lanyard. Nothing! He inserted the spare shell. Silence!

In desperation, he ordered: "Yell *'Boom'* at the count of three!"

"Nice job, sir," the sergeant commended.

* * * **Control** * * *

Lt. Walters sent an air-mail message to Lt. Allen's office across the hall, via a folded paper airplane. Allen's reply promptly sailed back into Walters' office.

Walters suggested stopping this nonsense and threw the airplane toward Allen's office. "Uh oh," Walters grunted as the airplane veered left, down the hall.

Clutching the airplane, Lt. Col. Davis said, "Lt. Walters, the tail must be straight for good control," and accurately tossed the glider into Lt. Allen's office.

*I enjoyed my two-year stint in the U.S. Army—had fun and worked hard. I received the Army Commendation Medal after a technical assignment to the Rand Corporation.*

# Trapped by a Mouse

*A glance, eye contact, and an extraordinary opening line starts more than a half-century of togetherness.*

After a hard day of graduate classes and experimental work in the laboratory, I sought relaxation in the music room at the University of Delaware's Student Center. My infatuation with the lyrical music of Robert Schumann was near its peak. This particular evening, I'd requested his beautiful piano work "Études Symphoniques". Schumann's inspiring chords, enhanced by the pianist's keyboard artistry, pulsed through my ears and almost into my soul. I quietly read the *Philadelphia Inquirer* as the music lifted my spirits. Some musically inclined coeds also frequented this place of contemplation, which partly motivated my attendance.

I should preface this story by saying my parents' generation dubbed me a "late bloomer." Hell, I hadn't even sprouted any buds! In high school, my passions were sports and books. Moving on to all-male Texas A&M did nothing to stimulate my awareness of the opposite sex. I became much more aware of girls while in the U.S. Army, but my consciousness really flourished when I arrived at the coeducational University of Delaware. I often sat on the front steps of Brown Lab, home of the Chemistry and Chemical Engineering Departments. My head would arc from left to right, as if I were watching a tennis match, tracking the coeds as they walked up and down the university quadrangle. I finally had begun to realize something was missing in my life.

In the music room, I was seated near a corner, enjoying the music and newspaper, when I heard a shuffle nearby. There she was again—the same cute girl I had admired in the music room the previous few days! She was a petite, blue-eyed blonde dressed in an attractive blouse and skirt (not the usual campus casual). Her neatly combed blonde locks barely touched her shoulders. She took a seat near me, against the adjacent wall. I sensed something special about this lovely young woman. She was a perky girl with a hint of mischief in her eyes.

I lost interest in the *Inquirer* and set it aside. I turned toward her and we made eye contact. My lips trembled as I waited for my brain to deliver something intelligent. I had little experience in these situations and considered potential topics. *Schumann? The nice day?* My pulse quickened with excitement at the prospect of meeting her, but anxiety reared its head with the fear I would once again mess up in getting to know an interesting, attractive girl.

My mental stammering lasted only briefly. Amazingly, the pert young lady leaned toward me and asked, "Would you get mad if I sent you a dead mouse?"

*What?* This brazen opening line excited my curiosity and at the same time eased my tension. We had started a conversation! But I figured I had better come up with a decent answer to her provocative question. A few brain cycles later I replied, "That depends on whether or not I deserved it."

That response seemed to satisfy her and we introduced ourselves. Doris Wild was a senior at the university, reluctantly majoring in Education; she was more interested in Political Science. I was a graduate student in the Department of Chemical Engineering, just recently arrived at the university after a stint in the U.S. Army and two years as a design engineer.

The Schumann piano sonata played on, but I no longer heard it. I was happily engaged in a conversation with the pretty girl I had just met!

Emboldened, I remarked to Doris, "Did you really send someone a dead mouse? That seems like a weird thing to do!"

With no hesitation Doris embarked upon her story about the unfortunate creature:

"My boyfriend and I were starting to break up. In a final effort to revive our relationship, I invited him to visit for the weekend at our farm near Dover. But the rat spent all his time talking in French with my very pretty older sister and hardly paid any attention to me.

"While studying one night the following week, a very distressed looking mouse limped feebly toward my desk. It stopped near my feet and keeled over dead.

"I looked at that poor creature and a lightbulb lit up in my head. This was a gift from heaven! I put the dead mouse in a box, wrapped it, and sent it in the campus mail to my ex-boyfriend.

"The next day after lunch, he approached me in the student center and irately accused me of sending him the defunct rodent. I feigned innocence and denied the charge. His face reddened with indignation and he stomped angrily away.

"That's why I asked you that silly question. By the way, I liked your response!"

Other music room patrons requested more music, but neither of us paid much attention. Instead, Doris and I busily chatted about the things we liked, and found we had a lot in common. My shy reluctance to social discourse contrasted with her effervescence. I was now much more relaxed in the presence of Doris and I wanted to get to know her better.

This was an important moment for me. The music room closing time was approaching, so I had to do something quickly. It was my turn to take the lead.

"Would you like to go into the city and listen to the Philadelphia Orchestra at the Academy of Music on Saturday night? Eugene Ormandy is conducting and that Philadelphia sound under him is luscious. Before the concert, we can have dinner at Bookbinder's Restaurant."

I was confident I could take Doris to these venues without incident, since I had gone to them several times while stationed at the Army Chemical Center in Edgewood, Maryland.

Doris responded, "I would be very happy to go with you; that sounds exciting."

We arranged the details for our first date and when we left, my spirits were soaring and my body glowed. I had finally succeeded in meeting a very interesting girl and had even arranged a date, without matchmaking "help" sometimes offered by my mother, aunts, and landladies. This time I had actually done it on my own—with just a little help from Doris!

Afterward, girl-watching sessions on the steps of Brown Lab ebbed as my interest in the opposite sex morphed from spectator sport to active involvement with a fascinating potential companion.

# Passing Muster

*Some male birds fluff up their feathers, display their colors, do silly dances, and strut their stuff to impress a prospective mate. Songbirds belt out colorful arias to accomplish the same goal. With homo sapiens, wannabe male partners face similar challenges—the multi-faceted hurdles of a weekend invitation to the parents' home.*

After the intense excitement of my first date with Doris had calmed down into the pleasure of a normal boy-girl relationship, I began dating her on a semi-regular basis. On some weekends, I'd ask her out for dinner and a movie, or for a picnic and a hike, or to travel the beautiful back roads of Maryland and Eastern Pennsylvania. I remember Angie's Pizza Place as a favorite spot for dining, especially for avoiding the "mystery meat" served on Sunday evenings at the university's dining hall. We even played tennis on some weekdays after school hours.

At this point, my dating skills had improved to, perhaps, the level of the average high school senior. I felt confident that I could navigate in this newfound space, and…I liked it. Really liked it! Just as the reformed alcoholic kicks the bottle and devotes himself to born-again religion, I started kicking the isolation of bachelorhood in favor of a compelling interest in being with Doris.

I tried to date her almost every weekend, often with no success. She had other interests and other friends. I quit eating breakfast with my fellow graduate students at the dining hall and pulled up a chair to the table of the 6:00 a.m. group of senior intellectuals—the place where Doris sat among her coterie of guy friends. I was an instant outsider, an older dude (four years their senior), and an engineer among arts and sciences students. At first, I was at a total loss during conversations—campus topics swirled around the table and none of them made sense to me. Some in the group probably regarded me as a parvenu in their lofty circle. After all, I was merely an experienced engineer with military service.

But I persevered and a few of Doris' friends begrudgingly accepted my presence, and even listened when I contributed tidbits of my experience in the outside world. Eventually, a few trickled away to other tables, telling Doris that it looked like I was serious about her.

Only about three weeks remained in the semester when Doris decided it was time for me to pay a visit to her farm near Camden-Wyoming, Delaware and meet her parents and sisters. I happily accepted her invitation for the weekend, not realizing until much later the significance of the events that followed.

On the fateful Saturday morning, I packed my bag and pointed my 1956 Chevy south for the hour's drive to near Dover. Doris had already gone home on Friday afternoon. Earlier, I had selected two bottles of the finest Rhine wine I remembered drinking at the Officer's Club at the Army Chemical Center; my mom had taught me to bring a gift when visiting someone's home. I felt some queasiness as I approached the Wild home, for I knew I was going to be inspected thoroughly. But I recognized the opportunity to learn more about Doris and her family.

Doris came out to greet me as I pulled into the lane and drove up to the house. She gave me a quick hug and proceeded to point out some of the features of the house, which was a modern, two-story, red-brick farmhouse. There were a few colorful flower beds and a large vegetable garden tended by her father. Azaleas and rhododendrons lined the nearby woods.

Just as Doris was describing the scene, a gray-haired, stubble-faced old man, in baggy gray pants held up by black suspenders, emerged from a dilapidated shack near the garden and shuffled toward us. Doris introduced me to Charlie. He extended a gnarled hand and grasped mine. His eyes sparkled as he flashed a toothless, tobacco-dribbled smile and mumbled something unintelligible.

"When Pop bought this farm, Charlie was among the leaning sheds, rusting equipment, and decrepit buildings that came with the deal," Doris explained.

My first impression: *What is this…a bunch of hillbillies?*

Doris led me inside and introduced me to the members of her family as they arrived on the scene. Her mother, Anna, was a warm and gracious person who welcomed me into her home and took what I felt was a genuine interest in me. Doris had told me earlier her mother was in the final stages of cancer and warned me not to discuss this with her. I sensed that Mrs. Wild must have been a very pretty young lady; years later Doris showed me a picture which confirmed this. Now, her face was almost cherubic, swollen by middle age and the effects of her cancer medication.

Doris was number two in a family of five girls. Her older sister was a graduate student at the University of North Carolina, soon to receive her MA in French, and be wed to a fellow graduate student. Sadly, Mrs. Wild died shortly after their wedding, at an unfairly young age.

Doris' three younger sisters sat at the kitchen table as Doris and I conversed with their mother. The older of these kept probing about whether or not I was a Catholic.

Morning had expended itself and presented us with lunchtime. That's when Papa Joe Wild came in from doing some Saturday morning farm chores. After Doris introduced us, he excused himself to wash up. When he returned, Joe was absent the stubble on his face, but still dressed in his undershirt and work shorts. Joe was short and extremely well built, perhaps in his early fifties. There was not a hint of gray in his blondish-brown, slightly receding hair. His intense blue eyes, muscular physique, confident mien, and angular face made it clear Joe was a fellow who could handle a variety of challenges. I certainly would not have volunteered to arm-wrestle him!

Joe and Anna Wild emigrated from south Germany in the late 1920s. They chose to speak English at home in their quest to be Americans. Anna spoke very good, slightly accented English, but Joe spoke with a curious mix of German and Brooklyn accents. I struggled to keep up with his comments.

He peppered me with questions about where I came from, my work experience, and what I planned to do after finishing my doctorate in Chemical Engineering.

Joe spotted the two bottles of Rhine wine I had placed on the kitchen table, examined them critically, and instructed his wife to put them in the refrigerator to be consumed with dinner.

"How did you select these wines?" Joe asked.

"These were my favorite Rhine wines. I drank them often in the Officer's Club when I was a lieutenant in the army."

Joe nodded his head in approval. Each time he asked me a question, I felt he was mentally registering check marks after my response.

Mrs. Wild laid out a light lunch, consisting of ham slices, Swiss cheese, sausages, and plenty of bread. I thought about trying to speak a little German, which I had studied while in the army, but I didn't dare.

After lunch, everyone went about their day. Doris took me on a detailed tour of their expansive farm—a 500-acre spread that Mr. Wild had built up over the past twenty years. The Wild potato farm was one of the biggest in this part of the state. As we drove back to the house, I reflected on the strong personalities of the family I had just met, and on the undisputed success of their family farming enterprise. I realized that my thought of hillbillies was misplaced, but there still had to be a story behind old Charlie—and there was[2].

Doris and I retired to the living room. She queued up a few records for background classical music, including some of my favorites. She approached me with a maroon, rectangular box in hand.

"Do you play Scrabble? Would you like to play a game with me?"

"Oh, yes," I replied, "That's one of the favorite games in our family. I would love to engage you in a Scrabble match!"

I didn't realize it then, but I had just been set up.

We spread out the Scrabble board on the coffee table and distributed the pieces—seven lettered tiles to both of us. Doris won the first play and made a nice

---

2   Doris Wild Zumwalt, *On the Wildside—A Personal Memoir*, Chapter 9 "Charlie," 1996.

six-letter word, which counted for several points. I responded in kind, then Doris added another big word. I was beginning to sweat a little, and then I spotted an opening.

There were enough words on the board that I could play just four letters and make three new words by interconnecting with existing words. Further, big-numbered letters fell on triple and double count squares, and two of the words fell on a double-word square. This amounted to one of the biggest one-play scores I had ever made.

"Oh, you scoundrel!" Doris shouted. "You just blocked me from making a great word!"

I made a similar play, for fewer points, but which thoroughly locked up the board. I could sense Doris' frustration. Her idea of fun in Scrabble—make big words—was at odds with my strategy of racking up points while denying openings to my opponent. So I relented and opened up the board with a big word for modest points. Doris pounced on this and made a beautiful word for great points. But this opened up the board for me, and I slammed a long word that covered a strategic double letter square and a double word square for more big points. We slugged it out for the rest of the afternoon; when the last tile was played, I had won by a substantial margin.

We stashed the Scrabble game and took a little walk around the near corners of the farm so we could look at things in more detail. Doris pointed out the old two-story farmhouse where the family had lived until recently; she recounted the days of no central heat, no electricity, and no indoor running water. She showed me the site of the "two-holer" privy not far from the house; the lilac bushes planted to camouflage the smell still grew there.

Doris showed me the sheds where she worked, grading and packing potatoes. Close by were the now unused living quarters for the migrant Puerto Rican workers who came each year to help with the harvest. She told me about driving a truck laden with produce to nearby packing houses. She was only fourteen-years-old, had no driver's license, and her feet barely reached the pedals. Her capacity for hard work impressed me then, and over fifty years later, I continue to be amazed at her dynamism.

The call to dinner came shortly after we returned from our stroll. Mrs. Wild had prepared a sumptuous meal, which we all enjoyed. We managed to consume most of the two bottles of Rhine wine I had brought. We took our time at the table, talking and laughing. Of course, I was the target for most of the conversation.

After dinner, we moved to the living room and sipped the remaining wine. Papa Joe and I continued our dinner table talk; he was especially interested in Texas. He wanted to know all about cattle, boots, horses, ranches, cowboys, and oil wells. I told him what I knew about my friends' and relatives' ranches, and that Texas was no longer a frontier state. I think he was a little disappointed when I said I had no boots and had ridden a horse only a few times. Thirty years later, Doris and I purchased the old family house in Hallettsville from my mother, which included a one three-hundredth share in a productive oil well. Imagine Joe's pride in telling his friends and neighbors, "Bob and Doris have an oil well!"

On Sunday morning, Doris demonstrated her cooking skills by preparing breakfast. After she washed the dishes, Doris beckoned me into the living room with a glimmer in her eye.

"How about another game of Scrabble?" she implored. "You can't go back to the university without giving me a chance to even the score!"

So we sat down to another tug of war over who could make the niftiest words. I noticed a change in her tactics. Now, she might forgo a nice word opening and make a short word that scored well but blocked me. My palms became a little sweaty as I geared up for a fight. It was nip and tuck for the entire game, and I barely eked out another win.

We finished around 10:00 a.m. and I felt I shouldn't outstay my welcome. After all, Doris had things to do before she could return to the university. I said goodbye and thanks to all the family members I could find. Doris accompanied me to the car and I thanked her profusely for the wonderful weekend in the country. She gave me another little hug and I climbed into my Chevy.

As I drove north, my mind vibrated with the diverse events of this incredible weekend. I had learned a lot about Doris. She was not just a bright college girl; she was very adaptable in a variety of environments and was not afraid of hard work—she could do many things, intellectual and practical. And she played a tough game of Scrabble.

Of course, I pondered what the family thought of me. I knew I had been under the microscope the entire weekend, but I hadn't a clue about their verdict. Did I pass muster?

After we were married, Doris confessed to me, "Remember that Scrabble game when you first came down to the farm? I gave that test to all the boyfriends I invited to the farm to see if they had anything behind their bluster. You were the only one to beat me, and you did it twice!"

She continued, "Pop was really thrilled when you brought that good German wine. He was impressed with your work and military experience and pleased to hear you planned to continue at the top levels of engineering. But most of all, I think he was impressed because you were a Texan!

"Pop told me I should marry you; he felt you would take care of me for the rest of my life. As follow up to this pronouncement, Pop intervened when one of my most serious former suitors came by to renew the relationship. He wouldn't leave us alone for even a minute lest we might foil his plans for his hand-picked son-in-law."

I indeed provided well for Doris and our family, but she took great care of *me* all our married life! Doris and I were evenly matched at Scrabble for most of our marriage. We play the 14-tile version of the game, which enhances Doris' joy in making long words. Alas, she beats me now almost every time we sit down to play. I fear the day is coming when I am faced with another unannounced test—is it time for Bob to move to the nursing home?

# Crossed Rites

*Interfaith marriages can be fraught with difficulty, usually because
of demands fostered by strong family religious beliefs.*

The spring semester at the University of Delaware had come to an end. Doris had graduated and went home to her family's farm near Camden-Wyoming, Delaware. She was seriously considering a scholarship in International Relations at the University of Denver. I remained at the university, working on my research project.

At least for the summer, Doris acted as the woman of the household, since her mother had just died. She cooked, cleaned, and did sundry chores for her father and three sisters. As the head of household, Papa Joe took care of any disciplinary matters in his unique fashion[3].

Although busy with my lab work, I couldn't keep Doris out of my mind and longed to see her again. We corresponded every week the old-fashioned way—by letters hand-written in cursive.

Doris expressed growing frustration in her letters to me. She was learning to cook and tried hard to please her Papa, but Joe complained often, "What is this shit? Give me something for a man!"

Graduate study at Denver seemed more and more appealing to her as an escape from this frustrating situation. I started coming to the farm on weekends, first only on Saturday, and later stayed for both days. Doris said my visits kept her from going insane during this difficult time.

---

3  Joe Wild, a German-American, was a strong-willed, complex character. Although he retained many of his European mannerisms, he readily moved forward in life without looking back. See "On the Wildside – A Personal Memoir," by Doris Wild Zumwalt, Chapter 9 "Pop."

Before I returned to the university, we often took a ride to get a snack or catch a movie. Afterward, we stayed in the car to say our goodbyes and perhaps steam up the windows. Papa Joe had his unique, European-based method for signaling to suitors it was time to go. He flicked the porch light a few times, came to the edge of the porch, unzipped his fly, and hosed away. Worked every time!

Doris and I became closer and closer as the summer progressed. We talked often of our separation deadline in September when she was to leave for Colorado. We recognized that a long distance romance of 2,500 miles would be difficult to maintain.

We developed a better plan. We would become married graduate students, and Doris would enroll again at the University of Delaware to pursue an MA in International Relations. No formalities, no classic on-my-knee plea for her hand! I returned the following weekend with a ring, although she didn't want one, and we informed her family of our decision. I don't remember asking Papa Joe beforehand if I could marry his daughter.

That's when the topsy-turvy, on-and-off specter of religious problems smacked us in the face!

When we met, I was a baptized Methodist who no longer went to church, and Doris was a confirmed Catholic who no longer went to mass, communion, or confession. We had no religious hang-ups, but some in her family did.

We had been thinking of a non-church, civil wedding, but two of Doris' younger sisters—I call them the "piety sisters"—were still devout Catholics and would have none of it. Doris remembered the family angst when her older sister married a non-Catholic a few months earlier and dreaded what was coming. The piety sisters demanded, "You've got to be married in the Catholic Church or we won't attend your wedding!"

They blocked every alternative we proposed. At first, I resented their devoutness, until I realized this was a result of years of church teaching. Papa Joe said little. He seemed mainly interested in marrying off another daughter (something important to a father of five daughters).

Doris and I reluctantly agreed to marry in the Catholic Church. Papa Joe intervened at this point and made an offer he knew we couldn't refuse. After bankrolling the older sister's larger wedding, he wanted this one to be much simpler and offered $500 to keep it small. This ended up furnishing our student apartment.

I chose to ignore my mother's remote protestation. She was the issue of an interfaith marriage; alternate siblings had been baptized Catholic, then Methodist. This was the same woman who as I was saying goodbye before leaving for my two-year army hitch had given me a big hug and implored, "Now Bobby, don't you marry a Yankee girl while you're away, and for Pete's sake, don't marry a Catholic!"

A simple wedding in Dover, Delaware's Catholic Church lay ahead of us, something that in principle should be easy enough. When we called Father Dominic he stated, "For a mixed marriage, both of you must attend our course of instruction. This could be only one session, but might take three or four if problems arise."

At our first session, Doris introduced me to Father Dominic and explained I was from a strongly Methodist family. Father Dominic warmly shook my hand and looked me over almost approvingly, like a car salesman eager to finish the deal with a likely prospect. Then he turned a steely eye to Doris.

"I haven't seen you at mass or confession lately. Are you still keeping the faith after you've gone off to college?"

I'm not sure, but I believe Doris blanched when the priest asked that question. She gave me a furtive, guilty smirk.

Father Dominic was about six feet tall, with silver-tinged, wavy hair and intense blue eyes. He looked very fit and youthful—maybe in his late forties. I thought he might even be a handsome dude if he took off that tight collar and wore normal clothes.

Father Dominic had a pliable face. It could be soft and welcoming when he explained things, pinched and red when he confronted an argument, and when faced with blasphemy, it would become deeply furrowed with narrowed eyes and mouth constricted in anger. His facial muscles got a good workout during our sessions!

The earnest priest explained his goals for the instruction, "I would like you to see the beauty of the Catholic faith and join our flock. And I want you to understand you must not hinder Doris in any way as she practices her Catholicism. Finally, you must agree you will raise all your children as Catholics and refrain from using contraception. For interfaith marriages, the Church requires that both you and Doris must sign a document stipulating the last two maxims."

Father Dominic looked toward me in vain for a sign of reaction to his goals. I sat there, implacable, as I ruminated over what he had just said. I thought to myself, *not a chance*, on the first item, *not likely*, on the second, and, *no way*, on the third.

Doris seemed equally unimpressed.

Our pontifical instructor explained some Catholic basics and asked questions to test our understanding. Finally, I awoke to the opportunity to turn this discussion into a two-way street, as I recalled the conflict between the Catholic and Protestant communities in my hometown.

"Father," I questioned, "as long as I can remember, my home town in Texas has been plagued with difficulties between the Catholic Church and the rest of the community. Like Doris and me, there were many loving couples who sought interfaith marriage. But a hardcore priest ruled against these couples without mercy by threatening to excommunicate those who didn't conform.

Occasionally, parents of the couple were just as stubborn as the old priest—families broke up and children were banished or disinherited. And a few waited until their parents had passed on before marrying."

Father Dominic was aghast at my heretical comments. His face dropped, then brightened as he prepared to comment.

But I beat him to the punch as I continued my harangue. "Father, why is it that your way is the only right way? It seems reasonable to me that you could marry us without my signing these documents. Who knows? Later on, I might see the light and become a solid member of some Catholic congregation."

On the way home I said to Doris, "I apologize for causing a commotion with Father Dominic."

She impishly grinned and responded, "You're doing great, keep it up!"

Back at the farm, we shared our experience with the rest of the family. Doris' faithful sisters were eager to learn our reaction.

I started, "I'm not a very strong churchgoer in my baptized religion, but I think the priest's demand that we should sign those papers is off the wall. Even if I signed them, I know in my heart I wouldn't obey them."

Papa Joe chimed in and expressed an opinion for the first time on this matter, "C'mon on, Bob, what's the big deal? This isn't some legal document. You are not promising anything about money. Just sign those papers and move on!"

Doris spoke up animatedly, "What do you mean, this is no big deal? It's a matter of principle! I don't want to be a hypocrite when I sign something. Maybe we should abandon the church wedding and get married by a justice of the peace."

The piety sisters started their mantra, "We won't come to your wedding if it's not in the church. We won't even see you again if you turn your back on Catholicism!"

I thought to myself, *My goodness, is this family going to break up because of a wedding?*

During the next meeting, Father Dominic answered the question I posed in our first session: "This has been Church law for centuries and we can't change it."

By now I knew where this struggle had to end and I begrudgingly accepted its inevitable conclusion. But I figured that I might as well poke a little fun along the way.

I remarked, "Father, I think the Catholic Church could stand a little more competition in Italy, where much of the church's dogma originates. Don't you think the Church would become a better institution if there were more Baptists and Methodists in Italy?"

No longer exasperated by my irreverent remarks, Father Dominic calmly replied, "Isn't that what we have now in the United States, in your hometown?"

Doris and I ended this meeting by saying we weren't sure we would sign the papers but were still willing to be convinced.

At home, the strident voices of the piety sisters dominated our family gathering. The loud ring of the telephone interrupted our arguments. Papa Joe answered and with a grim face handed the receiver to Doris, "It's Father Dominic!"

We craned our necks to hear both sides of the conversation.

Father Dominic sternly announced, "Doris, I've decided not to marry you and Bob. I'm afraid you two would not live up to your obligations to the Church."

All our faces hung with gloom.

For the first time, Papa Joe got really worried about the religious problem, since our wedding date was fast approaching. He took Doris and me aside for a private discussion, "Our family has suffered enough religious stress about marriage. I don't want to go through this again. Why don't you two just hold your noses and sign those papers? You know you don't have to obey those promises!"

At our next meeting, Doris emphatically told Father Dominic, "Bob and I have decided to sign the papers. We are ready to move on!"

The priest carefully considered our change in position, his face registering the various emotions he felt as he reflected on Doris' statement. Finally, he told us, "I've got to call the Bishop in Wilmington."

He said to his superior, "Monsignor, I talked with you earlier about this couple. I decided not to marry them because of their resistance to our teachings.

Now, they have come in and agreed to sign all our papers. But I really doubt their sincerity. What should I do?"

The Bishop spoke so loudly we could easily hear his telephonic response.

"Father Dominic, those kids are going to get married somewhere. Why don't *we* marry them and claim them on *our* rolls?"

And that was it—the hectoring was done—the insincere agreed to marry the hypocritical. We signed the papers on the spot.

Saturday was our big day. I drove down from the university, just a little bit nervous about what lay ahead. Doris told me later she was also nervous. After all, we had known each other for only six months and had seriously dated for only three. We were facing a lifetime together and didn't know where this would take us. Papa Joe gave me a shot of scotch to steady my nerves.

The small wedding party assembled at the Catholic Church. Doris wore a pretty blue suit, and I wore my only suit, in dark blue. We stood in front of Father Dominic. The guests were few: Doris' immediate family, her uncle and his family, and Doris' college roommate. Father Dominic conducted the minimum legal and clerical parts of the wedding ceremony—no music, no mass. At the end, Papa Joe, showing his displeasure at the controversy the Church had made us endure, threw a $100 bill at the priest's feet.

After dinner with the wedding party, Doris and I left on our "honeymoon"—to the married student apartments at the University of Delaware. We started married life running; both of us had to register for fall-semester classes on Monday.

Doris' professors jokingly referred to the married student apartments as rabbit warrens, where all residents practiced applied mathematics—multiplication. We quickly violated one of the major promises we had signed. At the first opportunity, Doris visited the local gynecologist to get a contraceptive device. But before prescribing it, the good doctor asked if she was a Catholic.

"No," she responded.

"Good," he harrumphed, "too many Catholics come for contraceptives and then admit it at confession. Then the priest knocks at my door and demands I stop corrupting his parishioners."

Our first son was born two years later.

Three months after our wedding, Papa Joe called early one Saturday morning and almost commanded, "Bob, you and Doris meet me at the mayor's office in Wilmington at 11:00 a.m. sharp!"

"Hey, Joe, what's up?"

"Anne and I are getting married and I want you two to be witnesses."

"Why in Wilmington?" I asked.

"I'll explain that later."

Doris and I knew he was very fond of a widow who lived on a nearby farm and had recently been dating her. But we had no idea they were getting serious. We cleaned up a little, put on dress clothes, and dashed to Wilmington's City Hall.

The mayor conducted a simple civil wedding ceremony, even simpler than our church wedding. We were the official witnesses and the only guests.

Afterward, the four of us celebrated at a nice restaurant in Wilmington. We couldn't wait to ask the question—why?

Joe filled us in, "We went to Father Dominic to arrange our wedding in the church. When he learned Anne was still of child-bearing age, the priest insisted we must go through instruction and sign those promises just like you had to do. I wasn't going to ask Anne to go through that and I didn't want to sign, either. Five kids is enough!"

Doris and I nearly choked on our salad. Joe never went to church. Questions ran through my mind. *Why did he go to Father Dominic? Were the piety sisters at it again? And why did Joe refuse to sign? Weren't principles something to ignore as a matter of convenience?* In his own way, Joe was just as hypocritical as we were. Later, Doris and I laughed many times over Papa Joe's conflicting advice. It was okay for us to ignore our principles, but he couldn't bear to do it himself!

# Engineer on Wheels

*A veteran engineer mentors a new employee and teaches about non-technical aspects of professional life. This story honors a remarkable person while describing an important but forgotten branch of computer technology.*

It was a hot Texas day in June and I had just finished with the personnel department and reported to my new supervisor. At last, I had finished my four years of graduate school and I was starting my career in mathematical modeling and dynamic simulation. My favorite graduate course at the University of Delaware was Differential Equations in Chemical Engineering, taught by Dr. Pigford, the beloved and nationally known head of the department. How wonderful that a refinery in a major oil company wanted to work those kinds of problems—and were willing to pay me to do it!

I was four years older and more experienced than the typical new engineer hired at the refinery. Almost twenty new engineers checked into the refinery around that time. That was when college graduates didn't take a year off after graduation or travel to Europe. They went right to work, instead. In spite of my experience and my newly earned Ph. D., I was still characteristically apprehensive about the new job, and probably more than a little bit naïve about how to do things in the real world of an oil refinery. I was just another one of the greenhorns, waiting to be picked on by the veteran employees.

My supervisor introduced me to most of the section members in the office building and then took me to the basement to point out my office and the enormous computer system I would be working on. *Wow!* This computer system could fill a warehouse—three big analog computers that could be connected together. With such a system, one could simulate the behavior of the refinery's process units and devise better ways to operate and control them.

Next, the boss took me into the adjoining office, introduced me to Tim Henley, and simply explained, "You'll be working a lot with Tim." I reached out to shake his hand, making sure to use my firmest Aggie handshake. Still, Tim's large hand easily enveloped mine and commenced crushing my knuckles! Tim was a big guy, with broad shoulders and thick forearms. He could have been a football linebacker. A wide big-toothed grin smiled out at me from a round, friendly face punctuated by big bulging eyes. He wore work pants and work boots, topped with an open-neck sports shirt.

Tim wheeled out from his desk and positioned his wheelchair in sociable mode, instead of in work mode. Often, when you see a person in a wheelchair, you see the wheelchair; but in this case, you saw Tim and simply remarked that he was in a wheelchair. Tim's presence, both verbal and physical, dominated that wheelchair!

As we engaged in small talk, my mind couldn't help wondering how Tim fit into the marvelous simulation projects I hoped to be working on. *Was he a technician? Was he the analog computing equivalent to a programmer?* Try to understand my confusion, because at that time the dress code for engineers was suit or sports coat with tie, and I couldn't relate that with Tim's dress. During Texas summers, we shed the coat but still wore the tie.

But it didn't take long for me to figure out how *I* was going to fit into *Tim's* world of large-scale dynamic simulation. Tim was an electrical engineer, a professional qualification which is often a misfit among the dominant species in a refinery—the chemical engineers. In fact, the refinery offered a course each year, "Chemical Engineering for Non-Chemical Engineers." Tim could have taught that course! He taught himself process engineering and worked on many projects that required chemical engineering skills. His electrical engineering background enabled him to move into the emerging field of analog computing. He was one of the first in the company to recognize that dynamic simulation of processes with analog computers could be very useful.

Analog computers calculate with DC voltages instead of the on/off bits of modern digital computers. I had played around with a mere toy analog computer at the University of Delaware, but it was not big enough to solve real problems. Tim pointed out the details of our computer—three consoles, each bigger than six refrigerators placed side by side, interconnected by several cables each as thick as a forearm (mine, not Tim's). Tim proudly said, "There are 400 operational amplifiers (the basic computing block) and each has seven vacuum tubes! We have dozens of square-root, logarithm, and non-linear cards. You can enter simulation constants from hundreds of potentiometers (knobs to turn)."

I asked him why we didn't use digital computers for dynamic simulation, and Tim explained, "Yes, digital computers work well for *very small* simulations." He continued, "But for the large problems encountered in the refinery, digital computers would take several hours to run just one case. Current digital computers are just too slow for large-scale dynamic simulation."

Tim showed me the patch panel for his current project—a large 2x3 foot aluminum slab with hundreds of red, green, and yellow colored holes. It was festooned with a rat's nest of multicolored wires plugged into the holes. This was the *program* for an analog computer simulation—not a deck of punched cards, punched tape, or a disk file as we use in digital computers.

The wires, called *patch cords*, connected the various analog computing blocks so the resulting electronic circuits would solve the differential equations for our project. Depending on the problem's size, a patch panel was needed for each analog computer console. To see the simulation results you looked at voltage readouts and at key variables plotted on a recording device.

"Let's start with a simple reactor simulation," Tim said as he started my instruction on practical analog computation. "Why don't you write the differential equations for this system?" Armed with my courses from the University of Delaware, I quickly wrote out the equations. Tim continued, "Now show me how you propose to magnitude-scale and time-scale those equations!"

"Huh," I reacted, "these are the equations. Let's not fool around; let's just solve them."

Tim patiently explained that the analog computer always represents process variables such as temperature or flow as DC voltages ranging from -100V to +100V, not in degrees Fahrenheit or barrels per day. Further, he convinced me it would not be good to solve the equations in *real time*, since some processes took hours to complete a change in conditions. "We use time-scaling to speed up or slow down the analog computation, relative to the process time domain," Tim explained, "and usually we speed things up."

Tim showed me how to incorporate the time and magnitude scaling into the values entered by the potentiometer knobs—the *pot settings*. I fastidiously drew a neat circuit diagram for the simulation, listed the scale factors and the pot setting calculations, and patched up the simulation. Naturally, I had some errors, and Tim showed me how to debug an analog simulation. He got a laugh when he showed me a method not recommended in the computer vendor's manual—kick the computer cabinet. One console had some quirky relays; a swift kick in the right place always fixed the problem.

I now understood the methods for setting up a simulation. I faithfully followed these systematic steps for all my future work. But I was distraught one day as I watched Tim work a modest-sized problem brought in by a field engineer. He was furiously patching away, without any visible reference to what he was doing. "Hey, Tim," I asked, "where's your circuit diagram?" He pointed to his head!

Tim's basic approach was to grab a fistful of patch cords and plug away. He had enough experience and innate engineering skills that he could build a simulation on the fly. When he got the simulation working the way he wanted, he would scratch out a messy looking circuit diagram for documentation purposes. Only Tim could do that!

Now it was time for me to start up a real, if small, simulation on my own. I was soloing, analog computer style. Tim wasn't there to guide me in case of uncertainty;

in fact, I didn't know where Tim was. I tentatively patched and unpatched wires, trying to remember Tim's instructions: "Always plug a wire into the green hole (input) first, and then into the red hole (output). That way, you won't risk grabbing a hundred volts and you won't be creating sparks!"

I was understandably nervous about shocking myself or zapping the expensive computing equipment. I paused a little to make sure I was following the proper procedure, and then confidently shoved the wire first into a green hole and then into a red hole. Imagine my distress when smoke started pouring from the analog computer console! In near panic, I quickly pulled the wire out, muttering, "What did I do wrong? How did I mess up?" I was really worried until I realized this was tobacco smoke and not the acrid smoke of burned electrical circuits. When I saw the two technicians behind me howling, I knew I had been had! Tim had wheeled his chair behind the console and, at the critical moment, puffed some cigarette smoke into the computer cabinet.

I was properly initiated now and could get on with some real work. My supervisor gave me plenty of interesting work, but I was secretly hoping that someday veteran field engineers would come directly to me with their problems, as they routinely did with Tim. That was the mark of real respect!

Tim was my mentor, and we became close professional friends as we discussed work items. We soon enjoyed a personal friendship as well. I was still very hesitant about discussing Tim's disability with him. Finally, I asked him and he readily talked. After many years of engineering work at the refinery, he contracted polio, less than a year before the vaccine became available. As only Tim could explain it, "I was lucky that only my legs were involved. I can get around well on crutches, and can drive a specially equipped van."

Around me, Tim never showed any bitterness about his plight, never complained. He was always concerned about the present and the future and never dwelled on the past or what might have been. He focused on what he could do instead of being frustrated with what he couldn't. Often, he found a way to convert the latter into the former. Tim, like the rest of us, had a family to love, a house to fix up, a mortgage to pay, and a ton of work to do for his employer.

Tim was a whiz in the wheelchair. He could stealthily sneak up on you and look over your shoulder, he could idle down the hallway as we were chatting, and he could bear down on a group like a bowling ball when he wanted to make a dramatic appearance.

Tim made sure I got a graduate degree in practical simulation as well. I recall a demonstration I gave for my supervisor to show him the nifty cat-cracker[4] simulation I had developed. Initially, everything worked fine, and then the overload alarm sounded. The simulation had crashed! Appalled, I checked the circuit in the vicinity of the alarm and found I had not connected a wire. I thought I had already done that, but I grabbed another wire, plugged it in, and got the simulation working again. I was greeted with applause from the supervisor, the technicians, and Tim, who was holding the missing wire and grinning broadly.

Everyone had a big laugh, but I was still a little agitated. "Why did you try to embarrass me in front of our supervisor?" I demanded.

Tim calmly replied, "Things don't always go right in this business, and Murphy's law seems to kick in when you are giving demonstrations. I want you to be able to handle such situations, and you did well this time!" Tim was teaching me and not trying to sabotage my work—he had created the fault so it could be easily found.

Sure enough, a few years later, I was demonstrating the new technology of computer control to the president of the company and several other bigwigs. The computer was controlling a cat cracker. We were demonstrating how the operator could change process conditions with the computer. As soon as he completed his moves, the computer crashed, accompanied by a very urgent-sounding alarm. The operator calmly left the computer console and went over to the backup panel to monitor the process changes. I quickly explained to the visiting dignitaries: "This unscheduled computer downtime demonstrates that a computer malfunction does not endanger normal process operations; if necessary, the operator can still monitor and run the cat cracker."

Thanks to Tim, I was prepared!

---

4  Important refinery process unit for making gasoline.

I learned analog computing for about a year at the knee of Tim Henley. He figured I could then handle the refinery's needs while he enjoyed a two-year assignment at the Central Engineering Department (CED) in New Jersey.

You can imagine the sparks when Tim hit New Jersey! CED was a very structured and orthodox organization, with a strict dress code. Converting Tim to a CED man was a force-fit at best. To their credit, Tim and the CED managers bent over backwards to accommodate this malaprop union. Tim even wore the occasional tie in the presence of visiting dignitaries. I was later transferred to CED and I asked my new colleagues about Tim. All agreed Tim was one of the finest talents at analog computing they had ever met, but he didn't document projects very well. All they needed was a brain dump!

Tim pushed through projects to replace the analog computers with hybrid computers (analog plus digital) and ultimately to replace the hybrid machines with all-digital computers. Analog computing, once an exciting gleam in the eye of an eager-beaver young engineer, is just a misty-eyed memory. Digital computers now rule the simulation world.

All of us who worked with Tim miss him dearly, for he's gone on to work at that great computer in the sky. I just hope Saint Peter kept his toes out of the way when Tim wheeled up that pearly ramp. I'll bet Tim was really scootin' along!

# The Baa's Motel

*Four city-slicker engineers on a business trip encounter a long-simmering feud between an old tomcat and a pampered pet crow, which explodes in a riot of commotion at this unusual Animal Farm guest house.*

I feel compelled to tell you about this trip, because, in my opinion, it sets the gold standard for bizarre business trips. None of my colleagues' war stories can top this one!

"Oh no," I groaned, after glancing at the meeting notice, "it's at the Pelican Refinery again." The notice gave details of Sluik Oil's Energy Conservation Committee meeting at this remote refinery on Canada's Atlantic coast.

The Sluik Oil Company operates five refineries, strategically positioned across the U.S. and Canada to serve special marketing or oil supply opportunities. All are small, since Sluik Oil has garnered only a tiny sliver of the gasoline and heating oil pie. The Pelican Refinery is the smallest, at 60,000 barrels per day.

This privately owned independent refining company survives in the hotly competitive refining business only because its tiny refineries, uneconomical in the mainstream, serve the nooks and crannies of the marketplace. Old Charlie Sluik, Board Chairman and CEO, is proud of how efficiently his lean staff operates those refineries.

His grandfather, Willem Sluik, founded the company in the early 1900s. Willem's enterprise survived the Rockefeller era only because old John D. couldn't be bothered by the peanut-sized operations in out-of-the-way places.

Charlie recruits top-notch technical and operations personnel and pays them well. He cross-trains his staff so each engineer and technician can do several jobs. Oil-industry union moguls have no hope in organizing these refineries.

I work at the Anniston, Alabama refinery. The other refineries are situated at Midland, Texas; Pueblo, Colorado; and Bellingham, Washington. Company-wide technical committees cover all facets of process technology, as well as economic planning. I am head of the Process Control Committee, but I also serve on four other committees. I was scheduled to deliver an important report on steam system operation at the coming Energy Conservation (Encon) Committee meeting.

Most of us don't like going to the Pelican Refinery on Pelican Egg Island in eastern Canada. The refinery is excellent, the people are friendly, and the island is rustic and scenic. But we deplore the lack of decent business accommodations.

Pelican Egg[5] is a large island just off the coast of Nova Scotia—not nearly so large as the neighboring island of Prince Edward. Pelican City is the island's only town. The island has a mainly agricultural base, with a small fishing economy. The only manufacturing is the Pelican Refinery, situated on a natural harbor on the leeward side.

I considered my hotel options: the SameOld Motel and the Pelican's Roost Inn. Neither appealed to me.

On my first visit to Pelican, I chose the Pelican's Roost because of its interesting name. Yes, its exterior was indeed rustic, but as a business-class motel the active description would be "rusty." It housed a very popular, noisy pub. The guest rooms were just above the pub and faced a central hallway. At each end of the hall

______________________

5   Local legend says the island got its name when a raiding crow dropped a huge pelican egg directly on the head of the Marquis de Cassetête, the dauntless French explorer.

were rooms labeled "Gents" and "Ladies," shared by all guests of the inn. I was conditioned to shared bathrooms during my years in France, but I hated having to stand in the hall in my pajamas, waiting my turn.

I tossed and turned on the sagging mattress, the thumping music below impeding my sleep. Although the food in the pub was good and the conviviality warm, the guest rooms evoked an air of seediness. I said to myself upon departure, "Never again!"

For my last three visits, I stayed at the SameOld Motel. Its founder, old Louie Sameson, proudly selected its now-unfortunate name. He thought the wordplay on his name was cute, and it was in the 1950s. Young Louie now runs the motel, and he has unwittingly bestowed its name with added relevance. The motel has perpetually been in maintenance mode since he took over.

Apparently, the motel's only upgrade has been a coat of cheap paint. Mr. Sameson thrives on a very simplistic but firm principle: if it's broke, fix it, but for Pete's sake, don't replace it. Mattresses are lumpy and unforgiving, bedspreads are tattered with cigarette-burn holes. The walls are reasonably soundproofed, and the private bathroom has 1950s fixtures—quirky but workable. What more could a business traveler want?

I apologize for boring you with all these details, but you must know what I previously endured to understand the desperation that led me into the next calamitous set of accommodations.

I telephoned my able colleague at Pelican Refinery, Pablo Canale, the host of this committee meeting, hoping he could recommend a better place to stay. Pablo is the son of a French mother and an Italian father; the family emigrated from the south of France to Montréal. His olive complexion and slightly accented English identify him as a foreigner—no big deal in Canada, but a rarity on the isolated isle of Pelican Egg.

With his Latin background, I hoped he could empathize with my desire for better accommodations.

"*Bon jour, Pablo,*" I said when he answered, "*comment* ça *va?*"

Pablo responded with a torrent of staccato French, of which I understood every third word. I protested, "Pablo, you know I can't understand Canadian French; why don't you speak the real stuff?"

He laughed, "You've been exposed to too much Southern drawl. I'm speaking French just like my highly excitable Mama taught me! I think you need some practice—why don't you take a vacation in Montréal?"

After we finished our usual good-natured banter, I explained my problem: "Pablo, I'm really looking forward to the coming Encon committee meeting, and I think the other members are, too. We have a couple of important issues to work that should help all sites in Sluik Oil save money. But I'm not at all looking forward to staying at either of Pelican Egg Island's not-so-elegant hostelries!"

"Tell me more," Pablo answered in a neutral tone.

I reviewed the shortcomings of the Pelican's Roost and the SameOld Motel. I could almost sense Pablo yawning, as I'm sure he had heard these complaints on my previous visits.

The line went silent after I finished my complaints and I feared Pablo was thinking up some diplomatic way to keep my problem off his back. Finally, Pablo's voice resumed: "Sorry for the delay. I just called my wife on the other line. There is a wholly different alternative you might like better. My wife knows an elderly couple who have converted their farm into a B, B&B."

"Wait a minute," I shouted, "I know what a B&B is. Are you stuttering, or did you really say B, B&B? What the heck is a B, B&B?"

Pablo laughed, "That's a Barn, Bed, and Breakfast! My wife says those are very popular for weekend getaways, especially for the big-city people. She says the place is booked solid every weekend until winter, but it's available on weekdays. Each guest cabin has its own bathroom *and* a small barn, with a domestic animal to care for. The lady is an excellent cook. My wife says people rave about her breakfasts. And she'll make supper for you if you wish."

I hesitated—my mind conjuring up images of travel in rural Switzerland, where the duplex barns and farmhouses always had a big, steaming manure pile in front.

"Hey, are these people Swiss, or something like that?" I asked, a bit skeptically. "Are we going to depend on a decomposing, smelly manure pile to heat our cabins?"

Pablo laughed and quipped, "No, the couple is as English as you can get. Don't worry about the smelly end of the domestic animal business; they keep the place very clean."

Still dubious about such arrangements, I told Pablo to proceed, "Okay, this sounds like it's worth a try."

After arriving at the Halifax airport, I sat in the waiting area for the commuter flight to Pelican Egg Island with almost an hour to kill. Since I arrived ahead of the others, I reviewed my steam system report. Every few minutes I scanned the room for my other committee colleagues. In principle, all of us would be on this flight; the next flight would be two hours later. Pelican Egg Island wasn't exactly a prime travel destination.

Carlita Sanchez arrived first, from the Pueblo Refinery. Carlita is a distillation expert; she plays a prime role on the Encon Committee, since distillation is one of the biggest energy consumers in a refinery. She is a petite, vivacious woman, with a figure you would believe impossible for a mother of three. Her efficiently coiffed short brown hair blends well with her dark brown eyes—eyes a fellow might like to peer into, but which could quickly cut into any engineer who tried to pull the technical wool over them. She is a highly respected engineer throughout the Sluik Oil circuit.

"Hi, Carlita," I greeted her and rose to shake her hand, "Did you have a good trip?"

"Everything was fine, except for the usual delay getting into Dallas. I was really sweating my connecting flight to Halifax!"

"Yeah, you don't want to miss the flight to Pelican Egg—it's a long wait for the next one. I sure hope the other two guys make it in time."

Just as we were seated again, both of the expected travelers walked into the gate area together. They had been on the same flight from Chicago. Tex

Richardson, from Midland, was hard to miss. He is a tall, lanky guy with an unkempt shock of reddish brown hair and an engaging, boyish smile. Tex was really duded up that day, sporting a wide-brimmed cowboy hat, blue jeans with a wide belt and buckle, cowboy boots, and a decorated cowboy shirt. He really likes to play the Texan role, especially on business trips, but I never saw him dressed like this when I visited Midland. Tex is a mechanical engineer, Sluik Oil's only compressor specialist. The poor fellow is on-call for compressor problems for the entire refinery circuit.

Andy Calhoun slightly trailed him. Andy is Bellingham's furnace expert and no slouch as a control engineer. He is the only committee member who doesn't look like he could run a mile. I'm not sure he could even make one lap. Andy is about five feet ten, and he must weigh at least 280 pounds. He wore his business suit with about as much aplomb as he could muster, and had unsuccessfully cinched up his tie to conceal his unbuttoned collar, which could no longer circumnavigate his neck. His slothful appearance could not detract from his mental acuity, however. Andy is the Encon Committee chairman, and the proud possessor of a letter from Charlie Sluik, commending him for running the most effective technical committee last year.

As we awaited our flight, we occupied ourselves with small talk, news about our respective refineries, and general discussion of the coming meeting. Of course, we poked a lot of fun at Tex Richardson, stimulated by his colorful garb—Texans always seem to attract a lot of kidding. But Tex was quick on his feet, and his nimble mind concocted some well-targeted insults for each of us.

All of us were silent on the prospects for our unusual accommodations on Pelican Egg—the Animal Farm B, B&B. Each of us harbored a lot of anxiety about caring for farm animals. None of us had grown up on a farm, shoveled manure, nor dealt with a balky animal. Probably, we had all fantasized about feeding the cute critters, petting them and talking nonsense to them—at least I had. Although our stomachs were knotted by worry and uncertainty, none of us wanted to expose our lack of confidence in handling these animals or to admit our total lack of experience in such matters. We covered up our collective anxiety with idle chatter.

The loudspeaker in our area barked loudly, shunting our animal farm anxieties into the background, "CanCommuter Flight 3031 for Pelican Egg Island is ready for boarding. Please have your boarding passes and picture IDs ready for inspection."

Good old Pablo, he had left a map and detailed instructions at the car rental desk, explaining how to drive to the Animal Farm B, B&B. Pelican Egg Island was big enough to get lost in, but not so big it could support a first-class system of roads. To me, each farm looked like the next, and the narrow roads were not graced with clear markings. I drove the first car, and with Tex serving as navigator, we followed the map to our destination. Carlita drove the second car, with Andy Calhoun in the jump seat.

Our small caravan arrived at the Animal Farm just before 5:00 p.m. The small, unassuming sign at the entrance said simply: 'B, B&B.' The name 'Animal Farm' was stenciled on the sides of the rural mailbox. We pulled up to a small farm shed labeled 'Office.' Next to it stood an old Victorian two-story, high-gabled farmhouse surrounded by a white picket fence—evidently the owners' residence.

We searched for the entrance to the office but saw only a large wooden door that looked like an entrance to a barn. I lifted the wooden latch, pulled open the heavy door a bit, and tentatively looked in. Sure enough, there was something resembling a reception desk on the other side of the large room. I tried to step over the threshold, but there was none; the floor was just packed earth, only slightly higher than the surrounding ground. I beckoned the others to enter.

As my eyes adjusted to the dim light, I took notice of my surroundings. The entire floor was earthen. Although it appeared relatively clean, there was a slight whiff of a fresh agricultural smell. I thought, *What kind of a line were you feeding me, Pablo?* There were two wooden benches fitted with plastic-covered cushions. Other than these, there was no furniture except a small TV stand in the corner; on it, an ancient-looking set blared out the evening news. The dim features of the news anchor barely shone through the blizzard of snow.

A big black bird sat on a shiny chrome hat rack in the other corner. I wasn't sure, but it looked like a crow. It shuffled nervously on its perch as it regarded the strange interlopers and then emitted a tentative 'caw.' Apparently, it didn't know what to make of the situation, and neither did we.

I approached the desk, on which sat a hand-lettered reception sign and a smaller sign that said, 'Press Button If No One Here.' Since no one was in the office, I reached for the button. But I was interrupted by a big mean-looking orange cat with pinned-down, battle-scarred ears, who looked up from his apparent slumber on the desk. He hissed and growled at me, threateningly. Reflexively, I jerked my hand back and said soothingly, "Nice kitty!" I didn't dare try to pet him. Before I could reach for the button again, a small door behind the desk opened and an authoritative lady hurried in.

She was just a little over five feet tall, but wow, did she have a presence! Her metal-framed bifocals gave her an old-fashioned, no-nonsense look. Her gray hair was pulled back in a bun and she wore a nondescript house dress that concealed whatever figure she might have had. Her bare arms seemed quite muscular, and I felt she knew very well what to do with the business end of a shovel.

"Good evening, folks," she announced. "Sorry to keep you waiting, but I was in the middle of something in the kitchen and didn't want to risk burning it. Are you the people from Sluik Oil?"

We confirmed her supposition, and she continued, "Welcome to the Animal Farm B, B&B. We aim to make your stay just a little bit different, something you can talk about for years to come. I'm Glynis Peters and my husband Lyle will be here shortly to help you with your bags and with your animals."

She turned out to be right on the years to come!

"We've already come in contact with two of your animals," I quipped and pointed toward the crow. "What's the story about that bird?"

"Oh, that rascal, he's a mess!" she responded. "That's Corky. We rescued him as a wee fallen chick. I put him in a box in the kitchen and fed him with oatmeal and table scraps. He bonded so closely with us that he never would join up with the wild crows. Every time we put him outside, he flew back into the house."

"We named him Corky, because he collected all our wine-bottle corks and stashed them in his nest." She continued, "Be careful with your jewelry, because he still likes to snatch shiny things for his nest."

Then she looked up to old Corky on his perch and beseeched, "Say 'hi' to the nice people, Corky."

The old bird cocked his head and looked us over with beady eyes. Seemingly, he approved of us and delivered two much more confident caws.

I noticed how the cat alerted, looked intently at the squawking crow, and started making those little yips so peculiar to cats when they see an enticing nearby bird.

"And what about this miniature lion guarding the desk?" I asked with a smile.

"That's Grumpy," Mrs. Peters explained. "He arrived at the door many years ago, tattered, hungry, and bloody. His face was all messed up. It looked like he was kicked—maybe by an abusive person or even a cow. That explains his almost permanent scowl."

"Doesn't the cat bother the crow?" Carlita asked.

Mrs. Peters quickly reassured, "No, dear, nothing serious goes on between them. They have a perpetual stand-off. Corky is always trying to steal the cat's food, and Grumpy makes sure the crow doesn't spend too much time at a low altitude! Also, Grumpy would slide down if he tried to climb the hat rack—I've seen him try that."

She patted the old cat on the head and said to him, "Say 'hi' to our guests, Grumpy."

The cat surely seemed to be scowling when he produced something that sounded like a cross between a grunt and a meow, officially acknowledging our presence. Then he rose, stretched, and started nuzzling Mrs. Peters' hand and arm, claiming her in feline fashion as his own. The crow was tracking the cat's movement and seemed to be staring directly at his rival. I could have sworn that old bird was giving Grumpy the evil-eye.

When we finished the usual guest registration formalities, Mrs. Peters announced, "Now it's time for you folks to get the special treat that you came here for, the farm animals!" The four of us looked at each other expressionlessly, not a hint of support showing for our hostess' enthusiasm.

She tapped out a semaphore with the buzzer button. Moments later, Mr. Peters opened the big door to the office and led in a beautiful horse, a mare with a gorgeous chocolate brown coat and a flowing black mane. She swished her tail idly at the flies that always seem to accompany farm animals. Aroused by the commotion, Corky shuffled his feet anxiously on his perch but said nothing. Grumpy opened one eye, then went back to sleep.

"Good evening, folks," Mr. Peters said deliberately. "I'd like to introduce you to Janet, who's been with us for over three years. She's a lovely, gentle horse who really likes people."

Mr. Peters was about six feet tall, with thinning gray hair. He was wiry, with a gaunt face that was lined and weather beaten. He might have had bad teeth, for he kept his mouth as closed as possible when talking or smiling. His blue work trousers would have fallen from his almost non-existent hips without the crucial support of a pair of bright red suspenders draped over a flannel shirt. He was a man of few words, who obviously preferred Mrs. Peters to do most of the talking.

She quickly took the cue. "All of you, come stroke her neck and see how loving and gentle she is," she invited, as she scratched the horse's ears and planted a little kiss on her nose. One by one, we dutifully came over and patted Janet's neck. I thought she was amazingly gentle. Tex was the last to come up. He was more apprehensive than the rest of us and tensed up a bit as he approached the horse. Janet sensed this and shied away, but Mrs. Peters quickly calmed the horse and placed Tex's hand on the horse's neck. Tex told me later this was the first time he'd ever touched a horse, and he couldn't believe how warm and relaxing it felt to him.

"Okay, big cowboy fellow," Mrs. Peters gushed, "how would you like to be the one who gets Janet?" Without waiting for an answer, she handed the reins to Tex, who just stood there stupefied and trapped by his regalia. His cowboy boots had never been introduced to the smell of manure, his fancy shirt had never been soiled by the dusty sweat of hard work, and his designer jeans had never straddled a horse's back.

"Way to go, Tex!" we kidded. "They know a real cowboy when they see one. We know you can uphold the honor of Texas!" Our levity was just a ruse to keep our minds off our own anxieties about taking charge of a big, real farm animal. Corky looked down at us curiously, as if he didn't quite understand what was going on.

While we were fooling around with Janet and Tex, Mr. Peters had silently disappeared and returned leading a small, somewhat balky goat. He tersely introduced the goat as Randy. "Randy is a little edgy today," he explained, "but normally he is very gentle and cooperative."

"Oh, I've always liked goats!" Carlita shouted. She couldn't contain her excitement. "I think they're so cute! Can I have him?"

Startled by the strident voice, Randy started to charge the visiting woman, but his inherently gentle nature quickly came to the surface and stopped him in his tracks. Mrs. Peters came to the rescue and put Randy's lead into Carlita's hand. She cautioned, "Try not to talk loudly or move suddenly. The old boy's really very gentle, but sometimes he gets overly excited. If he does, just drop his lead and talk softly and calmly." Randy relaxed completely and let Carlita rub his neck and scratch his ears, which also relieved a lot of Carlita's own tension.

Next, Mr. Peters brought in Cleo, the sheep. She was a beautiful ewe with bluish gray wool. "She won a blue ribbon at last year's farm fair," Mrs. Peters proudly announced, "and she is gentle as a lamb."

Mrs. Peters glanced at Andy and said, "You look like you would be happy to care for a nice gentle sheep, wouldn't you, young man?" Andy grinned sheepishly, not wanting to betray his inner apprehensions about taking charge of any animal. He meekly replied in the affirmative and Mrs. Peters handed him the lead.

Randy suddenly pulled at his lead, and Carlita instinctively pulled back, although she remembered Mrs. Peters' admonition. Randy dragged Carlita along as he went up to Cleo and started sniffing her hindquarters. The startled sheep pulled away from Andy, who immediately dropped the lead. Mrs. Peters came over and quickly restored calm by grasping Randy firmly around the neck and verbally scolding him. She helped Carlita bring the roaming goat to the far corner of the office, while Mr. Peters brought Cleo back to Andy.

Mrs. Peters laughed, "These animals! They're so gentle when they are alone with guests. But sometimes they get a little excited when they're together."

We weren't too sure this was very funny. During the ruckus, Corky's feet became quite agitated, but the old bird said nothing. Grumpy opened both eyes this time to scan the room for danger and then settled back into his slumber.

Finally, Mr. Peters brought in Sukie, a fine-looking milk cow, destined to be my animal. I was relieved to see she had no horns. Mrs. Peters showed me how to pat her neck, and then placed my hand on her head, between her eyes, and told me to scratch there. The gentle cow responded to my expression of affection by raising her tail and dropping a big malodorous brown pile right on the office floor.

"Way to go, Bob," my colleagues encouraged. "Just like at work, you've really got the touch!"

"We have one more bureaucratic formality, before you take your animal to its barn and you go to your room," Mrs. Peters proclaimed. She waved a sheaf of yellow forms and continued, "These are injury disclosure forms. You are responsible for the proper care of your animal, and your signature on this form makes you financially liable for any abuse of these gentle creatures."

"Wait a minute," I protested, "This is just like renting a car! How can we help if the animal panics and hurts itself? Where are the Abuse Waiver forms so we can have some insurance?"

"Don't get your knickers in a twist," she quickly reprimanded me. "I know when a panic incident occurs. I just want some protection against a guest beating or abusing these fine animals. Believe me, we get some weirdos visiting us from the big cities! Now, walk around your animals and inspect them for general good shape, so you can sign your form!"

So we very quickly walked around the animals. I had no ideas what to look for—dings and paint scratches? Carlita called out to Tex, "Hey, you didn't even look at your horse's teeth. I saw in a farm and ranch magazine this is the most important thing to look for in a horse!"

Tex promptly went over and peered into Janet's partly open mouth. "Yeah, he's got some!" Tex drawled. Mrs. Peters guffawed and a cautious smile broke out on Mr. Peters' face.

We signed our forms, and then Mr. Peters carried our bags while we led our animals to our respective abodes. Mr. Peters showed us the fundamentals of caring for the animals in the barns, gave us a few hints about the idiosyncrasies of each critter, and left us on our own.

Mrs. Peters had invited us for supper in the house that evening, by prior arrangement. She surely was a good cook!

We gathered around the big oaken round table in Mrs. Peters' kitchen at 7:30 a.m. the next morning. We sipped strong coffee and chatted, while Mrs. Peters cooked our breakfasts to order. Of course, we had all gotten up much earlier, to feed and water our animals according to Mr. Peters' instructions. Surprisingly, all of us enjoyed the opportunity to interact with these friendly animals.

The B, B&B is really an interesting idea, something that farmers in the USA should think about. This could add a new economic dimension to farmland near the big cities. The Peters had built six cabins, arranged around a few occasionally needed shade trees. Each cabin was duplexed with a mini-barn. I was relieved to see that the connecting wall was entrance-free and airtight, unlike the Swiss version I not so fondly remembered. And there was no manure pile in sight!

The cabin was outfitted much like a modern motel, with comfortable and attractive furnishings and a great bathroom. What a difference from the SameOld Motel! The TV reception was just as bad, but who wants to watch TV when you can go out and talk to your cow? The mini-barn attached to the cabin was very simply furnished for the intended use. There was room enough for the animal to lie down on the ground, a low rack containing hay that had been supplied by Mr. Peters, a feed bucket where the guest placed special feed for his or her animal, and a small watering trough with a faucet the guest could operate. In one corner was a little closet with a securely latched door, which held bags of feed and the tools the guest might need. Each duplex was fenced; the plot contained enough grassy pasture to keep the animal occupied during the day.

Carlita was so thrilled about her goat that she couldn't stop talking about him. "Randy was so much fun," she gushed. "I spent as much time as I could outside with him. He sure liked to have his neck and ears scratched, and he almost seemed to be listening as I talked to him. Of course, you might have thought I was a mental case if you had heard what I said! It was really cool to see him come into the barn when I called to give him his feed. He liked to nuzzle my hand and arm."

"I couldn't believe how neat it was to touch an animal and talk to it up close," chimed in Andy. "That sheep was real cool. Cleo was just as friendly and gentle as could be, especially when I was a little nervous being so close to her! We never had pets at home when I was a kid, and I always shied away from them at my friends' homes. Really, this is the first time I ever voluntarily touched an animal! I think I'm gonna buy a few acres outside of town and get some sheep."

Tex described his mind-shifting experience, "When Mrs. Peters handed me the reins for Janet, I nearly freaked. Back in Midland, almost everybody has something to do with cows or horses—usually both. I always cringed when friends wanted me to join them in horseback riding. You wouldn't believe the excuses I could generate for not doing it! Placing my hand on that horse caused a sensational transformation. Touching and communicating with a powerful animal opens up a new world for me. When you live in West Texas, being afraid of horses denies you a big part of life. First thing I'm gonna do when I get back is sign up for riding lessons. Who knows what might happen? I might even find a real use for my Western duds!"

We laughed heartily, including Mrs. Peters.

I started talking about Sukie, "That cow was so gentle and friendly, I spent almost all the remaining daylight hours outside with her. I sure satisfied a lot of curiosity about being up close to a cow. Mr. Peters said he would come by before dark to milk her, but I began to worry as the sun neared the horizon. She looked like she wanted me to milk her, after she sidled into the barn on her own. She kept looking back at me, swishing her tail, treading with her back feet. I almost panicked at the thought. I wouldn't have known how to start! Fortunately, Mr. Peters showed up. He gave me a lesson on how to do it, and offered me a chance to sit at the milking stool. I just shook my head and grinned. I sure like these animals, but I think I'll stick with cats!"

Mrs. Peters cracked: "How would you like an old crow with your cats? You sure seemed interested in that old bird yesterday!"

She brought some great-looking French toast and pork sausages to the table. "Tuck in your napkins and dig in! Eat heartily. You won't find a breakfast like this anywhere else on the island."

No one at the table would dispute that assertion. We took seconds, and one of us took thirds. We ate quickly since we still had some chores to do before heading for the refinery.

We rushed back, opened the barn doors, and let our animals out into their little pastures. We topped off the water troughs and put another measure of feed into their buckets. We cleaned up the barns by shoveling up the manure and placing it in the wheelbarrow placed at each barn's entrance. Mr. Peters would wheel these over to the main manure pile later in the day and hose down the wheelbarrows before returning them. After, we raked our barn floors smooth.

After finishing the morning chores, we pulled on our refinery work clothes and headed off for an intense day of discussion.

It was time to check out on Friday, after breakfast and the morning chores. We packed our bags and brought them to the office. Then we went back for our animals. We had to reverse what we did on Wednesday afternoon. I was very apprehensive about attaching the lead to her halter, but old Sukie helped me by holding up her head and keeping still. She seemed to know the drill!

One by one, we arrived at the office with our animals in tow. Carlita was the last to arrive. She apologized, saying, "Randy's a little ornery today. I had a hard time attaching his lead. Then he balked every time I headed toward the office. And he wanted to veer off at the least distraction!"

Mr. Peters shoved the balky goat into the crowded office and closed the door. A critical mass from the animal kingdom had now been assembled. Corky's feet began to twitch as the old crow looked down from the hat rack. The snoring orange cat was at his usual place, curled up on the desk.

Mrs. Peters assumed her official mien again and announced: "Mr. Peters will now inspect your animals, to insure you have treated them well. I'm sure you all were gentle with them and everything will be all right. When he is finished, we can do the checkout."

Mr. Peters dutifully walked around each animal, half-heartedly looking for something he knew he wouldn't find. When he inspected the goat, Randy became agitated and tried to butt the old farmer. "Yes, Randy is a little testy this morning," he said laconically.

I was the last to check out and pay my bill to Mrs. Peters. We exchanged a few homilies, and I expressed my thanks for the wonderful experience. When I reached for my cabin key, I also accidentally pulled out my rental car keys. The key holder had a shiny metal tab on it, and a glint of reflected light flashed across my eyes. I thought nothing of it and absentmindedly placed the keys on the desk.

What happened next was so quick you could hardly see it. The Germans have a great word for how fast it happened—in an *Augenblick*.

There was a resounding 'thump' near my elbow. Amazingly, my mind recorded exactly what happened, and I've played it back in my mind in slow motion many times.

The old crow had spotted the shiny tab. Obsessed with the prospect of adding another trinket to his collection, he dived pell-mell to seize it. Alas, in his excitement, he mistimed his landing and the keys slid over the far edge of the desk.

An orange blur flew over my motionless arms. Grumpy seemed asleep, but the savvy old cat had been tracking everything going on in the room. There was a long list of crow transgressions that needed redressing, and this opportunistic ambush seemed the perfect way to do it. The cat pounced, then bounced off the desk and seemingly achieved unpowered flight. How this big heap of lethargy could ever become airborne still boggles my mind.

The crow tried desperately to reverse his forward momentum as he slid across the desk. He beat his wings frantically to gain altitude. He tucked in his legs to reduce drag, spread his tail feathers to gain lift. At an excruciatingly slow rate, the big bird gained altitude—closer to safety and away from the attacking cat. Grumpy lunged with all his might toward the escaping bird. I can still see that orange paw, with a puff of white on the foot, as it tore into the crow's tail feathers.

Corky instinctively sounded his alarm with the most intense, raucous cawing I have ever heard. He was slightly deflected off his flight path by the cat's blow, but a couple of tail feathers pulled out harmlessly and started fluttering earthward. Grumpy's flight continued along a predictable ballistic trajectory, and he landed on the floor in a cloud of manure-tinged dust—on his feet of course. The cat looked up to see the feathers floating down and instinctively pounced on them.

But a dark Stuka dive bomber was circling above, not so stealthily cawing at the enemy below. It spotted the cat's preoccupation with the feathers and started its screeching attack. The crow delivered a punishing blow at the base of the cat's tail, which raised a big welt and a little blood. The poor cat screamed, with a yowl never heard during courtship, and raced for shelter under the desk. The triumphant crow seemed to laugh, with a succession of short 'caw-caws,' and then headed for his perch on the hat rack. He rearranged his feathers and looked down at the scurrying cat, smug with satisfaction.

This was the trigger; now comes the chain reaction.

The sudden motion and loud ruckus frightened the horse. Janet whinnied loudly and kicked out with her hind feet to thwart any attack from behind. This knocked over the TV stand in the corner, and the set came crashing to the floor. Miraculously, the picture tube did not break; the snowy image kept dancing around on the horizontal screen, in full view of anyone on the ceiling. Tex knew just what to do in this emergency—he dropped the lead and tried to disappear against the wall.

Usually, one person's problem is another's opportunity. This also works in the animal world. Randy was more than a little testy that morning. The lonely goat had been eyeing the cute little ewe for a long time, waiting for a chance to get to know her better. He figured that with all the distraction in the room, he'd better grab this opportunity. The goat tugged exceedingly hard on his lead, and Carlita dropped it—as instructed. The amorous goat bolted toward his intended unorthodox tryst and tried to mount the unsuspecting sheep.

Carlita screamed at the top of her voice when she saw what was happening. The additional noise and commotion panicked the horse even more than the first time. Janet reared on her hind legs, whinnying excitedly, and took off in hysterical flight.

Cleo moved forward to get away from the goat's assault, but she was restrained by the lead. Andy gallantly dropped it when he discerned the intention of the goat. The sheep took off in frenzied circles around the room, somehow managing to keep one step ahead of the goat's hoped-for union.

What a calamitous merry-go-round! The untethered horse lapped the almost humping couple several times. The racing animals knocked everything within reach to the ground in their frenzied running. Our bags were trampled, stressed way beyond the limits of what any airline baggage handler could inflict. Garments were scattered on the dirt floor. The hat rack crashed to the ground and Corky flew wildly around the room, squawking in protest about the loss of his perch.

Sukie was surely as panicked as any of us, but she stood still—perhaps in response to my firm grip on her lead and my admonitions to remain calm. Then the cow bellowed loudly and raised her tail to empty her bowel. Somehow, I sensed she was preparing for flight, so I let go of the lead and took shelter behind the desk. I grabbed Carlita's arm and helped her get out of the way. Andy was taking no chances; he had already clambered on top of the desk.

Mr. Peters realized the pressure in the room had to be relieved, and he lifted the latch on the  barn-like office door. The now-panicked cow bowled over the hapless farmer and headed for daylight. As if by centrifugal force, the circling horse spun off through the open door, narrowly missing Mr. Peters. The unlikely duo were not far behind. By now, the goat had given up on his ambitions. He ran to the left of the prostrate old man and the sheep to the right.

Before the dust had settled, I ran over to help Mr. Peters to his feet and asked if he was okay. As he dusted himself off, he stated tersely, "Son, I got no broken bones, but I know it will hurt like hell in the morning. I've had a lot worse in my time!"

Mrs. Peters expressed her concern: "It looks like a bomb went off in here. Look at this mess!"

"Yup," Mr. Peters agreed, "It must've been a big bomb!"

We adventurous business travelers gathered again in front of the desk. Andy nervously asked, "Where's Tex? Did he get trampled?"

I looked around and spotted him, still frozen against the wall. I called out, "It's all over, Tex. Come join us!"

The relieved cowboy was happy to rejoin his friends. I do believe his knees were still knocking.

We gathered our belongings and repacked our dusty bags. I looked at Mrs. Peters and asked anxiously, "I guess this was a panic situation, wasn't it? I don't think we're responsible for any of this, are we?"

"Now don't you worry about anything like that," our hostess assured me. "Mr. Peters and I should have paid more attention to having too many animals in the office at one time. You all were a real nice bunch of guests. I really appreciated how you felt about the animals, and how you cared for them so lovingly. Go finish up your meeting and have a good trip home!"

After we exited the office, I turned and looked back inside. I was rewarded with an image that will last a lifetime. Grumpy had come out of hiding and resumed his place on the counter, looking even more sullen than normal as he licked his wounds. Mr. Peters had just placed the hat rack upright in the corner. The haggard cat glowered balefully at the mean old bird when Corky settled back on his favorite perch.

"Okay," I shouted as we prepared to leave for the refinery, "where's the next committee meeting gonna be?"

"At Midland Refinery," Tex gleefully volunteered.

"Are you all ready to stay in a plain old West Texas motel?"

"Yes!" My colleagues bellowed in unison.

# Love Match

*A tennis-playing couple propose a bizarre wager which keeps some onlookers guessing.*

**B**ill Barnstable sat across the white metal patio table from his long-time mixed doubles partner, Jennifer Daly. The tennis players were enjoying a refreshing drink after an arduous afternoon of round-robin doubles matches. Jenny pulled very daintily from the straw in her Perrier on the rocks, but Bill gulped his Diet Coke straight from the can. Although the Westville Country Club stocked a large selection of beers and appealing alcoholic beverages from around the world, these two club tennis players preferred to refresh their sweat-soaked bones and to slake their thirst at this hour. There would be a time and place for a more relaxing drink later in the evening.

They were mildly fatigued after their exertions on this warm and sunny late September Saturday afternoon in suburban New Jersey. Most of their doubles opponents were sitting at the other umbrella-shaded tables grouped on the simple flagstone patio directly in front of the small, austere clubhouse.

Bill turned to his partner and said with genuine sincerity, "You really played great! We managed to win two of our three matches, in spite of my fumbly-bumbly play at the net. I don't think I could put away an easy shot today if my fortune depended on it!"

Jenny laughed, "Well, your serve and powerful forehand kept us in many of the games. I try hard now, but I miss too many shots. I'm not the champion player I was during my college years," she lamented. "Thanks to the one-set matches, we still should have enough energy to finish our normal Saturday afternoon—our one-set singles match. Speaking of fortune, you still want to invoke the usual wager, don't you?"

"You bet I do!" he replied, brimming with confidence, with a hint of a sly grin on his boyish face.

Then Bill turned toward the other players on the patio, waved his Diet Coke can in the direction of some distant trees lining the fairways, and announced in a strong mellifluous voice, "Look at those beautiful maple trees, their leaves starting their fall migration toward earth in brilliant yellow, soon to morph into flaming orange. What a glorious life we lead here, in this beautiful little corner of the Garden State! The daily grind of the long commute, the long hours at the office, the briefcase full of unread documents—all of this pays a dividend on the weekend. Long live the weekend!"

The other players raised their cocktail-filled glasses and joyfully agreed, "Hear, hear! To the weekend!"

One guy derisively interjected, "Bill, you sound just like a politician!"

Bill ignored the near insult and continued his big smile and observations.

Actually, Bill harbored a strong desire to enter the political arena and he was already doing the preliminary footwork. He had started with the West County prosecutor's office as an intern during law school, and he readily took their offer of employment after passing the bar exam. After a few more prominent cases, he might be ready to make a run for the legislature.

Jenny, on the other hand, qualified for the bar in both New Jersey and New York. She made the big bucks as a staff lawyer for a large financial house on Wall Street. They were a potent doubles team in tennis, but not well-matched in their legal talents and aspirations. The only court where they were likely to oppose each other had a net, not a judge.

With his free hand, Bill waved toward the horizon, exclaiming, "Look at those beautiful mountain ridges. The colors are already changing on the higher elevations. It looks like God has been at work with his paintbrush!"

The time-weathered ridges of the first Watchung Mountain scalloped the eastern horizon, offering only a hint of the grandeur it once achieved. But the interested observer could still find steep cliffs and wide-sweeping overlooks. On a clear day, you could see the stately twin towers of the World Trade Center. The second Watchung Mountain lay to the west of it. At an earlier time, this second mountain blocked the advance of suburban sprawl.

The country club was located just outside the New Jersey hamlet of Westville, nestled between the two Watchung Mountains. It was an old crossroads town with some original 18th-century buildings. Most buildings were relatively modern, but constructed in Victorian style with lots of built-in practicality. They housed a variety of boutiques and chic "shoppes," which appealed to well-heeled residents of the New York metropolitan area. The little village was about 20 miles west of the "Big City."

There would never have been a country club in Westville without the bedroom housing developments surrounding the village. These came in the 1960s and 70s, in the first big push into the outer suburbs of New York. At the time, this was considered luxury housing, unaffordable by the locals. But they were just right for the emerging upper-middle-class workers from the soaring skyscrapers of Manhattan and from the sprawling corporate campuses in the surrounding suburbs. There was street after street of two-story center-hall colonials—four bedrooms and two and a half baths—on half-acre lots.

They were not the elegant beautifully landscaped estates of Montclair or Summit, which were more established suburbs and better-connected via commuter rail lines. And they certainly were not the ersatz palatial monstrosities that followed later in the 1990s, built on three-acre tree-studded lots. The imposing, ugly developments swallowed up the remaining nooks and crannies of Basking Ridge and Peapack-Gladstone, and converted deer from wild creatures into backyard pests.

Westville Country Club came along at an affordable time, when real estate was reasonable and the charter members' aspirations were simple. The imported burghers of Westville could enjoy the affluent lifestyle on the cheap. The unpretentious clubhouse had a snack bar instead of a fancy dining room. The golf pro's wife tended both bars. She made a great bacon cheeseburger and brewed delicious coffee. But you had to mix your own drinks. She placed the needed bottles in front of the thirsty club member and depended upon the honor system.

The 18-hole golf course was the envy of many fancier country clubs. One of its charter members was a landscape architect, who donated much of his time and quite a bit of his workers' efforts into transforming the naturally lovely New Jersey terrain into a golfing garden spot.

Bill and Jenny occasionally played golf, but they much preferred tennis. There were four beautifully maintained hard-surfaced courts, with lush evergreen shrubs that hid the potentially confusing world behind the backstops.

A noisy patron on the patio, who perhaps had poured himself a jigger and a half instead of the one jigger in the cocktail recipe, shouted lustily, "Okay you two, it's time to get on with the main event—time for you guys to duke it out *mano a mano!*"

Bill turned to Jenny and said, "Are you ready? Shall we go out to the court and give them what they're looking for?"

Jenny rose and asserted, "Let's go! But first let's agree on the bet—it's still the usual deal, right?"

Bill nodded affirmatively and Jenny quipped, "But you gotta pay off if you lose; this time I'm gonna hold you to it!"

The rest of the players laughed gustily at Jenny's response and headed for the clubhouse for more drinks. Bill and Jenny picked up their gear bags and proceeded to the courts.

Physically, the two seemed well matched. Bill was a little more than six feet in height and stoutly built. His Wimbledon-marked cap struggled to cover his bushy brown hair. He had the fluent moves of a natural athlete and seemed to push his girth around the court with ease. Unfortunately, he had a little bit more to push each year. Bill only recently learned tennis, from a pro in a neighboring town. He overcame the hitches in his tennis form with inconsistent but powerful strokes he easily summoned from his muscular frame.

Jenny was also tall, five feet nine with socks on, but with a less muscular, although definitely not delicate frame. Her short blonde hair glowed in the afternoon sun, almost like the maple leaves. Jenny had played tennis since early childhood, and benefited from good coaching through her school years. She played varsity tennis at Brandeis and continued to play regularly since. Her smoothness of form and clean strokes from all positions compensated for the power disadvantage she suffered when playing against Bill. Anyone who hit a good shot toward her had better be prepared to see it come flying back over the net!

While Bill and Jenny warmed up their strokes, the other players were mixing their second round of drinks and discussing their own wagers. This was a regular feature for Saturday afternoons during tennis season. There was a lively round of betting on the outcome. If you looked at the long haul, the record was about fifty-fifty, but one never knew how a given match might evolve.

The active pair finished their warm-ups and met at the net for the ritual coin flip. Jenny won the toss and chose to serve. The sun was still fairly high in the sky and there was a stiff cross-wind from the west; an early but mild cold front had just blown in. Bill saw no advantage in picking the other side. Just as the other players straggled up to the sideline to watch, the first serve from Jenny whizzed toward Bill's backhand. He stroked it feebly into the middle of the net—fifteen-love.

He mis-hit the next serve—thirty-love. Then Jenny swung the serve far to Bill's right, forcing him to veer off the court to return it. Jenny dumped the ball into the open court—forty-love. Finally, she sealed the game with an ace to his backhand—one game to love in favor of Jenny. The sideline crowd politely applauded as the players changed sides.

Bill started with two powerful service winners, but it was all downhill after that. Jenny lobbed the ball over his head when he came to the net, returned his serve so fast he couldn't get his racket on it. Before he knew it, he had lost his serve. By now, Jenny's confidence was soaring and she unleashed more firepower on her serve. When they changed sides again, it was three-love, Jenny.

Mis-hit followed double fault and calamity ensued. At the next changeover, Bill was gasping for breath and trailing Jenny by five games to love. By now, half the onlookers were quietly lubricated. The other half, equally lubricated, were exhorting Jenny to bash Bill in a most unseemly way. "Bagel, bagel, bagel!" they chanted. They wanted the shutout, symbolized by the shape of a bagel.

Naturally, Bill was crestfallen at his circumstance. The ignominy of a 6-0 defeat at the hands of a woman was unbearable to his masculine pride. He steeled up his resolve to win his next serve. He paused to take a deep breath, bounced the ball innumerable times, and carefully tossed the ball into the air—mindful of the cross-wind. He reached high with his racket, concentrated on watching the ball, and gave it a mighty wallop. He got an ace. Encouraged, he repeated the actions—ace— and got an ace the third time. Now, he was up forty-love.

"I can't blow this one," he mumbled. "Let's get the damn ball over!"

Bill wanted that first serve to go in—desperately wanted it. He dreaded the thought of making a second serve under such pressure. He feared he would break down and dink it into the net as he had already done several times. He knew tennis is a mind game: negative thoughts usually lead to negative results. So he played psychological tricks on himself. He imagined that ball going deep to Jenny's backhand, where she couldn't do much with it. Calmly and confidently, he tossed the ball and hit a low-velocity spin serve into her backhand corner. When Jenny's return sailed way past the baseline, he thrust his arms into the air in exultation, as if he had just won Wimbledon. Five games to one for Jenny; no bagel to Bill this time!

Jenny joined the onlookers in cheering Bill's little success. Then she proceeded to serve out the set. Bill valiantly returned each serve and vainly tried to chase down her ground strokes from one side of the court to the other. The end of the final love game of the set brought both players to the net, where they warmly shook hands and perfunctorily embraced. They gathered up their gear and headed for home, satisfied with a Saturday afternoon well spent.

One couple among the spectator tennis players were guests; the woman turned to her hostess and asked, "What was all that hoopla about? The wager between those two players seemed like some kind of inside joke to you club members. How much were they betting? Are they rich, or something?"

She laughed and responded, "No, they're not rich—just typical Westville Country Club members. And their wager? The loser has to sleep with the winner!"

"Oh," the guest bemused, "I didn't realize y'all did those kind of things here!"

"Now don't get the wrong idea," the hostess assured her guest. "Those two have been married for over ten years…although they don't have the same last name."

# Footsteps in the Hall

*The mystery deepens as one misstep leads to another.*

I had just returned from a business trip and changed from suit and tie to jeans and t-shirt. That's when I saw them. Footsteps in the hall, leading into the bedroom. A chill shivered down my spine, one of my worst fears realized. Someone had broken into the house while both Doris and I were away.

Doris was in Texas, taking care of a project with our beloved second house that was my old family home. I was in New Jersey, earning the means to finance the Texas project. As luck would have it, I had to be away for a long business trip and I got back home the night before Doris was due to return.

Most husbands can relate to the anxious feeling about keeping the house in good shape while they are "batching" it. My mother always admonished me to wear clean underwear every day, lest some accident befall me and the hospital staff sees dirty undies. But my wife carries this one step farther, and insists that the house be immaculate before we leave on a trip—shining kitchen, sparkling bathrooms, freshly vacuumed carpets. "I want the house to smile at me when we first enter," she says.

So I was especially anxious as I investigated these strange footsteps. *Were some of Doris' treasures missing? Was the house vandalized?* A quick look showed that all was in order, but a closer look showed a certain freshness to the footsteps… *or was it earthiness?* The footsteps were brown and malodorous and some nimble detective work discovered that the bottoms of my recently shed shoes were smudged with the same stuff.

Imagine my distress as I realized I had stepped in some dog poop and tracked it throughout our clean house, with Doris due on the 1:00 p.m. flight tomorrow! I had picked up the mail in the dark, without concern about where I was stepping. But you know what wayward dogs do around posts. Unwittingly, I tracked the doggie doo through the kitchen and dining room, up the carpeted stairs, down the hall and into our bedroom.

*Doris is gonna kill me,* I thought. *I'll never get this cleaned without a trace.* My wife is the expert on cleaning, and I figured an improper cleaning job could be worse than a delayed one. So I called her in Texas, admitted the sorry state I had put the house in, and sought advice. To my relief, she did not yell at me, but just coolly said, "Put some Ajax cleaner in warm water, scrub well, and vacuum after it's dried."

I'm sure Doris spent an anxious three hours on that airplane, worrying about the house, but she wouldn't admit it. "What a clean-looking house!" she said as we entered. "It sure looks like it's smiling at us!"

Beside her stood a very relieved husband. Oh, and yes, she did clean it again to her exacting standards.

**Epilogue:** A couple of days later I wrote a humorous letter to the editor of our local paper, titled "Daring Do," which described my distress and urged the local burghers to observe the township ordinance requiring pooper-scoopers. I received many sympathetic phone calls, but a few days later observed something very strange. A Japanese fellow stopped his car by our mailbox and got out, looked carefully around the mailbox post, and drove off with nary a word.

Was he an expatriate trying to understand this strange Western culture, or was he the owner of the errant dog?

# What Have You Done With All Your Children?

*In a grueling interrogation, the subject admits to having more than
the disclosed number of children.*

I was squirming in my chair, fidgeting with unaccustomed nervousness. It was hot in the room and the bright lights shining in my face didn't help things. Sweat was rolling down my forehead in great drops, running into my eyes, blurring my vision. My brain was muddled and confused. Behind me, I could hear the snickers and murmurs of the witnesses, amused by my pathetic efforts to cope with the interrogation.

The technician recording the interrogation struggled to keep the camera focused on my face, for in my agitation I was bobbing from side to side as I strained to deal with the interrogator's questions. He had to swing the camera in great arcs, as if he were filming a tennis match.

I could see the shiny contours of the camera lens as it bore down on my face, trying to capture me in a moment of weakness. The intense light blurred my view of the interrogator standing directly in front of me—I could barely make out a dim outline of her features. It seemed she was a very pretty young woman. Her voice was soft and calming, although she spoke in her native language. *Ah, I thought to myself, they're trying to catch me off guard and lull me into giving the correct responses!*

She obviously expected me to handle this intense questioning in her language, but I blurted out some of the responses in English because those were the only words that emerged in my confusion. I tried to keep my wits about me and give plausible-sounding responses without revealing too much. But with my constant nervousness, I had totally blown it. After my last feeble response, I knew she was on to me. I realized too late that in my panic, I had given the answer to her first question as the response to her second.

*"Arrêt!"* she called out in French, *"Il faut recommencer!"* She had given up on my inadequate responses, and decided to trash this session and start over. No, I was not being grilled in the third-degree, I was just the poor sucker who had been chosen by his classmates as the interview subject for a French TV news program.

We were a group of expatriates, working in rural France and trying earnestly to learn a little of the French language. We met twice a week at the audio-visual language lab in the little Normandy town of Lillebonne. Our companies were very far-sighted about sponsoring this language training, as they wanted us to blend in as well as possible with the natives. It was also a practical matter for us, since most of our dealings with merchants, store clerks, doctors, and dentists had to be done in French. Many of the locals had studied English in school but they would freeze up and panic whenever you said something in English to them.

There were two American couples, along with British, Norwegian, and German couples. The French are very proud of their language and treat very kindly all attempts by foreigners to learn it. The regional French TV station learned that the étrangers were making good progress in French and asked to do a feature story. They wanted to interview a student in French, to demonstrate we could actually do it. They were pleased to get an American subject, as Americans were notoriously poor language students.

The bright lights were momentarily shut down and the interviewer and I went through the questions again and practiced my responses. Without the klieg lights, I could see that she was indeed very lovely. She spoke impeccable English. Obviously, she was destined for a great future as a TV *speakerine*.

When it appeared I had calmed down enough and had gotten my answers straight, we started over. I mopped my brow one last time and the klieg lights were switched on again. I waltzed through the preliminary questions, in adequate French. Despite my initial success, I was still a little nervous and a few beads of sweat had reformed on my forehead. Because I was somewhat calmer, the cameraman was now able to cope with my more restrained bobbing and weaving.

Now we got into the nitty-gritty of the interview. The nice lady asked me how many children I had, *"Combien d'enfants avez vous?"* I responded confidently and emphatically, *"J'ai douze enfants!"* I was puzzled why my classmates snickered at my response.

I didn't realize it at the time, but I had made the pronunciation error—a real no-no in French. Slight differences in pronunciation can make a gross swing in meaning. I knew I had two children, and everyone in the room knew I had two children. I knew the correct pronunciation, but I still unwittingly said *douze* (pronounced "dooz," which means twelve) instead of *deux* (pronounced "duz"). All of a sudden, I had acquired ten extra children!

The French TV people let this pass uncut, figuring it would be a quaint Americanism the TV audience would find amusing. They probably also figured that if they tried to correct me, I would just screw up something else on the next take.

A couple of weeks later, some of our American friends gathered *chez nous* to watch the broadcast. This was my first and only TV interview; I was quite excited, but very apprehensive. Imagine my discomfort as I viewed this obviously nervous fellow who resembled me trying to speak French, in a voice that only approximated what I thought I sounded like! There I was, my then un-bearded face dancing around on the screen—a talking and bobbing head!

The broadcast interview was finished, my family and friends applauded, and I was beginning to feel better about my performance as most of my French had actually been pretty good. I felt like celebrating, "A snifter of cognac sure would taste good right now!"

That's when the phone started ringing. Our French friends were calling to offer their congratulations and to joke around with us. But they all asked the same question: "Where are you hiding the rest of your children?"

# A Charlie Brown Christmas Tree

*A traveling family realizes that home is where the Christmas tree is.*

In the third week of December, 1971 our family bubbled with excitement because after living in Normandy for a year and a half, we were going to spend Christmas at home in Texas! As soon as the French schools finished for the holidays, we packed our bags and eagerly awaited the arrival of the limo driver, graciously supplied by the refinery where I worked.

Frazzled by long months of trying to run a computer project and learn French at the same time, I needed this homecoming. We carefully planned visits with friends and relatives, medical appointments, and inspection of our rented home in Baytown. We had not been back to the States during this period, and we longed for the taste of barbeque and Mexican food; the simple joys, such as talking with folks who said "y'all," and watching football.

"He's here!" our older son Fred shouted when he saw the limo, "I'll open the door!"

"*Bon jour,*" the driver politely addressed Fred, and the two commenced a mile-a-minute conversation in French. Our two sons spoke French fluently and often helped us out of linguistic tight spots, much as modern kids help their parents with computers.

Our driver delivered us to Air France's door after a three-hour trip to Paris, and we were soon on a non-stop flight to Houston. During the long plane ride, we talked about what we might feel once we set foot on Texas soil again—all useless speculation. Our most striking impression upon arrival—the people were huge, tall in height and wide in girth! Months of living in France had accustomed us to small people, who stayed that way in spite of the rich Normandy cuisine and the very drinkable French wine.

We stayed at an uncomfortable motel, convenient to all the places and people we had to see. We didn't want to inconvenience my brothers; their families were plenty busy with their own holiday doings.

After a hectic week, we had seen our relatives, done the required business, and had been thoroughly poked and prodded by doctors and dentists. On December 23, Doris asked me, "Why are we still here? Why don't we go back to our house in France where we can be more comfortable and feel a little more of the Christmas spirit? This just doesn't seem like home anymore."

I felt the same way. Luckily, we found seats on that night's Air France flight. Fred helped us with our biggest challenge, changing the pickup schedule by telephone with the French limo driver. We apologized to Mom for our premature departure, but she understood that home is where the heart is.

Our plane touched down at Orly Field in Paris early on December 24. We were so pleased to see our limo driver after our long-distance negotiations in French!

"We're back in the land of the little people!" Doris exclaimed, "I'm home!" We felt refreshed by the brisk December air of northern France. It had been unseasonably warm in Houston, and we were no longer accustomed to such muggy weather.

Soon after arriving at our small house in Notre-Dame-de-Gravenchon, we headed straight for the *marché* (the farmer's market). We knew the stalls would be closing early on Christmas Eve. We needed holiday provisions and, of course, we wanted a last-minute Christmas tree.

By this date, shoppers had picked bare the Christmas tree merchant's stock. All that remained were two bedraggled specimens: scrawny and scrawnier. "Nobody's going to take that poor tree," Doris lamented. "It really needs a friend."

I looked at it carefully. It was a mere skeleton of a spruce, pulled up by its flimsy roots, a few tattered arms pointed out haphazardly, and its top tilted askew. "Looks like a good one to me," I replied, "We oughta be able to make this look real pretty." I thought of Charlie Brown, the comic strip hero who had a knack for choosing dilapidated Christmas trees, and said to Doris, "I bet Charlie Brown would really be proud of us!"

We amazed our boys by bringing home such a tree; they thought we still must be jet lagged. The limbs were too flimsy to support Christmas lights and other ornaments, so we made balls of tinfoil and attached them with string. I approximated a five-pointed star, and Fred and Andy cut out and colored some paper decorations.

We ended up with a cute little tree. It was not exactly a candidate for Rockefeller Center, but we adored it. We had fun opening our Christmas presents as the little tree looked down upon us from the table where it sat in all its tinfoil splendor. We were home again! We felt the Christmas spirit was with us again as it always has been in our little family. I think this was the most remarkable Christmas we ever enjoyed.

Before leaving for the Texas vacation, we had not realized that France had become our home. It was folly to think Texas was still "home," as several of our more experienced American colleagues later explained. Our strange feelings at that Texas motel and our joy upon returning to France were perfectly normal. Such feelings illustrate "reverse culture shock," experienced by most expatriates working abroad upon returning to their home environments.

Oh, Charlie Brown Christmas tree, we still think of you. We smile at how your emaciated arms struggled to hold up our humble decorations. Thanks for helping us learn a lot about ourselves.

# Through the Lens
# and Beyond

*Superstitious people keep an old myth alive, as the writer revisits a beguiling but almost lost region of rural France.*

The sleepy village of Quillebeuf-sur-Seine reclines serenely on the left bank of the famous river, as the postcard-pretty water of Paris courses down the wide channel en route to its rendezvous with the salt water of *La Manche* (the English Channel). The waters quickly appear brackish, as the tide plays hide-and-seek at the feet of the charming little town. The water here is dark, rippled by an evanescent breeze and the predations of white sea birds. The birds punctuate the moiré pattern of reflected sunlight induced by an oily film—created by discharges from passing ships and from the massive petrochemical complex across from the bucolic 17th-century town.

Our little family sat in our antique Simca *voiture*, a small company car provided to us by my employer, awaiting the Quillebeuf ferry. I was an engineer on loan to the big refinery across the river from Quillebeuf. Although it could be balky at times, the little car faithfully transported us on weekend excursions to many delightful nooks and crannies in Normandy. It was a French car with built-in Gallic pride: each time we took it to a foreign country, it coughed and sputtered.

The boys amused themselves in the backseat by punching each other and bombarding us with impatient questions, "When is the ferry going to come? Why do we have to cross the river?"

We could see the ferry on the opposite bank—immobile. On weekends, the ferry captains took a *laissez-faire* attitude toward the posted schedule and timed their passage perhaps by the temperature of their strong coffee. Also, the ferry had to take its turn in the maritime traffic, still surprisingly heavy on a Saturday afternoon. We watched as big cargo ships chugged their way between the Channel and the interior port city of Rouen. We also saw shiny pleasure cruisers, headed toward the rich suburbs of Paris, and the occasional oil barge as it slipped into the refinery docks.

Finally, the ferry's horn reverberated across the immense river, and we saw a puff of black smoke as the captain revved its engines.

Our younger son Andrew shouted in alarm, "But it's not coming to us!"

Fred, the elder, punched Andy on the upper arm and informed him, "Stupid, don't you know the tide is going out? The pilot has to aim upriver to get to us when he crosses over!"

I couldn't add anything to Fred's terse explanation and let it pass.

The ferry shook the dock as it arrived, then let down its loading ramp with a thunderous clang. We watched as the cars and trucks unloaded, marveling at how such a small vessel could carry so much. At the signal from the man on deck, I shifted into gear and nervously edged the Simca to a place at the very front of the ferry. The man insisted I move forward even more, but I desperately feared we would end up in the river. I silently vowed never again to be first in the ferry queue!

I watched in the rearview mirror as the deck man made his way from car to car, occasionally stopping to chat with friends. He was a burly, barrel-chested fellow of medium height, with thick forearms. A small ticket machine emphasized his ample girth. His sandy hair suggested Viking ancestors, and his ruddy face showed his Norman heritage. He wore the traditional blue work clothes. When he came to our car, I was overpowered by the aroma of the cheese and wine he had consumed for lunch.

The ferry was supposed to be free for residents of the area, so I was surprised when he demanded payment. He explained the situation in the thick accent of the region, but I could hardly understand him. Fred translated, "He says your car is registered at company headquarters in Paris, so you have to pay a little, even though we live here. Two francs."

When we arrived, we debarked and headed down Quillebeuf's riverfront road, on our way to the day's ultimate destination—the primitive area called the *Marais-Vernier*. We admired the town's riverfront restaurants with their sidewalk tables and peered down the narrow side streets as we passed. We were amazed at the ancient buildings in the town, made of half-timbered masonry construction. Some were unbelievably narrow, and a few were canted at a perilous angle.

Many years later, I sat in front of the slide viewer, peering at about twenty slides from the years we lived in France. These were all from the *Marais-Vernier*, some from the trip just mentioned and some from later excursions. Once again, I was trying to organize my huge collection of French slides into something coherent, something we could print and put into a more easily viewable album. Alas, I was again sidetracked by fond remembrances of those wonderful years in France, as evidenced by my reverie on the ferry ride across the Seine.

There was a picture of Doris and the two boys standing in front of the Simca, smiling as they gazed at the rustic countryside that surrounded them. We had stopped on a wide spot in the narrow one-track road, barely paved and built above the surrounding ground, which encircled the large expanse of small country plots. The interior was interlaced by a network of rutted dirt roads, mere driveways, which we dared not attempt. The edges of the road fell rapidly toward deep ditches, which drained the continual rains that dampened Normandy. The word *marais* means swamp, and that's what this region was a long time ago, before hardy peasants drained and cleared it. Don't even ask me what *vernier* means!

One could look in almost any direction and be rewarded with a jigsaw puzzle view. A ramshackle fence surrounded each mini-farm, patched with an odd assortment of wires and occasionally plugged by a piece of corrugated iron. Apple trees, whose beautiful white blossoms of spring gave way to drooping fruit-laden branches in summer, and then to a pile of apples in the fall dotted the landscape.

Apples run a close second to bread in sustaining life in Normandy, as anyone who has partaken of *tarte-aux-pommes* (thin apple pie) or calvados at restaurants can attest. The brandy called calvados does to apples what liquefaction does to natural gas—it makes a burning source of energy available to be enjoyed in distant locations. I still have a few bottles!

Almost all of the houses were quaint old stucco and stone cottages, half-timbered in traditional Normandy style and covered with a foot-thick layer of thatching. These were called *chaumieres*. The thatching was made from special reeds grown in the *Marais*, which supplied much of the thatching needs throughout France. Most of the thatched roofs were heavily weathered; a few showed badly decayed portions and some showed patches of fresh reeds. These thatched roofs pulsed with the rhythms of life, for many sheltered birds' nests and no telling how many rodents, and most had a row of bulb plants growing at the ridge line.

Many of the houses leaned in disparate states of disrepair, but they were solidly built compared to the barns and other outbuildings. Some barns were thatched, but most were roofed in corrugated iron in various shades of rust. Vegetable gardens abounded, but there were few flower gardens. Instead, the peasants liked colorful window boxes.

There were no garages, although many peasants now had *voitures* — almost universally they were beat-up Citroen *Deux Chevaux* (two horses), a 1950s equivalent of the Model T Ford. These were well-suited to the region: lightweight, mechanically simple, with a high wheelbase for rutted roads. If you got stuck in the mud, just ask someone to help you lift it out! Some places had a *Deux Chevaux* propped up on blocks, Ozarks style.

Each little farm had its complement of one or two brown-spotted Normandy cows, a few goats, and free-range chickens. One had to be careful when driving through the *Marais*, for you were responsible for any chickens you ran over. Chipped and rusted pieces of assorted junk adorned many farming plots, perhaps used as chicken nests or for storing farm supplies.

If you cast a narrow and critical look at the place, you saw a junkyard. But if you relaxed a little to understand what this place was all about, you saw a charming bit of isolated country life juxtaposed on the wonderful tapestry nature had provided.

The peasants were descended from a hardy stock, which had endured centuries of isolation. They were now in transition between the nineteenth century and modern life. A few houses sported television antennae; almost all had electric wires leading to them. Some of the men drove their *Deux Chevaux* each day to Quillebeuf to catch the ferry and then worked at the refineries on the other side.

But some lacked the mental skills for such work and toiled in the *Marais* fields, poisoned in their infancy by well-meaning, but ignorant parents. These individuals had suffered brain damage from the old folk medicine practice of putting a little calvados in the bottle to calm a restless infant. The French government only recently mounted a campaign, aided by television, to inform the people of the dangers of such ancient practices.

The traditional superstitions of the *Marais* people lingered even into modern times. I knew they didn't want to be photographed—my French colleagues had warned me of this. They were afraid their spiritually distorted image would be inverted as it passed through the lens, polluted by the chemicals used in developing, and ultimately cast into silver halides on a flat plane, which would disturb their soul and interfere with their afterlife.

Still, I couldn't resist the urge to stop at a delightfully dilapidated *chaumiere*, with a beautiful Normandy cow reposing under an apple tree, and a woman peering out a second-floor window. I whipped out my camera, fiddled with the focus and the settings, and tried to compose a good shot. The woman shouted an unintelligible but well-understood epithet and slammed the window shutters closed. My picture showed only the house and cow. I hightailed it out of there before some angry peasant could confront me!

I looked again at my slides, and each affirmed my impressions of that charming little corner of Normandy. Most were furtively snapped by Doris from the car window, as I slowed or paused when we spotted a memorable scene ahead of us. They were all keepers. I didn't have enough shots from this era to find any discards.

Almost thirty years after our sojourn in France, Doris and I once again returned to our beloved former home territory in Normandy. We had many happy reunions with our friends and enjoyed their warm hospitality and fine cuisine. We reserved a day for revisiting some of the charming byways across the river that we had enjoyed so many years ago. I chose to drive our rented Renault toward the Tancarville bridge, instead of heading for the Quillebeuf ferry. We wanted to see more of the countryside without having to wait for the ferry. Yeah, I know you're thinking: I was just chicken about driving a car onto the ferry!

The road on the other side of the bridge was now, much to our dismay, closer to a superhighway than a lane. Doris buried her head in the map and suggested I, "…turn off here…, no…,wait…, turn off there." Finally, we got onto a smaller road that looked promising, but definitely not familiar. We came to an intersection with a sign that pointed toward the *Marais Vernier Circuit.*

I was ready to pull onto this road when Doris shouted, "Wait! This road's too big! It can't be our little road around the *Marais.*"

So I reached for my bifocals to peer at the map. Nothing made sense. We knew intuitively that the *Marais* lay in that general direction, so we agreed, "What the heck, let's move on and see what happens."

After a short time, we came to a raised section of the road, but this stretch was two lanes wide and even had a suggestion of a shoulder. It was nicely paved with some of the refinery's finest asphalt. We could tell by the general lay of the land that we were indeed on the circuit road.

But we sure couldn't tell by the houses! Yes, the *Marais* was still full of *chaumieres*, but these were not the thatched roof cottages of old. These houses were enormous! They were fitted with half-timbering in Normandy style and the thatching was in pristine condition. Even the dormers were thatched! A dense row of flowering bulbs decorated the ridgeline of every roof. Of course, we couldn't go into any of these, but we guessed that the kitchens and living areas were beautifully fitted, as were the new houses of our friends across the river.

It seemed the houses got bigger as we drove down the road, as if each resident were trying to keep ahead of the deClercs. The cows and chickens were gone, as were the ramshackle fences. In their place were neatly painted wood fences and the occasional horse. Separate three-car garages, thatched of course, offered plenty of room for the Mercedes, Volvos, and huge Citroens we saw parked in the driveways. Surrounding the houses were lush lawns that would make a New Jersey suburbanite green with envy. Carefully tended apple trees still looked beautiful as they blossomed, but we doubted the fruit from these would ever see the inside of a calvados bottle.

Only a few people stirred at this mid-morning hour. We saw some older, well-dressed people puttering around in their extensive flower gardens, apparently retirees from the big city. We saw some women walking to their cars, dressed as if they were on their way to club meetings. Laborers repairing potholes in the road wore the only blue work uniforms we saw.

In the old days, as we remembered it, many mongrel dogs roamed the neighborhood. Now, we saw only a few fine canine specimens lounging around the yards. Clearly, the *Marais Vernier* had gone upscale!

I turned to Doris and asked, "Where are all the quaint old, run-down *chaumieres*? Have they all been overrun by progress?"

She looked at the map and responded, "We're coming up to the point where the circuit road turns sharply to the left. There used to be a bunch of dilapidated old places there."

Wrong! We rounded the corner and came upon some even more imposing new *chaumieres*, surrounded by huge parcels of well-manicured land. What used to be the low-rent district was now the estate region!

We even tried some of the interior roads, still small, but now paved. The entire interior was now built up. So I turned the wheel toward Quillebeuf and suggested, "Let's grab some lunch!"

The restaurant that faced the Seine remained as charming as before, and the entire town still looked like it could tumble over at any time. The waitress placed us at an outdoor table, where we ordered a *croque monsieur* (toasted ham and cheese) and a glass of wine. We enjoyed the passage of several large ships up and down the river, waved to the crewmen, and marveled at the daring gymnastics of the seagulls as they pounced into the wake in search of their lunch.

We carried on a halting conversation with the waitress, a pleasant young woman, in our fractured French. She surprised us with her patience to listen as we brutalized her beautiful native language with our rusty American accents. We found we could communicate fairly well.

"We lived in Normandy thirty years ago," I announced to her, "and we visited the *Marais Vernier* many times. Now, everything has changed. What happened?"

She didn't answer right away, and I feared I had violated some sacred space by mentioning this place.

"I used to live in the *Marais*," she answered, "as did my parents and grandparents. I tended the cows, goats, and chickens when I was a girl. I loved that old place and now it's gone!"

She turned from us momentarily and appeared to be wiping away tears.

"It's all because of those rich people from Paris with their digital cameras!" she blurted.

Puzzled, I asked, "What do digital cameras have to do with this?"

"Because those people started buying houses in the *Marais*. They tore them down, saved the old timbers, and built big new houses. They took pictures of the new houses with their digital cameras—and they are pretty houses—and sent them to real estate agents and newspapers all over France." The waitress continued, "Soon, other people came and just bought up all the houses. They offered good money— too good to refuse. My parents got enough to buy a nice apartment in Le Havre."

"Did anybody not sell, in hope of waiting for more money?" I asked.

"Oh yes, several people did. Now, they relax in the sunshine of Provence[6]."

Finally, I asked, "How long did it take for all the old houses to disappear?"

"About two or three years!"

We paid our bill and left a generous tip, then headed upriver through the scenic Forest of Brotonne to find the bridge to Caudebec, where we had rented a hotel room.

6   Provence is a beautiful, rustic section of south France, gentrified long before the *Marais Vernier.*

As we drove, I said to Doris, "Looks like the camera really is bad news for the *Marais* people! Of course, I don't believe any of that superstitious hocus-pocus!"

Doris reflected a moment, then stated with genuine gravity, "Don't discount that camera thing. Cameras might well have had an evil influence on those people. Some very strange things have happened in Normandy. If you don't believe it, just read Victor Hugo!"

# The King's English

*Can't find the right word? This humorous tale explores*
*a common problem.*

We almost take our language skills for granted. Ever since we were small tots, we have been modulating our voices and tuning our ears to share in that wonderful person-to-person activity—conversation. And if we work at it a little, we can even convince ourselves we are communicating with our pets! We don't even have to think about it; formulate any thought in our minds, straightforward, abstract, or mundane, and the words just come tumbling out. Until we reach a certain age, of course.

Once we reach that indeterminate milestone, many of us may sometimes find ourselves in a brilliant line of conversation, and then our mouths open, there is a pregnant pause as the thought lodges in the mind…and nothing comes out. In that moment, mouth agape, we stammer and yammer as our brains dig to excavate just the right word.

For example, we might have thought a neat little word like "prescient" would suit the flow of our brilliant conversation. We know there's a word out there that fits—old Mr. Webster made a thick book full of them. Our brains know it too and search desperately through our most remote memory banks to find it. Nothing. The neurons spin from cycle to cycle, but they don't really click on the answer. Finally, out of embarrassment, we say something, anything, to get the focus away from our painfully silent mouths. We blurt out a do-nothing word such as "bright," and instead of the hoped-for effervescence of our thought, we end up with stale fizz.

Our brains usually keep searching, even in the background. We might wake up at 2:00 a.m. and find it has placed that word right on our tongues!

Trying to learn a foreign language as an adult exposes you to the verbal challenges encountered later in life. But there is an important difference—with a foreign language, you flat don't know the word you are seeking, and your brain sure as heck doesn't know it either! After the embarrassing pause, you blurt out the word in your native tongue. As a refinement on the technique, you can say the word in yet another foreign language you might know.

When we moved to our apartment in France in the summer of 1970, there were a lot of things to acquire for managing life in our strange new quarters. We bought most of the stuff locally, which gave us some practice in using the classroom French we had endured in the weeks prior. We even began to have a little confidence in our language skills—prematurely, I might add!

Our carpets were dusty and we had no vacuum cleaner, so we set out to the fairly big Normandy city of Rouen to find one. We went to the big department store, *Galleries Lafayette*, where I asked the sales girl, "*Je voudrais acheter un…* embarrassing pause…vacuum cleaner?" This resulted in a look of total confusion on the hapless clerk's face.

I realized this was not getting through to the young lady, so I repeated the question with the same embarrassing pause. This time, I relied on a tried and true Yankee tactic—I said "vacuum cleaner," much, much louder.

The confused look on the sales girl's face disappeared, replaced by a totally blank look.

I knew I was in big trouble, so I dug down deep to solve the problem. I carefully constructed a French sentence that would clarify the situation. Fortunately, I knew all the words to complete the thought.

With lots of Gallic-Texan gesticulation, I carefully said in French, "I want to buy a machine, an electric machine that you plug into the wall so you can clean the carpets."

Immediately, the girl's face brightened with recognition, and she exclaimed in a delightfully French tone of voice, "*Ah, un aspirateur!*"

"*Oui,*" I affirmed, "*Un aspirateur!*"

This scenario was repeated many times while we lived in France, and certainly when we returned on visits. Now, we are dually afflicted. Sometimes we flat don't know the French word and other times we suffer the age-induced embarrassing silence as our brains struggle to find the word we know we know.

Ten years after we returned from living in France, Doris and I headed overseas again, this time to jolly old London, England. No language lessons for us this time, no siree. They speak English just like we do. In fact, they invented the stuff, so they oughta be able to do it purty good!

Guess what? Our house in Wimbledon needed a vacuum cleaner. So we went to John Lewis on Oxford Street in London to procure just what we needed.

Filled with confidence, I said to the sales girl, "I would like to buy a vacuum cleaner."

A look of total confusion overcame her plain English face.

Clearly, I was not getting through to her, so I repeated the question…much louder.

This was getting nowhere fast. Then my French experience came to my aid, as I remembered how I had solved the same word puzzle at that department store in Rouen. Inspired, I asked, "I want to buy a machine, an electric machine, that you plug into the wall so you can clean the carpets."

"Ah," she exclaimed, "a Hoover!"

"Yes, I would like to buy a Hoover!"

Doris and I proudly carted our new possession to the car park[7], where I carefully placed the Hoover into the boot[8] of the car. Then, I opened up the bon-net[9], to make sure I was no longer leaking oil in my four-year-old company car.

---

7  Parking lot
8  Trunk
9  Hood

On the way back to Wimbledon, I had to stop for some petrol[10]. Before I could reenter the main road, I had to wait as a long queue of lorries[11] passed. On the road again, I tapped my fingers impatiently against the steering wheel, as I peered through the windscreen[12] at the huge traffic tailback[13] at the roundabout[14] ahead of us.

I didn't say too much as I negotiated the heavy traffic while driving on the wrong side of the road. But I was able to observe to Doris, "It sure is nice my company moved us to a country where we can speak the same language!"

She responded wryly, "Yes. Now I can aspirate my carpets, or I can Hoover them. That oughta keep 'em real clean!"

---

10   Gasoline
11   Trucks
12   Windshield
13   Traffic jam
14   Traffic circle

# Cawporate Takeover

*Avian mobsters hostilely take over a peaceful family's food supply.*

We enjoyed the services of a small family-operated enterprise for many years. They were a group of three—Mr., Mrs., and (presumably) Mistress—who operated their business efficiently and reliably. In late spring, Junior helped them out. They knew us, we knew them, and each thought the other was predictable. But now they are gone, the victims of a hostile takeover, and we must deal with a larger corporate-like entity.

Their services satisfied a real suburban business need—removing from the premises kitchen waste such as chicken skins, bones, fat, and table scraps. With this group on the job, there was no need to put such stuff in the freezer until garbage collection day, lest it stink up the garbage can. We didn't have to clog our sewers with stuff put down the garbage disposal. Never mind that these business operators were crows—they did a great job in an environmentally conscious manner.

Our three crows showed up early each morning to check on business. It was my job to put our kitchen's edible wastes in the backyard, before breakfast. The threesome would descend upon the table scraps almost as soon as I turned my back. If I ran late, the crows would fly to other neighborhood offerings, but they always managed to keep a watchful eye on our backyard. The minute I went out the door with plate or pot in hand, there would be some distant "caw-caws" and our faithful group would soon appear.

The crows worked fast with a new collection of scraps. They might sneak a few bites of a particularly crow-appetizing tidbit, but mostly they would disperse and hide the scraps, to keep them from the clutches of wandering cats and dogs or marauding blue jays. They carefully put their respective morsels into small depressions in the lawn and covered them with nearby leaves or grass clippings. They came back to the yard during the day, at their leisure, to find and consume the food stashes.

Because of the way they handled the food scraps, we considered the crows to be intelligent. If some scraps were hard, such as bread crusts, they hauled them over to the bird bath and dunked them. The crows competed with the neighborhood squirrels for last year's Texas pecans that we put out during the winter. Squirrels will chase crows away, but a pecan-hungry crow just retreats to a tree, watches as the squirrel buries its pecan, and then steals the pecan when the squirrel goes back to the nut pile.

We often wondered if the crows really enjoyed the stuff we put out, since some scraps were from gourmet cooking in the French style. Perhaps their preference was for road kill since they handily took care of the occasional mouse we trapped. But we had no doubts about that on Saturday (pancake day). We always cooked a few extra for our feathered friends. The crows gulped several pancake bits before cramming their beaks with disgraceful amounts to stash away.

It was a mutual relationship. We felt they were *our* crows and they felt our yard was *their* turf—turf they defended vigorously from alien crows. During fair weather, we often set up a lunch table under a shade tree. Our crow friends would hang around in the trees, hoping for a small reward. Even when we were gone for a week or two, the crows would greet us on the first morning of our return.

And it was a family thing as well. In late spring, Junior showed up with his elders, newly fledged and with an appetite as big as any teenager's. It was an amazing sight to see this big gawking young bird, flapping his wings, encouraging his mom or pop to put something in his garishly open beak. It was interesting to watch the older crows teach Junior how to hide and cover his food and how to dunk morsels into the bird bath. But Junior's gravy train was over at the end of summer; he grew up and now had to find his own way. The older crows chased the reluctant young adult away, something many suburbanites can relate to.

We were eventually confronted with a paradigm shift in the crow world. Our comfortable business relationship with our three-crow group was shattered—and in quite a rude way. We heard a big commotion, with raucous cawing and vigorous aerial combat—sounds and actions usually reserved for an intruding hawk.

Alas, the friendly waste removal business had been taken over by a corporate gang of six crows. The new bunch didn't know us, and we didn't know them... yet. Initially, we were offended by their lack of trust in us because whenever we tossed out some food scraps, they cautiously danced around it until some brave bird made a stabbing peck at it. Our old threesome knew the menu we served and went right in. Now we felt as if we were dealing with a cold corporate entity.

What went wrong in our three crows' business? Maybe they got a little long in the beak and could no longer defend their turf from corporate raiders. Maybe some well-placed opportunists were feathering their own nests. Or maybe the crow world was undergoing the same corporate aggrandizement pressures we have witnessed in the human world, with more aggressive and larger flocks grabbing the small guys' turf.

We recently witnessed the specter of the ultimate corporate raider: turkey vultures. Three vultures descended on our scrap place and quickly scarfed down the chicken skins and chicken fat while the corporate crows sulked in the background. Our old bunch never let that happen. We concluded that if these corporate predations were to continue to escalate, then perhaps the avian world would discover that sometimes business arrangements must come to an end.

We certainly didn't have enough scraps to support a group of six. Rather than doing business with a new group of birds, it might benefit all concerned for us to just put the scraps in the freezer and precipitate an avian downsizing.

We worried that our old crows might be relegated to spend their golden years dining by the side of a road. I also wondered about the new Junior. *Would he grow up to be the crow version of Dilbert?* Such sentiments may have arisen because we, too, are an older couple, enamored with the old-fashioned way of transacting business.

Business just ain't the same anymore!

# Has Anyone Seen My Mama?

*This tale about a blackbird emphasizes we should never*
*underestimate the bond between outdoor critters and people.*

I sipped again from my coffee cup, knowing full well it was empty, and coaxed from it one final drop of caffeine-laced nectar. *The London Times* was strewn asunder on the breakfast table, each of its sections folded open to an interior story—that's where one finds all of the interesting stuff. I never could fold that paper neatly at the seam. It was always crumpled and dimpled, almost as badly as one of our refolded road maps.

All but one of the pancakes were eaten, victims of our Saturday morning ritual breakfast—a tradition that persists through the decades and endures the rigors of foreign residence. Doris sat beside me, oblivious to my presence, thoroughly transfixed on the intricacies of the *Sunday Times'* crossword puzzle. Yes, it was Saturday, but the delivery people were nice enough to package the *Sunday Times Magazine* with the Saturday paper.

My tummy was full, and my spirits were soaring. Last week's travel schedule was numbing: meetings at the home office on Monday; then off to Gatwick Airport for a flight to Marseilles and its nearby refinery; then to Paris and three days at the Normandy Refinery. Fortunately, I finished sooner than expected and caught an earlier flight back to Heathrow. And the limo driver was there waiting for me! A joyful reunion with my wife and a delicious home-cooked meal immediately put me in a good mood. I was happy to be home!

I stepped idly over to the dining room windows (they were really swinging glass doors) and looked down onto our small backyard. I was curious about what kind of day was in store, but I really shouldn't have been. In England, it's going to be mostly sunny, with cloudy periods, and a spot of rain; or, it will be mostly cloudy, with sunny periods, and a lot of rain.

There was a flutter in front of the window, and a blurred grayish-brown form morphed into a bird as it came to rest on the outside handle of the swinging doors. She twisted her head to look up at me, and I could almost hear her imploring, "You're late this morning! I'm hungry! Please bring my pancakes now!"

This was Mama Blackbird, who was our good friend and backyard companion for over two years.

I grabbed the purposely leftover pancake and headed downstairs toward the back patio door. As I approached the door, Mama quickly flew over and sat on the patio door handle, somewhat impatiently awaiting her reward.

Up close, I peered at her through the glass to admire her fine lines. The long delicate toes of her feet skillfully grasped the doorknob as she adjusted her balance. If you were color blind, you would swear this was an American robin. Her size and bodylines were a perfect match with our native robins. Her thick and fore-shortened beak looked much the same. Her choppy flight mannerisms resembled those of the North American robin. Her lyrical, almost quizzical, song sounded much like the birds that visited our New Jersey backyards.

Alas, the color was all wrong! Her back and tail were grayish-brown, not grayish-black. Her protruding breast was light brown and tinged with yellow, not red.

I had questioned some of my English friends, who informed me this was not a robin. They all had assured me, "That's a blackbird!"

Although I had protested, "Blackbirds are supposed to be black. That bird is grayish-brown," my friends insisted this was a blackbird—no matter its color.

They went on to inform me, "We do have a robin here, the English robin. It's a small bird, about the size of a sparrow, with a vivid red breast."

"Yeah, I know," I had responded, "I almost stepped on one as it sat on my shovel when I was digging in the garden. It was waiting for me to unearth a worm." Those little guys were almost as tame as Mama Blackbird.

I cautiously opened the door, allowing Mama to make an unhurried escape from her possibly perilous perch. I strode briskly down the path in the backyard, not wanting to slow until I'd reached my destination. Otherwise, Mama would be underfoot.

When I stopped, there was a familiar "plop" near my feet. The Mama had landed! She looked up at me expectantly until I broke off a few pieces of pancake and tossed them nearby. Mama gobbled those down voraciously. Those were for her. I broke off a lot more pieces and tossed them. Mama started stuffing her beak with them, piling them in until crumbs spilled out the sides of her beak. These were for her babies.

I awaited her return and started the process again. She kept carting off the delicious morsels until the pancake was finished, then she sat around and looked at me, hopefully. I simply put my palms in the air and said to her, "Go find a worm!"

When she continued looking at me, I knew what I had to do. I opened our little ramshackle tool shed and pulled out a shovel. After I turned over some soil in our small flower bed, she immediately came over to look for more natural prey.

We never saw her babies, but we could hear them peeping from their nest in a neighbor's tree. We thought surely that Mama would bring them over to dine with us, but she never did. Instinct probably told that bird to teach her babies to be self-sufficient. She didn't want her little birds to spend their lives on the dole! Maybe I attached too much nobility to her actions—she might have just wanted to keep such a good deal all for herself.

We followed this routine for over two years. Mama especially loved pancakes, but she would eat almost anything. We brought her leftover bread, meat scraps from the table, and crumbled cookies—she loved it all.

Honestly, we had to be careful walking around the backyard, for fear of stepping on Mama. She followed us around like a chicken, eternally hopeful we would toss her a tidbit or unearth a succulent grub.

Once, Doris opened the dining room windows to air out the place, since we were expecting guests for dinner that evening. Good old Mama, she came right on in the house, no doubt expecting to get at the source of all this manna. Doris had to chase the disappointed bird out. Mama would have probably joined us at the table if we dared leave the dining room windows open, which we never did after that incident.

Mama was a tame and gentle bird, but not shamelessly tame like the sparrows of Green Park or the pigeons of Trafalgar Square. She was very close to us but kept her distance. Many times, I tried to coax her into eating from my hand, or taking things from my fingers. She would come within an inch of my fingers, but she would not touch anything if I still held it. When I dropped the food particle or worm, it was gone in a flash!

After our fourth year in Wimbledon, we had to move because the landlord wanted to sell the house. Luckily, we found another house in the same subdivision, just a stone's throw from our first house. Dutifully, we fed Mama plenty of pancakes on our last Saturday in the house. We hoped we could induce the bird to follow us. We hung around the old house a few times, with her favorite food morsels, hoping she might spot us, but we never saw our friendly bird again.

As an exercise in fantasy, I started composing an advert for the local Wimbledon paper. It started with, "Has Anybody Seen My Mama?"

# Queuing for Court

*Two down-home Americans negotiate the portals of one of
England's most hallowed institutions.*

The sprawling, green-splashed grounds of the All England Lawn Tennis and Croquet Club lies on Church Road, just off St. Mary's Road in Wimbledon, London. This is the home of Wimbledon, the only one of the four Grand Slam professional tennis tournaments with grass-covered courts. The French Open is played on red clay, and the Australian and U.S. Opens are played on hard-surfaced courts.

Wimbledon is the most prestigious tennis tournament in the world. Minor players fight through special tournaments to qualify for the event. Star players enter minor grass tournaments during the brief two-week period after the French Open to accustom themselves to the slippery surface. And fans from all over the world flock to this Mecca of tennis.

We lived in Wimbledon for five years as expatriates while I worked for an international oil company. We resided in a row house on St. Mary's Road, less than a ten-minute walk from the All England Club.

As a long-time tennis player, I wanted desperately to attend this illustrious tournament, but obtaining tickets at face-value prices is a challenge. Methods for getting tickets include: know somebody with connections; belong to a group with special ticket privileges; enter the ticket lottery (the normal way); or line up (queue) for a few available same-day tickets. Failing these methods, there is nothing to do but pay whopping prices to ticket scalpers.

We submitted lottery forms during our first year of residence; amazingly, we were rewarded with tickets to the Ladies' Semifinals on fabled Centre Court.

What an exhilarating experience! We recognized all four players in the two matches —highly ranked players we had seen many times on TV, clad in regulation all-white tennis outfits. We stood along with the British fans as they sang their national anthem, *God Save the Queen*, and we quietly sang *My Country 'Tis of Thee* to the same tune.

The lush green tennis court spread out before us with regal majesty, surrounded by a dark green wall sprinkled with bold yellow advertisements and scoreboards. A royal box filled with "Royals" and their friends lay far below our seats (we recognized none of them). Uniformed linespersons stood stoically at their assigned positions, ready to call a shot in or out with hand signals; they never flinched when an errant ball struck them. The ball boys and ball girls, dressed in colored outfits, knelt on the sidelines, ready to dash out and retrieve balls no longer in play. The British fans applauded politely when a point was won, with little of the cheering and jeering so common at other grand slam events. Between matches, we circulated around the grounds, inspected vendor offerings, and of course, ate the traditional and expensive strawberries and cream (not ice cream).

Watching a tennis match on HDTV presents a sharp but two-dimensional picture of play. Watching from home shelters you from the vagaries of weather, but blurs the impact adverse weather has on the players. At Centre Court, you learn to suppress the urge to relieve yourself until breaks in action where movement in the stands is acceptable.

Attending the live event unfolds a spectacular, multi-dimensional panorama —the three spatial dimensions augmented by the extra dimensions of people, color, crowd noise, and distractions. On TV, the camera does the panning, but at the stadium, your neck pans the field of view to get a satisfyingly complete image of the event. For example, we chuckled at the antics of the few remaining pigeons at Centre Court, undaunted by the trained hawks that patrolled the grounds before play began.

Thoroughly thrilled, we wanted more of Wimbledon. Attending the real event, with all its rich color and pomp and circumstance, made the back of my neck tingle—much as one might feel while attending a World Series game or the Super Bowl.

One of my British colleagues told me, "You have a much better chance of getting a ticket to the stadium courts by queuing at the main gate. But this takes a bit of time and endurance."

"I'm not about to camp out overnight just to get tickets, even for Wimbledon," I demurred. "You must have seen on TV all the tents pitched along the club's fence at the last tournament."

"Ah, but that's only on the first day," my friend clarified, "if you join the queue on the second day through Wednesday of the second week, there should be no problem if you get there early enough."

For the next four years we enjoyed Wimbledon tennis, sometimes for several days at each tournament. I usually scheduled a week of vacation for the first week of the Wimbledon fortnight, and sometimes took single days off when I could. Doris attended the tournaments at her own pace, usually with her good friend—a Mexican lady married to a Swiss diplomat.

The key to getting stadium court tickets (Centre Court, Court 1, Court 2) was to hit the queue before 6:00 a.m. The London Underground starts up at 6:00 a.m. and dumps hordes of tennis fans at Wimbledon Station shortly after. I always got there early enough to secure my choice of stadium court. While sitting in line, I reviewed the order of play for each court to decide what ticket to buy.

But that requires over four hours sitting or standing in line. How does one cope with the ennui of queuing for such a long time?

Unlike in many other European countries, the British treat queuing very rationally, and the All England Club members pride themselves at maintaining an orderly queue. First of all, one has to earn the privilege of buying a face-value ticket; the club requires only one ticket is to be sold per person. British queue standers take a very dim view of anyone who tries to hold a place for late-arriving friends or relatives.

The club members steadfastly guard the practice of keeping a quantity of stadium court tickets available for same-day sale. This practice has come under pressure by American financial managers who have taken over the profit and loss aspect of the tournament in recent years.

To endure the queue, I dressed comfortably, usually wearing jeans and sneakers. I always carried a bag that contained contingency items: umbrella, peelable layers (sweaters, etc.), a windbreaker or raincoat, a hat with sunshade, suntan lotion, sunglasses, snacks for the queue, and reading material. I had to be prepared for rain, sun, wind, hot, and cold—and sometimes experienced them all!

I never had time to read as much as I thought, for I soon started talking with fellow queue standers, mostly British. It was interesting to trade "war stories" and tennis talk with these strangers in waiting.

Of course, I needed a restroom during the wait. Fortunately, the All England Club provided excellent portable facilities across the street. The tradition of the queue dictates that your neighbor in the queue will hold your place when you have to go.

As I waited, I watched the tennis day coming to life—players arriving (some driving, some driven, and some pushing baby strollers), hawkers in action, and the parking lots filling with cars. At 10:30 a.m. the main gate opened and as the queue began to move forward, my pulse quickened with anticipation.

When I reached the gate, I dashed toward the ticket booth for the stadium court I had chosen, where of course I had to negotiate a mini-queue. Finally, I reached the moment of fulfillment: a Wimbledon ticket clutched firmly in my hand, with no large sum paid to scalpers!

This ticket entitled me to a reserved seat in the chosen stadium court for the entire day, and I settled in to watch the start of matches. If a match proved dull, as early-round matches often were, I could get up and walk around the grounds and take in the action on the outside courts. In the early part of the tournament, many excellent matches took place on these courts. The view was much closer than in the stadium courts; one felt almost part of the action, dodging as a player crashed into the fence near you, laughing as a player muttered to himself or cursed the officiating under his breath. Occasionally, a player might even joke a little with the fans. When I tired of standing, I headed back to the stadium court and reclaimed my seat.

Doris and I have watched Wimbledon on TV for over twenty-five years after leaving our "fairy land" assignment in London. It's certainly not the same as being there, but nostalgia still overwhelms us when the cameras pan over the stadium and the far away surroundings. We marvel at the things that have changed (London skyline) and the things that haven't (St. Mary's Church, the apartments across the street). We laugh at sights we've seen before as the camera zooms in on a red fox in a hedge near St. Mary's Church.

The Wimbledon ticket queue continues to operate today, in spite of economic pressures to curtail it.

# Frequent Flyer

*A carry-on bag reduces a business traveler's anxiety and tells many tales.*

Hi, my name is Nifty, and I have a fine story to tell you. I've got to tell this now while there is still time, for I fear my days are numbered. I met Bob one bright summer day at the John Lewis department store on Oxford Street in London. I had languished at the store for many months, and no one had paid any attention to me until Bob came along. He looked at me from different angles, to see the effect of light on my features. He also looked at some of my more glamorous and popular colleagues, but his eyes kept coming back to me.

Finally, he took me in his hands, felt the softness of my sides with his gentle hands, checked all my zippers, and explored my various compartments. Satisfied, he said to his wife, "This is a really nifty carry-on bag! It will be perfect for my business trips."

I was so thrilled that I decided from now on my name would be Nifty.

Bob took me to the checkout desk, where he became my official master. We have been almost constant travel companions for over fifteen years. Bob acquired me because his first business trip for his new London job had ended in sartorial disaster—he successfully flew to Hamburg, but his checked suitcase went to Corsica. In the U.S. people would have wondered why Bob wore the same shirt to work for three days in a row, but in Europe, this was not noticed at all—everyone did it. But Bob didn't like it and vowed he would never check a suitcase again unless absolutely necessary. When he had to check a suitcase for longer stays, he always took me along to make sure he had the traveling essentials.

I'm talking to you now because someone left the closet door open. Unfortunately, I have been consigned to a back corner in the closet for the last few weeks, gathering dust as Bob travels with a newer bag. I know he doesn't like this new bag as much as he liked me. I heard him mutter several times as he packed for trips, "I can't pack as much stuff in this bag as in the old one. I sure wish I could use that nifty bag again."

I'm feeling a little like Humpty Dumpty now—my grip handle fell off and now rests inside my main compartment, waiting for an able craftsman who can put me back together. Bob took me to several leather specialists, and they all just shook their heads. There was no way to reliably reattach my handle. Bob was really dejected with this news, and he had no choice but to get another carry-on bag for his next trip. Remember Hamburg!

Enough of feeling sorry for myself. Let me tell you of some of the wonderful trips Bob and I took. Our first trip together took us to the refinery in Normandy, France. After a one-day meeting, Bob rushed to Charles de Gaulle Airport in Paris, desperately hoping he could make his flight to Rome in spite of slow going on wet and busy roads. Out of breath when he reached the British Airways check-in counter, Bob learned he had missed the flight, but he could catch the Lufthansa flight that left in ten minutes. Clutching me in his right hand and his briefcase in his left, Bob ran to the Lufthansa gate and just barely made the flight. He couldn't have done this with a suitcase!

I really gave Bob a lot of flexibility in his travels. When necessary, he could take longer on his business meetings and catch a later flight. If he were lucky enough to finish early, he could try to get on an earlier flight. Either situation usually required fast and deft moves to get to the available flight, with no time to fool around with a suitcase.

Flexibility was paramount on Fridays. The traveling business community in Europe always headed home Friday afternoon or evening, the earlier the better. For frequent travelers, it was a cardinal sin to spend part of the weekend on the road! I recall one trip where Doris accompanied Bob to Paris; she was to stay with a friend in Paris while Bob went on to a two-day meeting in the Normandy refinery. As usual, Bob carried only me.

As they left the airplane, Bob told Doris, "Be sure to get back to the airport in time to check your suitcase. And don't fret if I miss the plane. Just board the plane and go back to London. I'll get back somehow."

I was in the front seat of Bob's rental car; he fumed while nursing the car along at a snail's pace on the *Boulevard Périphérique*. Friday afternoon rush hour traffic had completely choked the five-lane thoroughfare. There was no alternative route; the side roads would have been much worse. One could only stop and go and hope. Bob nervously glanced at his watch, checking how close we were to flight time. Foolhardy motorcyclists distracted Bob as they roared by on the white line between lanes on both sides of the car.

Bob had resigned himself to a later flight as he ran with me directly to the flight gate 15 minutes late. But the British Airways plane was still there! Bob rushed on to the plane, gripping me tightly as he worked his way along the crowded airliner, and sat down next to Doris. She told him, "The pilot held the plane for you! Well, maybe not just for you. He said traffic was brutal on the *Périphérique* and was sure many passengers had been caught up, as he had."

All the passengers gave a cheer as we roared into the early evening air. Those who had been stalled on the *Périphérique* cheered the loudest. As was the usual for Fridays, passengers and the crew were in a festive mood. Both groups were members of the traveling community and they all wanted to get home for the weekend.

Paris was the site of yet another travel adventure, again on Friday evening. When he checked in, Bob learned that the French air controllers' strike was still in progress, but British Airways fully expected to leave—allegedly, the controllers would give them a pass. Many passengers hopefully checked their suitcases, and these were ultimately loaded on the plane. But Bob still had me resting by his foot as he sat in the lounge, reading. We waited and waited for our flight to be announced. After more than an hour, British Airways said we wouldn't fly after all.

At this news, Bob jumped up, grabbed me and his briefcase, and dashed for the taxi line outside the terminal. He knew there would soon be a heavy demand for taxis. "*Gare de Lyon*," he told the taxi driver in heavily accented French. He requested this railway station because he knew that we could catch the boat-train to London. We spent the night tossing around on the English Channel and then picked up another train to Victoria Station in London. Bob was happy to get home Saturday afternoon, even if this violated the "no weekend travel" rule.

I also was exposed to culture during my travels. Sometimes, Bob took his concert or theater ticket with him on a trip; that way, we could go directly to the event upon returning to London. Unfortunately, they wouldn't let me in, and Bob had to check me along with the coats and umbrellas. But I could still hear a little of the wonderful Royal Festival Hall music.

Bob always kept a nervous eye out for fog, especially when he was going to Holland, Belgium, or Milan. During bad fog, he informed himself of travel alternatives and was always seeking another way back home. Sometimes there was no way out because the pea soup was just too thick. We were hopelessly fog-bound in Brussels when British Airways gave us the good news: we had hotel rooms for the night. And the bad news: there weren't enough rooms, so we would have to share.

Bob met his random roommate; he was a very pudgy middle-aged fellow of Indian extraction who reeked of tobacco smoke and curry. Secretly, Bob hoped it would be a sweet young thing; this was not exactly a dream match-up! This guy snored even louder than Bob, and my soft sides vibrated to this nocturnal duet.

Tobacco smoke reminds me of volcanic plumes from Mt. Aetna. We went to the Sicily refinery many times, but sometimes we were turned back by an eruption from this volcano. Whenever we went to Sicily, Bob spent extra time packing his things. I knew full well that he was an expert in cramming a lot into my three compartments! Doris often wondered how he could put so much stuff in such a small bag. One had to be prepared for contingencies in Sicily, so Bob usually packed a week's supply for these trips. The Alitalia airline workers were thoroughly unpredictable in their work habits. You never wanted to be in Sicily on a Friday. They often went out on wildcat strikes that day—probably to ensure a long weekend undisturbed by work. You really had to be flexible in the face of threats from Mt. Aetna or Alitalia.

Bob always stowed me well in the overhead baggage bins. If he could not find enough room to do it, well, he just put me under the seat. I remember once that a passenger in the seat directly in front of Bob was bopped on the head by a poorly placed briefcase that fell from the overhead bin during some turbulence. This accident gashed the bald head of this unfortunate traveler. Luckily, a physician aboard treated the wound. Bob promised he would never endanger a fellow passenger with his carry-on items.

I have suffered violent turbulence, missed landing approaches, aborted takeoffs, and several engine failures. I tried to remain calm during these departures from the norm, much as Bob did. I have a feeling he took comfort from my calmness, though, for he usually reached down to touch me when we were bumping and veering. I suffered the indignity of being rudely sniffed by drug dogs in Italian airports. In Sicily, the dogs trampled all over the bags in their search for contraband. One miserable creature even peed on me.

There's not enough time to relate all the strange things I experienced during my travels, for here comes Bob with a determined countenance. I would like to think he's going to take me to a leather shop that can fix me, but I fear this is just hopeful dreaming.

As Bob carries me outside, I keep hoping for the best; but there is a certain strangeness in his demeanor. "No, Bob," I want to scream, "Not the dumpster!"

He gives me a violent swing and turns loose of me, "B…o…b!!"

# Insects Anonymous

*Two men, hooked on activities related to their work, seek the comfort of their peers.*

It was slightly before the appointed weekly 7:00 p.m. meeting time and most of the attendees had arrived. A blue haze of tobacco smoke had already gathered over the conference table, and the excited din of multiple conversations drowned out any hope of expressing a coherent thought. This looked like a business meeting from the old days—all attendees were middle-aged men, all were white. Most of them still worked for the company, some had retired, and a few had been involuntarily retired. Uncharacteristically, none of the men sported big bellies and all appeared to be in superb physical shape.

Raymond Parker, the leader of the group, tried repeatedly to call the meeting to order. He was good-natured about it, as he realized the men needed to relax with personal conversations before grappling with the problem at hand. Ray still worked for the company and represented the management viewpoint at this series of meetings. Just as Ray was succeeding at quieting the jabbering throng, Joe Uphill rushed into the room and found a place at the table. He apologized sheepishly for being late, citing the press of retirement activities. Shortly after, Mike Battle sauntered into the room and sat in the last empty chair. He didn't even bother with an apology.

Ray opened the meeting by leading the group in the Pledge of Allegiance to the United States, as he did in all of these meetings. He reminded the group of the reason for the meeting, "The company values the contributions you guys made over many years. You worked long, hard hours at great personal sacrifice and took many risks to accomplish our objectives. You kept apace of the latest technology and you knew when and how to use the company's sophisticated equipment."

Ray continued, "The company stands beside you for the things you did on our behalf, and we will continue to help you overcome the serious addiction you acquired while working for us.

"This series of meetings is really a form of group therapy to help you deal with your addiction," he added, "and our behavioral scientists believe you must do this from now on, or risk a relapse."

The company's management decided to model the program after the famous alcohol addiction program, since the staff psychologists claimed the addiction mechanism was much the same. The company wanted to handle this addiction internally, with as little publicity as possible. The potential embarrassment to the company was just too large to let the problem fester on its own.

The company was the CIA, and the "business men" were present and past field agents—members of the elite Whispers Section of the covert intelligence group. Whispers was a code name for all activities using electronic surveillance. The men used "bugs"—electronic surveillance devices—to get the information the company needed. They used tiny microphones and sophisticated digital filters to capture conversations from very noisy backgrounds; miniature cameras to transmit video pictures of subjects in the dimmest of light; and computer equipment that could crack encrypted e-mail and remotely read the internal computations in a subject's PC. They were all trained for surreptitiously breaking into homes and offices. The Watergate scandal provided them with a strong incentive for competence. All section members had degrees in electrical engineering or in computer science; some had advanced degrees.

The Whispers Section succeeded in numerous covert operations, gathering vital intelligence to help fight terrorists, foreign spies, organized crime, tax evaders, and other practitioners of illicit activities. An executive order after the 9/11 attacks allowed only the highly specialized Whispers Section of the CIA to work on domestic cases. A similar organization in the FBI grudgingly cooperated with them. They were strictly legal and constitutionally correct; court orders were always necessary for an operation. Yes, they sometimes got carried away with their activities, and this is the reason for Insects Anonymous.

A small percentage of the secret operatives became obsessed with the power to watch people in the most intimate of activities, to listen to conversations dealing with strictly private matters, and to pry into the personal finances of their subjects. These affected individuals lingered over assignments while gratifying themselves with bits of irrelevant sleaze. They extended the scope of the operations, sometimes illegally, to friends and relatives of the subjects, especially to young pretty females. One extra-curricular foray led to another and could quickly cascade into addiction. Seriously affected men carried their perverted activities into retirement.

Ray started the "confessional" phase of the meeting, where individuals acknowledged they were addicted, cited recent temptations they had been confronted with, and talked about any backsliding into now-forbidden activities. As in alcohol addiction, one had to face the demon directly. The first few men called upon described relatively minor temptations and no backsliding, and the group offered strong encouragement.

Joe and Mike were the last to be called upon, not necessarily because they were the last stragglers to arrive at the meeting. Each in the group knew these men were the most seriously addicted of the lot. They had been an operations team for more than fifteen years before retiring. Uphill and Battle, they were quite a team, recognized by their superiors and highly respected by their peers. The likeable duo were often the victims of good-natured gratuitous jokes. Because of their finely honed skills, they were assigned the most difficult of break-ins and buggings. They handled dangerous foreign assignments as well as high-profile domestic cases.

Joe specialized in micro cameras and miniature microphones. He could plant them in strategic locations and camouflage them so they were virtually undetectable. But his most-treasured skill was in devising means for transmitting the surreptitiously detected sounds and images to remote recording devices. He had earned a master's degree in electrical engineering during his early days with the company, and put this technology to good use during his operations. Each case posed a different challenge and required custom equipment to transmit a low-level radio signal that could avoid bug scanners, yet still be received by the surveillance team.

Unlike many such break-in and planting specialists, Joe also liked to join the surveillance team, ostensibly to monitor how well the devices were working. He found it great fun to listen to people when they thought they were talking privately, and to watch people in deliciously private moments. This ultimately led to his downfall. Joe's crash in the company came when he was monitoring a prominent senator for suspected organized crime connections. The senator's wife was a vivacious blonde, whom Joe discovered was having an extramarital affair with a defense contractor. Joe became more interested in the wife than in the senator, and collected voluminous tape recordings of her sexual exploits. He even re-entered the senator's home to plant more strategically placed cameras for a better view.

Aware of what Joe was doing, the other technicians on the surveillance team talked about it among themselves. A new member of the surveillance team overheard some of this small-talk and reported it. The section head had assigned a new person because Joe's intelligence reports on the senator's activities contained successively less useful information. When the section head confronted him with his dereliction of duty, Joe promised to stop this wayward behavior.

But it didn't stop. Company management decided Joe had an unfortunate obsession with snooping and could no longer be trusted on sensitive operations, for fear of embarrassing discovery. Watergate was never far from the managers' minds; they slated Joe for early retirement and enrollment in Insects Anonymous.

As with many retired covert operatives, Joe found that a steady regimen of golf and gardening soon became boring, and he gravitated toward private detective work. Unfortunately, this was like handing a bottle of vodka to a recovering alcoholic. Joe entered a downward spiral with his obsession, dallying for days on simple divorce cases where he could spy on pretty young women. Soon, his marriage was in shards, and his job was no more.

Again, this didn't stop Joe. He persisted in electronic voyeurism on his own, with simple devices he constructed from components bought at Radio Shack. He selected his own subjects who best suited his perverted needs.

Mike Battle's story was much the same. Mike was a real computer jock, with a degree in computer science from Case Western Reserve University. While Joe was hiding cameras and microphones, Mike was planting electronic devices and worm-like software on subjects' computers. The "worms" were similar to the e-mail viruses so popular now. But they were much more sinister. The worms intercepted the transactions within the computer so that all activities in the computer could be read by knowledgeable surveillance operatives. The worms communicated with tiny electronic devices, which transmitted the computer information via radio signals or existing power lines to remote surveillance stations.

Mike was a master at developing worms that could evade the most expensive virus scanners. He was also highly trained in cryptography, and he had access to an arsenal of computer programs that could crack so-called, "unbreakable encrypted e-mails."

Mike's downfall was a case involving a Wall Street executive and the Vice President of the United States. The "Veep" was supposed to have placed his stocks into blind trusts to avoid any semblance of conflict of interest. Capitol Hill rumors about frequent e-mail traffic between the two suggested otherwise, so the Whisper Boys were called in. Mike soon found that the rumors were groundless and that the Veep's steady stream of e-mail with the executive dealt simply with old college ties and mutual volunteer activities.

The executive proved to be much more interesting for Mike, so interesting that it caused him to descend into unanticipated early retirement. The executive had many gay friends, with whom he had some delectable e-mail sessions. That didn't get Mike's attention as much as the executive's e-mails with other financiers. The executive was involved in a huge network of inside information sharing, where the participants traded company secrets; he also discussed confidential information with some Hollywood and television stars. Mike's weakness was the rush he felt when he could read the private communications of the subject. The power to know what important people were doing gave Mike all the high he needed.

Again, Mike's efficiency dropped because of his obsessed, extra-curricular activities. Company management forced his retirement, fearing embarrassment if the beautiful people involved learned of Mike's illicit probing. Retirement proved as boring for Mike as it did for Joe, so he also worked as a private detective. Different agency, same result.

When Joe and Mike had their turns at confession before the group, they only half-heartedly talked of the things that obsessed them. The leader, Ray, knew, as well as the other men at the meeting, that Joe and Mike were still deeply troubled. The Insects Anonymous methods didn't seem to work for them. All tried discreetly to get Joe and Mike to talk more openly, but they were not forthcoming.

When the meeting broke up, the guys again picked up in amiable chatter. "Let's go to the Lizard's Lounge, have a beer, and trade a few spook stories," one of them suggested. Unlike their role model, the Insects Anonymous group had no compunctions about drinking. In fact, a little alcohol actually relaxed the tensions felt by the group members. "Come on, Joe and Mike," Ray shouted at the departing duo, "Why don't you two join us at the bar?"

Joe just waved his hand at the group as he headed down the street. He didn't have the least intention of wasting time with this group. "No," he replied, "I have to meet a client."

Mike smiled as he turned toward the group and shouted, "I can't really join you tonight. I have an important report to read and digest." Then he headed off in the opposite direction.

Ray and the remainder of the group relaxed comfortably in a corner of the Lizard's Lounge, quaffing a few beers and chatting about old times. Cigarette smoke billowed above their heads as they recalled humorous episodes about past operations, often laughing boisterously.

But then the conversation took a more serious turn when Ray said, "I'm really concerned about Joe and Mike. No matter how hard we try to help them, they seem stuck in their old perverted ways."

"Yeah," responded one of the group members, "we all know that Joe's client is probably an unsuspecting victim of his voyeurism."

Another member piped up, "And we're pretty sure that Mike's report is a set of financial transactions of some celebrity."

Ray reflected on this a moment and then observed, "The methods of Insects Anonymous work very well for just a few of us, and offer some help for most of the rest of us, but some will not be helped for a long time, if ever. Joe and Mike are consummately obsessed with spying on others, for their own personal gratification. We know it's wrong, they know it's wrong, but we can't help them until they are ready to be helped. Someday they might sink so low that they really want to regain a normal life. Let's be ready to support them when that time comes!"

With that, the group drained their beer steins and stood to leave. "See y'all next week," Ray shouted to the departing group.

# Herding Lizards

*A simple anecdote about a green lizard turns into a*
*championship tall tale.*

I sat at a quiet table in one of those old-fashioned looking, but really quite new, brew pubs that have popped up in downtown Austin. My old buddy Josh sat across from me as we munched peanuts and sipped some very good beer, an amber creation with a name I quickly forgot.

Henry Wilhelm Reinhardt, "Josh," as all of his friends called him, was a retired policeman from Fredericksburg. Yes, I agree there is no logical connection between his nickname and the names his mama gave him. I don't know for sure, but I've been told by members of our club that he got this sobriquet because he never could tell a truthful story, or anything even close to it. Makes sense to me, because many is the time I have tried to talk straight with Josh, but I have never been sure I succeeded—I always felt he was pulling my leg.

"Josh," I said after wiping foam from my beard, "that was really some kind of a story you told the group today. About how your father planted what he thought was a dead cow, and the next day he found the cow had popped up from the ground, with a calf to boot, just like growing crops. And that was how he started a whole new approach to the cattle business. How did you ever dream that one up?"

"Who said I dreamed it up?" Josh grumped, seemingly put off because I dared challenge the veracity of his unlikely story.

And then he continued, "A good story always starts with somethin' real, maybe only a smidgeon of it. Then the storyteller starts embellishin' the facts, adds color, injects good folksy humor, greatly enhances the action, makes the situation ridiculous, and finishes up at the height of hyperbole."

Josh had turned philosopher king and I could do nothing about it now except sip beer, roll my eyes, and let him rant on.

"What about Paul Bunyon?" Josh challenged me, "Do you think he was just a silly liar, with no basis for his stories?"

I shrugged my shoulders, gripped my beer stein firmly by its handle, and confidently answered, "Everybody knows those are just tall tales. We don't expect they have any semblance to reality. We don't want them to. We like them as they are, for what they are."

Josh leaned forward, narrowed his eyes, and placed a hand on the table; his fingers almost circled my beer stein, as if daring me to drink while he was talking. "Don't think for a minute that his stories aren't based at least a little on stuff that actually happened. Greatly exaggerated, yes. Life was tough in those pioneerin' days, and people had to find imaginative solutions to real problems. They also liked their beer, just as we do, and their stories always sounded better with beer. Frontiersmen were macho by nature, so they embellished their stories to flaunt their manhood. The stories were augmented and passed on from generation to generation, and before you know it, we had Paul Bunyon!"

I wanted to argue, but I knew I was out of my element. I was facing an expert. We were in Austin for a two-day meeting of the Lone Star Liar's Club, a venerable institution with origins from J. Frank Dobie's time. Josh was always very competitive in the storytelling sessions. Just a couple of years ago, he won the blue ribbon. And today, his story about planting cows brought him honorable mention. I tried nobly, but my feeble fib the day before didn't make the cut. I could lean back and enjoy the second day. No need for sweaty palms!

Both of us opted to spend an extra night in Austin instead of risking a nighttime drive home. This is a good way to visit with your buddies, swap stories, and disappear a little beer. Lots of attendees do this. Heck, it only happens once a year!

The philosopher's blood was still boiling and Josh kept railing at me, "The trouble with you is that you don't really git committed to anything. You don't let your true self come out when you tell a story. Take a look at my face. What do you see? Any whiskers? And what color are they?"

I forced myself to take a long look at Josh's visage. His was an active looking face, of a guy who had spent plenty of time outdoors. The skin was tanned and weather-beaten, with wrinkles furrowed deeply enough to supply him character for the rest of his life. His shock of pure white hair perfectly matched the stubble that emerged from his chin. Old Josh shaved every morning, but he always looked like he needed a barber by noon.

"Yeah, you've got enough whiskers to make a second lieutenant jealous, and their whiteness is a whole lot purer than your soul!"

Josh laughed at the insult and exclaimed, "See! I know I'm an old fart, and I let my grayness show. I'm proud of it. That's me!"

He continued, "If you looked at yourself in the mirror, what would you see?"

I shuffled around to see if one of the beer decorations on the wall had a mirror.

"Don't bother," he added, "I'll tell you what you'd see. You'd see the face of a man who cain't make up his mind about who he is after all these years."

Josh kept on his roll, "Look at that salt and pepper beard, at that pitiful excuse for hair you have on top! You cain't decide whether you want an old-guy image or the looks of a virile dude! Obviously, the old look doesn't bother you, otherwise you woulda done somethin' about that hair. But don't be half gray. Talk to your barber. He can advise you on getting all gray or all black. Either would look okay on you."

"What I'm tryin' to tell you," Josh continued, "your story tellin' reflects who you think you are. Be yourself!"

By now I was thoroughly on the defensive. I am comfortable with how I look and I damn well know who I am! I hemmed and hawed, desperately searching for a useful reply. That's when I noticed our beer steins were empty. I signaled to our waitress, Anna. She filled a fresh pair of steins and started walking to our table. My eyes carefully tracked her approach.

When she left the table, Josh leaned over to me and spoke softly, as if reading my mind, "Isn't it amazing how the look of Russian tennis star Anna Kournikova is showing up all over the place! Form-fitting black pullover, thigh-hugging shorts, blondish hair forced back into a ponytail. Our Anna is quite a looker."

Josh kept on in mischievous mode, "You're a tennis nut. Why don't you ask her to help you with your forehand?"

"Hah!" I retorted, "She'd probably backhand me across the face."

Thankfully, the philosopher mode was over, which gave me a chance to salvage something. I desperately wanted to earn Josh's respect.

"Hey, Josh," I ventured, "do you remember those green lizards that always hang around the house? The ones that proudly puff out their scarlet pouch under their neck?"

"How can I not?" he replied, "I still have a lot of fun watchin' their antics. Those are Anole lizards, not chameleons as many people call 'em. Texans have a funny way of callin' things the wrong name, like buttercups for evening primrose."

I forgot my inborn nervousness and started up in storytelling mode. "Josh, I'm gonna tell you a nice story about how I herded one of those lizards down a trail, just like your dad might've done with his planted cows."

This caught Josh's attention, and he eased back in his chair. He had switched to listener mode. He sipped his beer silently as I told my tale:

"I had seen this little green fella several times in my office over the garage where I do all my writing. This made me very nervous."

I paused briefly, as I imagined his mind, thinking, *What writing?* But Josh didn't react. He was deeply into listener mode.

"You wonder why a little green lizard would worry me. Well, I'll tell ya. I've always had a very active imagination. When I look at one of those green reptiles, I imagine a magnifying glass in front of me and I see an alligator. How do I know he cain't get big on his own? I get this overall panicky feelin' when I see a little lizard today and think how he might be an alligator tomorrow. If that guy's gonna turn into an alligator, I want him to do it outside, not in my office!

"One day, I strode into my little bathroom and there he was, on the toilet seat, his blushing pouch pushed out to the fullest. He cocked his head toward me, daring me to lift that toilet seat. I decided I could hold my water.

"The next day, I saw him near the stairway, not far from where I sat typing a story. I wheeled the chair around to get a better look at him, and his head rotated toward me in response to my potentially threatening motion. Once again, I worried about how he got into my office, if he found enough to eat to turn into an alligator, and how in the heck I was gonna get rid of him.

"He was on the floor near the stairs, the way I get outta the office. Inspiration struck. I was gonna herd that fellow down the stairs and out the garage door.

"But how do you herd a lizard? I didn't have any lizard dawgs. All I had was my hands, and that thought got me worried. Lizards can leap better than NBA players. This guy might just jump over my hands and dash back up the stairs.

"I would have to keep my hands close to him, to urge him along the trail. And I could deflect his jump and keep him heading in the right direction. A chilling thought made me think twice about using hands. *What if he bites?*

"Just a couple of weeks ago, I saw two big green fellas duke it out on the porch banister. One grabbed the other's snout in his mouth, struggled a bit, and then dangled him over the precipice, Godzilla style. The lizard in distress flailed around until he caught hold of a banister post. This gave him enough leverage to pull himself back onto the banister top, where he immediately assaulted the first brute and dangled him in space.

"Those guys have powerful jaws, and I betcha they could nip your finger real hard. And who knows about teeth? Ugh! I shivered a little but remained convinced it would have to be hands. There was no other way.

"I got on my hands and knees and tentatively approached my adversary. He looked at me warily, waiting for me to move first. I cupped my hands and slowly placed them to cut off his upstairs escape route. The only direction he could go was down those stairs!

"The guy wouldn't budge. The only way to get him moving was to touch his tail. By now, he knew I was seriously aggressive. He took one step down in a lizard leap. I went after his tail again, but he scooted to the side and ran up onto the baseboard. Uh-oh! He was gonna do the jumpin' thing! I girded myself to deflect his upward leap, but he jumped to the next lower step, instead.

"Things worked okay for a while. My routine got him down several steps. Then he disappeared. Like gone for good. *Where could that rascal be?* I wondered *Was there a crack or hole in the stairs?* I couldn't find an obvious escape route, so I screwed up my courage and put my nose in harm's way. I remembered how lizards could change color, so I lowered my face close enough to see. There he was, very still, his color almost perfectly blended with the dark carpet.

"So we got things moving again, one slow step after another, until we reached the ground floor. This lizard was thoroughly bamboozled. He had used up his defense mechanisms, except for his bite, and I was still on his tail. I reached up to turn the door handle, while keeping the other hand strategically positioned. I urged the lizard onto the threshold. When he caught sight of daylight, he took a flyin' leap almost to the edge of the porch and scampered into the green sanctuary of one of my wife's flower beds.

"I slammed the door shut and stood to savor my triumph. I had herded that lizard right down the trail I wanted him to take!"

Josh came to life and clapped his hands in genuine applause. "That was really a good tall tale!" he exclaimed. "You oughta tell it a few more times to get it embellished real good, and come back here next year with it. I bet you could win a prize!"

I looked at him curiously and explained, "But, Josh, that wasn't a tall tale. That actually happened. It was a mealtime anecdote I told my wife!"

"Oh come on," Josh retorted, "I know a good lie when I hear one. Ain't no person gonna herd no lizard. Those guys can jump over your head if they have to!

"It's just like I was sayin' earlier," Josh continued, "each tall tale has an element of truth. Did your story start with a little of the truth? And maybe you embellished it a little?"

"Yeah," I admitted, "but you wouldn't have listened to me if I had just told the simple facts, like I told my wife!"

Josh pushed back from the table and rose. "That's my point! You polish up that story and come back here next year. We're gonna get you a prize!"

Then he exclaimed, "Let's get outta here! I need some sleep. If I drink any more beer, I'll spend the rest of the night runnin' for the loo."

"Me too," I agreed. I pulled out a five-dollar bill and tossed it on the table for Anna, or whatever her name was.

I enjoyed a warm glow of satisfaction as I thought of my success with Josh. Then a sobering thought dampened that glow, "You wouldn't be joshing me now, would you?"

# Keystrokes of Destiny

*Footpads on a keyboard torture a consulting engineer with angst*
*and legal hazards.*

I sat alone at our old round oak table in the kitchen eating area, trying to take my orange juice in small sips, instead of the huge gulps my exercise-depleted body demanded. This was a Friday, an ordinary Friday. I had started the day around 5:30 a.m. with my usual two-mile run at the excellent track in the high school stadium. I had to cool down on the front porch for at least half an hour, before my sweat-soaked bones could dare face the air-conditioned chill inside the house.

After breakfast, Doris went outside to hit some good licks in her flower gardens, before the South Texas heat and humidity would drive her indoors to her bath and to her quilt sewing. I remained at the table, sipping orange juice and idly reading the Business and Technology section of the *Victoria Advocate.* In the background, I heard the NPR news program, but I didn't pay a lot of attention to this. I was more interested in the newspaper story about the latest computer virus attack. I read all about the ghastly potential it had to create havoc among computer users. When I finished the article, I enjoyed the smug satisfaction of already being prepared—I had downloaded the latest protective software patch from Microsoft two days ago.

My agenda for today was nothing, absolutely *nada*, in spite of Doris' plea for me to erect a small decorative fence in the backyard. I had just finished a big consulting project yesterday afternoon for a chemical plant. When I clicked the SEND button on my computer screen, my beautifully formatted product of weeks of intense engineering effort was reduced into simple zeros and ones. These were divided into information packets, then electronically shoved into a thin wire and sent bouncing among the myriad nodes constituting the Internet. My client was only a hundred miles away, but my report might have toured the entire U S of A before it got there.

E-mail is a wonderful tool, perhaps the most productive of the tools offered by the Internet. It enables consultants like me to live and work in pleasant but out-of-the-way places like Hallettsville. What a shame it's become corrupted by spam, viruses, worms, and hackers!

I put down my newspaper to listen to the 8:00 a.m. news summary, and to the local news that followed. The local news really lassoed my attention: "A spectacular fire has darkened the sky over Midland, Texas. A spokesperson for the Sluik Oil Company Refinery said this was caused by a leak in a heat exchanger in their new catalytic reforming unit, which makes gasoline components. There are no injuries, but the fire is not yet under control."

This news set my heart pounding and jolted my previously relaxed body with a torrent of adrenaline. My brow furrowed with worry and concern; my muscles tensed in anticipation of imminent reproach. Instant angst pervaded my entire being. All of a sudden, my stomach sensed the acidity of the already ingested orange juice and sent clear signals to my brain not to drink any more. The follow-up NPR news stories faded into a distant background murmur; the print on the newspaper in front of me dissolved into a gray blur.

I had worked on the design for that process unit as a chemical engineering consultant! I had designed some of its heat exchangers. *Did I work on that one? Did I screw up in its design?* One frantic question after another flew through my brain and whipped my burgeoning state of agitation into a total frenzy. I had to get more information about this accident and fire!

The relaxed day I had anticipated had already disappeared and had been rudely replaced by a consulting engineer's nightmare scenario—the defense of one's professional reputation and the conservation of one's financial future.

I left my newspaper strewn across the old table my grandfather had lovingly built for his family. I stepped onto the back porch and pulled on my battered garden clogs and strode purposefully toward my garage office. This plastic footwear served as a marker beacon, used by Doris, our cat Laci, and knowledgeable visitors to track my exact location.

Laci ran up to greet me, her tail happily held high, as I marched down the walk with grim determination. Overcome with my professional concerns, I totally ignored her. With her front paws, she grabbed me around the leg. "Let's play!" her impish face and imploring eyes told me.

"Not now, Laci," I replied. "I've got a big problem to work!" I patted her on the head and marched on. The disappointed cat stopped cold and flopped on the walkway. That cat was over three years old, but she still wanted to play at every opportunity.

Doris greeted me on the garage porch where she was repotting some plants. "Look at how this cutting from a chicken gizzard plant has taken root and flourished! I've got to repot it now before it gets root-bound!"

I looked at it and nodded blankly, totally incapable of generating a coherent reply. "Excuse me," I apologized, "there's a problem with some work I did for Sluik Oil and I've got to get some more information, quick!"

I disengaged from my clogs and opened the door to enter the office. Doris looked at me quizzically, her face expressing momentary concern, then went about with her repotting. Laci chased happily after a grasshopper, not worried in the least about grumpy old Bob.

My feet skimmed up the stairs. I hit the On button, and then waited impatiently for the computer to boot up. I drummed my fingers on the desk in rhythm with the intergalactic noises that emanated from the modem, waiting for the slow dial up connection to link to the Internet. I quickly found some news service stories about the incident, but these didn't tell me anything more than the NPR story. Finally, I found a website for one of the Midland TV stations.

Their website had some spectacularly disastrous looking photos of the fire. My whole body groaned as I viewed the flames that leapt a hundred feet in the air, billowing dense black smoke toward the city. I flinched at the thought of all the housewives complaining to the refinery manager about their laundry getting soiled, before I remembered that people didn't hang wash out to dry any more. Still, the environmental impact of this incident would be huge, and would likely result in large fines by regulatory agencies.

Then I shivered at the direct cost to Sluik Oil. Part of their new and profitable unit was being reduced to cinders, its steelwork twisted into grotesque shapes. With gasoline at over two dollars per gallon, the lost production cost would be hundreds of thousands of dollars per day—and it would take months to put this unit back online again.

Desperately, I tried to determine from the photos what part of the unit was burning. I saw flames licking around the reactor preheat furnace. Furnaces often suffer leaks, fires, and even explosions, but there was still too much of the furnace intact for this to be the problem. *Could it have been the preheat section?*

I dug into their news story and found what I dreaded. An uninstructed, but probably very excited refinery employee had spoken directly to a wily TV reporter, before the refinery spokesperson could intervene. The news report read, in part:

"Informed Sluik Oil Refinery sources tell us there were some pressure fluctuations on the preheat train to the main reactor furnace. The last heat exchanger blew out, releasing hot oil and hydrogen gas. This ignited and caused the huge fire, which enveloped the surrounding area, including the furnace. Quick work by refinery firefighters prevented serious damage to the expensive reactor vessel."

Cardiac arrest almost claimed me at that dire moment, while I completely digested the content of this news story. "That's E-501!" I shouted to the computer, "I designed that heat exchanger!"

I rushed downstairs, stopped at the garage porch, and slumped into a chair—distraught. Doris put down her pot of the moment and came over to see what was wrong.

"You look like you had just read your own obituary," she blurted out. "What's wrong?"

"We're ruined," I groaned. "I might even end up in jail. One of the heat exchangers I designed for Sluik Oil blew up and caused a huge, expensive fire. I musta screwed something up!"

Doris reflected on this a moment and then tried to console me. "Just because you designed it and it blew up, doesn't mean it blew up because of a mistake you made. You might have designed it perfectly and something else caused the explosion!"

"Oh no," I retorted, "exchangers just don't blow up. There had to be something wrong with the design!" I knew that was a ridiculous assertion, but I insisted on focusing the blame on me.

"Think, Bob," she countered. "You sent the design by e-mail, didn't you? No telling what might have happened to it on the way, what with all those viruses and hackers!"

I knew she had a good point, but I still felt queasy about the possibility I had goofed. Too many disastrous fires and explosions in petrochemical plants had ultimately been traced to faulty design.

I glanced up and saw Laci trotting up the walkway, proudly carrying a grasshopper in her mouth. Like a good cat, she deposited the hapless insect at my feet, and immediately chased after it when it tried to escape.

"That's it!" I exclaimed loudly and jumped up from the chair.

Doris looked at me strangely in view of my newfound animation. The startled cat jumped a foot in the air and looked toward me in alarm, the fur on her tail bristling with apprehension. She lost her grasshopper in the commotion.

I sat back down and spoke excitedly, almost babbling, "I remember one day when I was working on the Sluik Oil project. It was raining cats and dogs, with lots of thunder and lightning. Normally, I would have shut down the computer and stopped work until it cleared, but I had to get those heat exchanger spec sheets into the equipment fabricator. You had let Laci in earlier, when you went grocery shopping.

"She slept for a while, then wanted to play. I got down on my hands and knees and played with her for a few minutes, then sat back down at the computer to complete my task.

"She jumped into my lap and moved around until she had found just the right position. I stroked her calmly with one hand and stroked computer keys with the other. Of course, the movement at the keyboard was too much for her to endure. She batted my finger, then got up and marched almost deliberately across the keyboard so she could sit on the desk and watch the action on the screen. She musta hit every key, usually more than one at a time.

"That computer was beeping like a pinball machine in the clutches of a pimply faced whiz-kid. I was bombarded with more protests from the computer than I normally get in a month. I looked at the screen, and instead of solid engineering data on the spec sheet, I saw nothing but gibberish.

"I had worked nearly an hour on E-501 and was almost finished. Unfortunately, I hadn't saved my work. I normally save every few minutes, but I musta been distracted by that cat.

"I was ready to ditch it all and start over when a brilliant thought hit me. I started clicking on the Edit/Undo menu. Each time I clicked, more gibberish disappeared, and was replaced by reasonable-looking data. Soon, I was able to look at my almost completed spec sheet. I finished the design, and then carefully reviewed the numerous entries on the spec sheet to be sure each contained the correct data for this exchanger.

"That's how I screwed up," I moaned to Doris. "I musta missed something important and a terribly wrong number ended up in one of the entries!" I slumped and buried my face in my hands.

Doris remained calm and thoughtful during my moments of distress. She always relied on intuition when she got into sticky situations, and she insisted on following the same path in handling my mental anguish. She didn't know a thing about designing heat exchangers; in fact, she wouldn't recognize one if I set it right here on the porch.

"I still think there are many things in the plant that can cause an explosion—not just bad design," Doris proclaimed. "Why don't you go back upstairs and check your records about the design for that specific exchanger. At least, that should make you feel a little better; it should reduce the guilt you insist on assuming."

I pulled up the design calculations and spec sheet for E-501. I looked at my files with a macro view, and compared what I found with my experience. All seemed reasonable. Then I focused on specific details. There are several design considerations for heat exchangers, but two things come to mind when one thinks of explosion causes: design pressures and materials of construction. The pressure consideration is obvious, and both shell and tube-side design pressures were okay. This puppy wasn't going to blow because of pressure!

Material of construction is a much more subtle consideration. In hydrogen service at high temperature and pressure, one has to worry about cracking and corrosion. A special steel alloy is required for this service. With the wrong type of steel, a disastrous leak or explosion can occur.

I looked at the type of steel I had specified—this jibed with my experience. To be sure, I consulted Sluik Oil's Design Basis Memorandum, found the Materials Section, and confirmed my choice. It was right on!

When I rushed back down to my chair on the porch, Doris could see my outlook had improved. She set down her watering can and muttered, "I think I see an engineer who designed a certain heat exchanger correctly! I think we need a cup of coffee to celebrate!"

This was coffee time, about 10:30 in the morning. Laci appeared at the porch on schedule, awaiting her cat snack. Normally, coffee perks me up and fortifies me for the remaining tasks of the morning. But today I could take only a few sips. The black liquid, with just a touch of milk, tasted just like it looked: like crude oil. Just a few sips had sent my blood pressure up; the entire cup would have put me over the red line.

I set my unfinished cup down and turned to Doris, "I'm really too juiced up to drink coffee this morning. I feel a lot better now, but it still ain't over. There's gonna be an investigation. They're gonna be lookin' for a fall guy, wherever they can find one!"

"We're gonna have to watch our cash flow the next few months, just in case. I do have some professional liability coverage, but you know how much lawyers cost. We'll have to delay projects like that fence you want so much, until the coast is clear again."

Day after day, week after week, month after month, I waited and hoped—hoped I wouldn't hear from anybody about this terrible incident. I dreaded that subpoena, which might send me packing into court and scrambling for my professional liability insurance policy.

I could drink coffee and enjoy the simple pleasures of life in Hallettsville again. By now, I could sit in the swing on the front porch and relax, just as two generations of Zumwalts before me had done. When the incident first occurred, I had worried about keeping this old house in the family—the house my grandfather had built, which first my parents, and then Doris and I, had restored. With each passing day, I felt better about the prospects.

Every day, I called up the Midland website, to follow up on any news about the incident. Usually, there was nothing. One day, I read a news story about a court proceeding that caused me to hoot and holler loud enough to be heard outside. In part, the story read:

"The Sluik Oil Company presented its case in District Court today against the AirTite Construction Company. Sluik Oil sued AirTite for negligence relating to a serious explosion and fire at its Midland Refinery. As evidence, Sluik Oil presented a specification sheet for heat exchanger E-501, prepared by a qualified consultant, R. E. Zumwalt, for Sluik Oil. This was followed by testimony from expert witness Dr. Charles Waters, who pointed out the correct specification of materials for the exchanger. He then testified he examined the wreckage of the exchanger and determined it was fabricated from an inferior grade of steel. In his opinion, the sub-standard steel cracked when it contacted hydrogen gas at high temperature. This caused the leak, which led to the explosion and fire. After this testimony, AirTite lawyers approached the bench and announced they wanted to negotiate a settlement with Sluik Oil."

Joyfully, I ran down the stairs and claimed my chair from Laci. Doris soon arrived, with coffee for us and a snack for the cat. "It's over. It's finally over!" I shouted with glee. "They've settled the court case and the fabricator was at fault. I'm off the hook! At least I think I'm off!"

Doris leaned back in her chair and flashed a big smile. "I had faith in you, Bobby. I knew you had done a good job!"

The phone rang, so I set down my coffee cup and went in the garage to answer it. I was on the phone for many long minutes.

"What was that all about?" Doris asked. "Is the Chamber of Commerce looking for tour guides again?"

My drawn face must have shown a little concern, for she quickly asked, "It wasn't about Sluik Oil and that fire, was it?"

"Yes, it was," I grimly announced, and watched as her face reflected my concerns.

"They want me to do the design work for rebuilding the unit damaged by that fire."

Her face visibly relaxed and she asked, "When do you start?"

"I told them I wasn't taking any more consulting jobs. It was time for me to really retire!"

"Great!" Doris shouted, as she almost leapt to her feet. She embraced me and then gave me a little peck of a kiss. "Now we can get started on that fence project!"

# The Erector Set

*An anxious middle-aged man finds that careful reading of instructions is important.*

Jake Slocum and his wife, Maggie, sat across from each other at the kitchen table, sipping coffee and reading the newspaper after their traditional full-course Saturday breakfast. Their son and daughter were off to college and the couple loved to relax on weekend mornings. Maggie seemed bright and alert, intently reading the national news section. But Jake felt demoralized and dispirited, maybe even a little depressed. He peered at Maggie from behind his sports section. He thought how lovely she looked, her auburn curls still neat after a night's sleep, her natural face radiantly beautiful even without makeup.

*How can anyone look so young and pretty when they are pushing 50?* he asked himself. Jake had already passed that milestone and looked and felt it. He was six feet in height and a solid 200 pounds…well, maybe not so solid. His only exercise was cutting the grass, and he made sure he didn't fertilize the lawn too heavily. He still ate all those foods the papers and doctors said were bad; he felt he could always cut back later. More and more of his forehead was getting a tan, and his bifocals tended to slip down his nose.

The visible shortcomings weren't what was bothering him today, no siree. Jake had had plenty of time to adjust to those. Maggie had made fun of him this morning, and that wasn't the first time. Actually, she had just gently kidded him in good fun, but it had the same effect. He knew he was no longer the virile male of his youth, and now Maggie knew it well enough to talk about it (as if she didn't). Last night's episode was really a flop, and that's what was bugging Jake.

Jake had a plan, but he was disappointed his hoped-for solution had not yet arrived in the mail. He learned about this from a group of guys at the office. "This stuff makes you feel like a lad of nineteen, and it really works," exclaimed a gray-haired office veteran. "You can order it straight from the Internet." Jake and colleagues earnestly took notes as the old-timer shared his knowledge.

Jake logged on to the Internet that evening and pulled out his notes to make sure he had the website spelling correct: www.youdadoc.com. *Strange name for a website,* he thought. But he understood after he got into the mechanics of this cyber enterprise. Literally, Jake was writing himself a prescription for Viagra. Yes, there were shill doctors on the staff to make it technically legal, but the only numbers they examined about Jake were on his credit card. He ordered a three-month supply and anxiously started counting days to the estimated two-week delivery time.

*That stuff was supposed to be here yesterday,* thought a disappointed Jake as he finished the sports section.

That afternoon, Jake was alert for any sound of the postman. He wanted to beat his wife to the mailbox so he could retrieve his eagerly awaited reinforcements. Luckily, Maggie had gone out shopping when the mailman delivered a small package wrapped in plain brown paper. His help had finally arrived!

Jake ripped open the package and skimmed the instruction booklet, looking for the high spots, not the stupid details. He carefully noted that, "if one pill doesn't do the job, try two," but ignored the warning, "don't take more than two." Jake was in no mood to be disappointed; if those guys thought one might not work then he better make sure he had enough. Jake popped those little blue pills like M&Ms. He was going to be ready for tonight.

When Maggie returned, she noticed Jake was no longer wearing his depressed-looking face. In fact, he seemed to have a bit of a sly look on his handsome visage. "Hey, Jake," she said in jest, "you've really perked up since this morning. Got something up your sleeve?"

"Not exactly," he replied with a little glimmer in the eye that Maggie understood so well.

After dinner, a shower, and a couple of hours watching TV, Jake yawned and said it was time to head upstairs. He brushed his teeth, pulled on his pajamas, and eased his Viagra-laced hulk between the sheets, eagerly awaiting his lovely wife.

The next morning, Sunday, the two sat at the breakfast table, even more silent than the day before. Jake was thoroughly disconsolate—last night was again a disaster. *This stuff was supposed to help!*

"Don't worry, Jake," Maggie consoled, "it's going to be better. You will outgrow this. It's probably just too much stress."

Jake had made the mistake of relying entirely on miracle chemicals. Had he paid more attention to the instructions, he would have learned the importance of tenderness and passion.

Maggie broke the awkward tension by announcing, "We'd better get moving if we're going to church this morning. I'll hit the shower first."

As the nattily dressed couple entered the church, they noted the throng already inside. More were streaming in. "Why so many people?" Maggie asked.

"I guess a lot of folks got up this morning feeling guilty!"

Maggie and Jake sat near the aisle end of the nearly full pew; they left some room for latecomers. Almost right away, a younger couple sat beside them. Everyone moved down a bit, while keeping a comfortable social distance. As Jake inched to the right, he glanced at the young woman who was taking a seat to his left. *What a gorgeous blonde!* She flashed him a naturally engaging smile that would have warmed Frosty the Snowman. His nostrils caught her perfume and the enticing aroma enveloped his entire being. A warm glow flashed through his body and a tingling sensation crackled to his extremities.

Just as the services began, another person arrived at their pew. Everyone shifted to the right again to make room, but this time the social distance had completely evaporated. They sat elbow-to-elbow, thigh-to-thigh. Jake's tingling sensation sharply increased, rapidly heading toward the critical point.

Jake glanced at the young woman's knee, not quite covered by her tightly stretched skirt. He knew he'd better be careful when turning pages in the hymnal, lest his hand brush against that luscious knee. He involuntarily shifted his hand to the right and averted his glance, as those sensations kept building.

The pastor intoned, "Please rise and sing Hymn 496 along with the choir." Jake hesitated, for he had already started rising. Maggie nudged him and he reluctantly stood up, holding his hymnal strategically low.

As the liturgy progressed, so did Jake's distress. He fidgeted, he shifted what little he could of his bulk within the compressed space on the pew. He kept holding the church program as low as he could in his lap. Maggie noticed his agitation and kept watching from the corners of her eyes. Then she saw his problem—Jake was experiencing a monumental erection. The damn thing was bulging his trousers!

"Oh, Jake!" she groaned to herself. "Why in church, why not at home?"

Neither Maggie nor Jake understood what was happening. Jake's body was hostage to the overly concentrated chemicals, whose effect was unfortunately delayed for this first-time user.

The preacher was into his sermon and Jake tried to focus on his voice. He hoped if he actually tried to follow the sermon for once, he could get his mind off this pressing problem. Just as Jake picked up the thread of the story, the preacher boomed, "Do not be tempted by your voluptuous neighbor!" This admonishment wasn't going to help.

Then he thought of showers, cold showers. That tactic always worked when he was a teenager. He added ice—heaps of ice cubes, icicles, icebergs. The thing still wouldn't retreat. It had its own agenda and nothing Jake did or thought was going to make a difference.

As the services came to an end, Jake was still shuffling to maintain his composure and reduce his visibility. The final hymn was sung and the congregation rose for the benediction. The ushers took their positions to help the people file out. The usher at Jake's pew was also a deacon. Jake dreaded the moment, but knew he had to leave. As he turned to exit the pew, the deacon immediately spied the obvious problem. Amazed, he shouted for all to hear, "Praise the lord! That was truly an uplifting sermon!" A chorus of "Amens!" responded.

A man leaving the opposite pew also noticed. Since this was a strange place to have such a problem, he quickly came over to Jake and took him aside to a less prominent location. He spoke very softly to Jake, "Excuse me, sir, I am a physician and I can't help noticing the big bulge in your trousers. I don't mean to intrude in your personal life, but is it possible you've taken an overdose of Viagra?"

By this time Maggie had joined them. Jake nodded his head sheepishly, too ashamed to utter even a word.

The kind physician decided he'd better deal directly with Maggie; she was likely to be the calmer half of this distressed pair. "We better get your husband to the emergency room right away. This situation could be very dangerous. I'll go with you and see that your husband gets the help he needs."

When the trio entered the emergency room, the physician explained the problem to the admitting nurse. This hard-bitten veteran of many a life-threatening emergency shouted into the ER's public address system, "Another case of *rigor erectus*. Roll out the Erector Set. And hurry, the patient looks like he took way too many pills!"

Even this ego-puncturing exchange had no effect at deflating Jake's single-minded problem. The resident on duty huffed up to Jake's side just as the medical techs wheeled up the trolley with "Erector Set" emblazoned on both ends. This contained all sorts of syringes, needles, flasks, and other medical accouterments.

Some ER wag thought up this appellation last year, based on the construction kit used by generations of kids. With the collection of clinical components on this trolley, a skilled doctor could flatten the most refractory dream castle.

With considerable difficulty, the techs succeeded at removing Jake's trousers and undershorts. Before proceeding with treatment, the young doctor paused to admire Jake's titanic totem and wisecracked, "Wow! I bet Alexander Graham Bell could have strung wire on that!"

Jake groaned and slunk farther into his ignominy. *Here I am, in the most compromising of positions, and they're making cheap jokes about me?*

The resident asked how long this crisis had endured. Maggie responded, "Only a little over an hour, thanks to the good Samaritan who helped us at church."

"That's better." The resident relaxed a little. "We don't have to take the most drastic action—just give an antidote to relieve the problem."

He retrieved a large syringe, slowly filled it with a noxious-looking amber fluid, and attached a thick needle. Jake watched intently and nervously. Up to now he hadn't said a word in the emergency room. He instinctively tried to shield his privates and rasped, "That thing's big enough for a horse, what are you gonna do with it?"

"That's because you have a horse of a problem and we have to relieve it quickly before it does you serious damage. We have to inject a bunch of this stuff into your nether regions to counteract all the pills you took." He continued, "The good news is, you will soon be able to walk without embarrassment."

"And the bad news?" Jake anxiously inquired.

"You won't be of much use in bed for about a month!"

They kept Jake in the ER for over an hour to observe his reaction to the injection. Everything worked normally, and Jake's problem quickly wilted. Maggie drove him home in respectful silence.

Jake, though much relieved to be heading home after his tumultuous bout of tumescence, kept reflecting on the perverseness of things. *Ponce de Leon tromped all over North America searching for the fountain of youth,* he mused. *And we millions who follow keep looking!*

# Having a Fine Time!

*A very lucky kitty reports on her new home after dodging a bullet.*

Dear Victoria Animal Shelter Folks:

Remember me?

My name is Laci, and you cared for me for a few days, until these people from Hallettsville came down to adopt me. My folks read about how much you love your homeless clients, so I'm writing to let you know everything is okay and I am doing well in my new home. I am eating well and I have gained a lot of weight. My new people, Doris and Bob, take real good care of me, show me plenty of love, and play with me often. It's really fun in their house!

The day after I arrived in my new home, they put me in the cage and started up the car. I was afraid they didn't like me and were taking me back. They took me to a man they called "The Vet," who jabbed me with needles, shoved a thermometer up my rear, dropped pills in my mouth, and squirted stinging stuff into my ears. I was really worn out when I got back, so I crawled into the bottom part of my new double-decker cat bed and slept and hid the rest of the day.

Doris and Bob are really nice to me—maybe even crazy about me. Bob holds me in his arms when I want to be cuddled, and talks to me as he carries me around. They talk to me often and tell me how cute I am—even if Doris thinks I look like a possum! So I talk to them too, about going in and out of the house, wanting to play, and of course, telling them I'm hungry. Sometimes, I just talk to myself, when I'm outside and see a lizard in the flower bed. You might remember, I'm quite a chatterbox!

When I first got here, I was all skin and bones, and really hungry. They said I ate like a horse. But I didn't give up any of my feline dignity just because I was hungry! They feed me different kinds of dry food and canned food. I like some of it, but I try not to be too critical, since they are still learning about my sophisticated palate. I think the best thing is the food Doris cooks. The smell of cooking drives me nuts! But she is an easy touch when I cozy up to her and cadge a sample. Then, when they are eating, all I have to do is blink my eyes real cute and nuzzle Bob's leg, and he will slice me a few tidbits.

Bob plays with me two or three times a day, sometimes late at night when he's tired, but when I'm ready for a good time. He can really look silly! He gets on his hands and knees and tries to act like a kitten. I try not to laugh and just enjoy the play—he can fake the kitten stuff pretty well. He gives me great toys: cardboard boxes, shopping bags, pieces of string, wadded-up paper balls, pecans to kick around, and even a battered toy mouse. He likes to show people how high I can jump to catch things. We play hide-and-seek, too.

They have a great house for me with lots of rooms to hide in, stairs to tumble on, closets to explore, and cool places to sleep. Bob even takes me over to his office above the garage, where there are more boxes and toys to play with. I love to step on his computer keyboard and lie on top of his papers!

They let me outside during the day, when I want to. They have some real good climbing trees, and lots of flower beds where I can chase lizards. It's funny how more and more of those lizards don't have tails, now! A neighbor cat, a former Tom named Tucker, comes by to beg snacks when Doris and Bob take coffee. He's interesting and I follow him around, but I don't let him come too close. Yesterday, I chased a stupid dog.

But they make me come in when it gets dark. They say all sorts of bad critters like skunks come at night. I tell them how badly a cat wants to be out at night. But they just say, "No!" So I grab a few bites of dry food and find a good place to sleep while they read or watch TV. Sometimes, I sit on one of their rocking chairs and watch with them. *Pirates of the Caribbean* was exciting! But the one about taking care of cats was a real sleeper. Maybe they'll learn something from it!

Dear folks, as you can read, I lead a sumptuous lifestyle—not bad for a "throw-away kitty!"

I send you this snapshot, so you can see how much I'm growing and filling out and how beautiful and sleek my fur looks now. Thanks very much for rescuing me from the street and caring for me lovingly while I stayed at the Victoria animal shelter. And thanks for helping me find Doris and Bob. I'm so glad they selected me to share their home.

What happened to the mama cat with the four black kittens? Did anyone take them to a good home? How about the long-haired old female cat with no claws? Or that nice-looking orange Tom?

I'm having a great time. Wish you were here.

Gotta go, Doris just called "Din-Din!"

Love,
Laci

# Sleek Young Thing

*This love letter will keep you guessing!*

Dear Bob,

I knew you were dissatisfied with me, because I could tell from the way you acted. But for the life of me, I couldn't figure out why. I have always tried my hardest to do what you wanted and to make you happy. We have had some good times together, with lots of productive output. I am really proud of the things we've done.

I noticed how your head turned when sleek and glamorous new models came onto the scene. I tried to ignore it when you became impatient with my few shortcomings and when you said bad things to me. Although I know I'm not perfect, and I'm no longer a spring chick, it still hurts when you treat me that way.

But now you've done it—abandoned me for the comely new kid on the block. Yes, she runs a lot faster than I can, remembers more, and has a bigger smile. I just sit here, alone, watching you make a fool of yourself over this racy young thing. You make me sit here by the two of you, in case you might need me from time to time. You just let me agonize over all the fatuous attention you used to show me, which now goes to her.

It pains me as I watch you struggle to do familiar things with your new lady. She has her own ways of doing things, and you have to figure out how to please her. I've seen you get exasperated as she repels your usual moves. I chuckle as I remember that I also taught you a thing or two a few short years ago! And I've noticed the longing glances you make at me when she's really giving you a hard time. I just sigh as I think of how much more easily you could have done that with me instead of her.

Okay, I know you will soon get things smoothed out with your new lady. I resign myself to going on to my new life, whatever that might be. I just hope you will remember me. And I hope against hope that I can please you if you turn once again to me.

Still love you,
Your Old Computer

# Cyber Boots

*The intrusion of new technology into a drowsy computer user's session turns into a nightmare.*

I was comfortable and relaxed after a great dinner and a nice glass of wine. But I couldn't just slump down on the couch and nod off while watching TV, because the project deadline was approaching. It was time for the evening shift to kick in, although I had hit some good licks during the day. This was the down side of the exciting life of the work-at-home consultant.

My long engineering experience brought me many clients who had more problems to work than regular employees to handle them. The current project was lengthy, tedious, and boring. It was not very challenging, but it paid well. I typed away at the keyboard, peered into the monitor to verify I was doing everything right, and slowly chipped away at it. I typed in one mathematical formula after another, fighting drowsiness all the way.

I was working on my new GEN-1000 computer; it had all the latest in hardware and software features. For decades, the computer industry made machines with more power than business applications could intelligently use. Multi-megabyte and multi-megahertz were mundane commodities now—all manufacturers had them. Cutting edge machines now had silicon sensors on the keyboard and monitor, with state-of-the-art software for tracking the computer user's performance. The GEN-1000 had it all, including advanced software I hadn't even looked at.

Fumble fingers is the bane of all serious computer users, a distraction that interrupts the train of thought. Hitting the wrong key might just cause an error; but sometimes it completely locks up and freezes the machine. Then you have to restart it and reenter lost work.

But this time it was me, the computer user, who froze up.

An observer would have seen me transfixed in a curious position with the computer. My fingertips were locked on the keyboard in standard Qwerty position. My head slumped forward until it rested against the monitor screen.

I had mistakenly hit Alt-F6 instead of Control-F6. I didn't know it, but the key combination Alt-F6 was a short cut for the CyberSelf™ program.

CyberSelf™ is one of the many opportunistic spinoffs of the human genome project. Critics had long predicted that the collection of genetic data would be exploited for self-serving purposes, and this program was a good example. CyberSelf™ was intended to analyze one's genetic history and profile, but it went a few steps farther than competing programs. It actually collected data from the individual and then tried to impose behavioral modifications consistent with that person's genetic background.

Only a small part of CyberSelf™ resided on my computer; it was just an emissary for the application's main workhorse on a gigantic supercomputer in Portland, Oregon. When I inadvertently started the program, telephone lines between Portland and my office crackled with communications between the supercomputer and tiny silicon sensors on my keyboard and monitor.

The keyboard sensors sampled the skin secretions from my fingertips, looking for the telltale components needed for DNA analysis. The main computing module in Portland cranked up a Fourier-series analysis, seeking to map my DNA. Only a supercomputer could handle this calculation.

But the arteries of the Internet were scaled up with fatty deposits left by a multitude of hackers. All but one of these did no harm to the calculations in progress, they just slowed up the process. Unknown to the makers of CyberSelf™, one of these hackers was an evil genius—a cybernetic psychopath. He was smart enough to crack the code of CyberSelf™, and focused his malevolent skills on the behavioral modification part of the application.

The CyberSelf™ authors intended behavior modification to be a very innocent psychological approach to small personality defects detected during the DNA analysis. It used the huge human genome database to determine DNA norms and calculated the user-specific exceptions. For example, if the user's DNA indicated a tendency to anger, the application would use bio-feedback by sending corrective signals to his brain through the monitor sensors. This was not an automatic process. The application informed the user of what it intended to do and why it should be done, and then asked for his permission to proceed.

Alas, the hacker had corrupted this part of the program in a most deadly way. Strangely, in my sleep-like trance, I could actually see the behavioral modification code as it executed. The most critical part of this code for me looked something like this:

```
IF user has DNA Type Z THEN
   Message: "The user has inferior DNA"
   IF user wants to be terminated
        type "Y"
ELSE
        type "N"
```

I trembled as I watched the behavioral modification code jump into this part. Evidently, I had Type Z DNA. Then the dialog box for permission to terminate came up on the screen. Naturally, I had no intention of letting this proceed, so my right index finger reached for the N key. Or at least I thought it was reaching for N.

Instead, I cringed as I saw my finger reach for Y. *No,* I silently shouted to myself, *hit the N key!* I willed my finger to hit N, I mentally coerced the errant digit to do what I wanted. But to no avail. The finger kept moving, paused above the Y key and firmly pressed it. I had no control over what was happening.

I soon realized what was in store for me. The rogue program started a series of commands to my brain through the sensors on the monitor. These were instructing an orderly shutdown to my bodily functions. My blood pressure, heart rate, and respiration were all being slowly lowered. No rapid movements were made to prevent any spasmodic jerking that might interrupt the flow of commands.

*My gosh*, I drowsily thought, *they're trying to do genetic cleansing through the Internet! Is this some kind of Nazi conspiracy?*

My wife abruptly entered the room and shouted, "Bob! Wake up! Get off that computer and come to bed!"

In response to this strident stimulus, my head jerked upright, breaking the lethal connection with this malevolent bio-feedback. I gasped for breath and shook my head to clear out the cobwebs.

"You really had me worried," she said. "You looked like you had just died with your computer boots on!"

"Yeah," I muttered to myself, "I thought I was just about to do that!"

I still don't know whether I had dozed off at the computer and had nightmarish dreams, or whether I was really in mortal danger. But I do know I was not going to take any chances. The next day, I deleted CyberSelf™ from my computer and traded in the fancy keyboard and monitor for plain-vanilla versions. From now on, my GEN-1000 was going to work *for* me, not *on* me!

# Hobson's Choice

*Enjoying a forbidden pleasure leads to a difficult decision.*

At last I did it; I booked a two-week vacation trip to Mexico. I had traveled all over the world and lived in two foreign countries, but all I had to show for Mexico was a couple of youthfully misspent one-day border crossings. Many of my friends had talked very glowingly about their vacations in Mexico; a couple of them even had second homes there. I figured I must be denying myself a vital experience by shunning Mexico. I always worried about stories of criminal acts against *gringos* and of course there was the fear of "Montezuma's revenge."

I found myself at the bar in *El Gaucho Loco*, an upscale drinking establishment across the road from my resort hotel on the Pacific coast of Baja. The owners intended it to look like a Mexican bar, to impart a local ambiance for the target customers: American tourists and vacationers. Beneath the Mexican veneer was a typical American bar atmosphere. No Mexican local would be caught dead here, unless he were trying to arrange a business deal with a visiting American.

The bar even had an ersatz Mexican bartender named Manuel. Manuel Rodriguez was indisputably Hispanic. To me, he spoke Spanish like a native, but all the villagers knew he didn't. He spoke flawless American English, with what sounded like a mid-Western accent. When I asked him about this, Manuel explained that he grew up in Detroit. His father was a migrant farm worker with valid papers, a highly intelligent *hombre* with more education than the typical migrant worker. Through a farmer with big-city connections, he got a job at a Ford plant in Detroit.

Not many Mexicans worked in Detroit's auto industry. Manuel's father decided he would try to be as American as possible, so they mainly spoke English at home. For Manuel, Spanish was a second language. When he finished college with a degree in business, he didn't know what he wanted to do—he felt aimless and rootless. That's when he answered an ad seeking a Mexican national who spoke "good" English. An American resort in Mexico, seeking an American who looked Mexican, and a Mexican-American in search of his roots—what a topsy-turvy but copacetic combination!

Excitedly, I told Manuel of my wonderful experience in the out-of-the-way tourist attraction, *El Splendoro* cave that day. Manuel had recommended this to me during an earlier visit to the bar. But he had cautioned me, "Don't go past the barrier fence you will see in one part of the cave. Beyond it, the cave drops steeply to ocean level. Because the cave is at the head of an inlet positioned at a critical angle to ocean and wind currents, the tide rises much higher here, similar to the Firth of Forth or the Bay of Fundy."

I went on and on, describing the beautiful stalactites and stalagmites and the glitter of the crystalline coating deposited on the cave's ceiling. Although it was a small cave, its beautiful features and remarkable proportions gave it an aura of grandeur, rivaling better known caverns in the States. When I told Manuel I had pulled back the barrier fence and stepped in to take a peek, he pounded the bar with his uncalloused fist and reprimanded me. "You idiot," he shouted, "you could get yourself drowned in there!"

Actually, I had gone even farther into the forbidden zone, but I didn't tell Manuel. It was delightfully pretty in there; little tidal pools glittered from the light on the miner's cap I had rented at the cave entrance. The rocks were coated with multi-colored algae and lichens. Small crustaceans rested in the tidal pools, awaiting the next high tide to replenish their oxygen and nutrients. The passageway dropped steeply toward the sea. I went down about half way, until I remembered Manuel's caution and hastily retreated. I was nervous about a rapidly rising tide. Besides, I didn't even know when high tide was due.

"I sure would like to see more of what's beyond the barrier fence," I said to Manuel, after I told him of how wonderful that region of the cave seemed to be. "Can you tell me more about what it's like down there?"

"No, I can't," he replied. "I would never go past that fence." Manuel pointed to a man sitting at a table in the corner. "Talk to Peg if you want to know more about the forbidden zone. He's one of the few who have gone all the way to the bottom."

"Yeah, what's with that guy?" I asked Manuel. "Every night I've been here I've seen him sitting at that same table."

Manuel hunched up a little closer to me and spoke much more softly. "He's a Vietnam war vet who's been here since way before my time. He told me he came to Baja to get away from the American public's reaction to the war. No one here knows how he makes a living; I guess it doesn't take much of a pension to live in this village. He seems like a loner, but he's really a pretty good guy—in a blunt and direct way."

"Will he talk to me, a total stranger?" I asked.

"Of course," Manuel responded, "just bring him a Shiner Bock beer and he's guaranteed to talk with you."

So I approached Peg's table with a couple of bottles of Shiner Bock and a whole lot of apprehension. Peg was a big well-built guy who looked disgustingly fit. His nose was juxtaposed on his square face at an odd angle, as if he had seen a bar room brawl or two. His cauliflowered ears were framed by a graying but still robust crew cut.

"Howdy, Peg," I said as I extended the beer. "Manuel sent me over. My name is Bob and I'm looking for information on the forbidden zone in *El Splendoro*."

Peg crushed my effort at a firm handshake and indicated I should sit down.

I still don't know why I said this—one less beer at the bar and I'm sure I wouldn't have. I blurted out, "How did a guy that looks like a paratrooper get a girl's name like Peg?"

Peg just laughed and started talking. "Actually, I was a Green Beret. My real name is Roosevelt Hardin; they used to call me Rosey. Either way, Peg or Rosey, it's still a girl's name!" He dug a thick finger into one of his huge ears and continued, "Served two tours in 'Nam with nary a scratch—now look." He shoved his chair out from the table, pulled up his left trouser leg a little, and pointed to the prosthetic device that served as his foot. "That's why they call me Peg!"

"Oh, I'm so sorry," I lamented. "How did that ever happen?"

"*El Splendoro* and stupid curiosity, that's how it happened." Peg pulled long and earnestly at the Shiner, and then started his story.

"Many years ago, I explored *El Splendoro* and thought it was really beautiful. I was about ready to leave when my eye caught the sign on the barrier to the forbidden zone. It wasn't too long after I returned from Vietnam and a sign like that was more of a challenge than a warning. Besides, I could see some of the neat stuff just inside the barrier. So I pulled the fence open a little and went in. Never in my life have I seen anything so wonderful. The bright little tidal pools, the many shades and hues on the rocks, the creatures of the tide. It was at the same time fascinating and compelling, urging me to descend further toward the sea."

I motioned for Manuel to bring two more Bocks as Peg continued with the story: "I must have gone down 10 or 12 feet in elevation. I was picking my way downward over the rocks, at the same time drinking in the amazing sights. Never have I seen so many spectacular things bunched together like this. The dim light of the miner's lamp added an element of mystery to my fascination. By then, the sea was just a little below me, and I could see the waves rolling in and hear the 'brrump-brrump' as they slapped the rocks."

Peg upended the beer bottle and drank lustily from it. He wiped his sleeve across his mouth and looked me straight in the eye. "I was looking at this little crab in a tidal pool, and noting how his shell had iridescent colors like the surrounding rocks. At this point, all the rocks were covered with thick coats of algae. I should have paid more attention, but I kept stepping downward. Whoosh! My left foot slipped on the algae as if I were treading an ice-covered step in New Jersey."

By now, we both needed another Shiner, and Manuel brought some more. After a big drink, Peg kept talking. "My left foot hurt like the dickens, and I figured I had a bad ankle sprain. But I couldn't pull my foot up to examine it because it was wedged firmly between two big and immovable rocks. I could wiggle my toes, but that was about it. I pulled, I strained, I wriggled, I moved every which way, trying to dislodge my trapped foot. *Surely, I can pull my foot from my boot*, I thought. No luck. I guess the trauma of the fall caused my foot to swell up and trap me even more firmly. By then, the waves were getting closer to my feet—the tide was coming in! That tide was going to come in fast and it was going to rise way above my head."

Manuel was hanging around the table, listening to Peg tell his story. He had heard the story many times, but it was a fascinating story and nobody could tell it better than Peg. This time, Manuel had brought three beers. All of us purged the dryness in our throats and Peg continued.

"By now, I was more than a little desperate, if not panicked. For the first time, I could appreciate the desperation a trapped animal feels. I reached for my trusty hunting knife and cut away the top of the boot, which should've freed up my foot. Not a chance. I tried cutting farther down the boot, but couldn't reach the bottom part because of the rocks. I was hopelessly trapped. The tide was going to be above my head in 15 or 20 minutes; I would soon have flooded lungs to go along with my sprained ankle."

We all paused to relax our breathing a little and to make sure our beer bottles weren't too full. I was aghast when Peg finished the story.

"I was a little panicky, but I could still think clearly enough to realize I only had two hard choices—drown like a rat or hobble like a crip. The water already covered my left foot. I quickly decided I didn't like rats and turned my hunting knife on my balky ankle. It hurt like hell, but I sawed and severed until my leg pulled free. I won't sicken you with the gory details, but I scrambled up the rocks a few feet to gather my composure and stop the bleeding. My Vietnam experience really helped as I had treated many comrades with more grievous wounds than my missing foot. In spite of my trauma, I still had enough spunk for a ghoulish laugh. I hoped the crabs enjoyed what I left them!"

Manuel fetched some bar napkins so we could mop our brows. By now, we needed something stronger than Shiner Bock. I asked Manuel for some cognac, and he produced a bottle of really good 20-year-old stuff, with three glasses. No one had come into the bar during this time, so Manuel could join us without feeling guilty. We traded war stories of all types until the cognac bottle was drained and it was time to close the bar.

I awoke with a tremendous hangover the next day—my last day of vacation. I washed down my last aspirin tablets with lots of strong black coffee. In spite of my throbbing head, I set out on an urgent mission—I had to visit *El Splendoro* again.

I went straight to the barrier in front of the forbidden zone and looked in with my feeble lantern light, trying to see what lay beyond, down that glorious passageway to the sea. If a trooper like Peg could get carried away with such beauty, what would it do for a sensitive fellow like me? The fascinating sights Peg described tugged at me, trying to pull me into the forbidden zone. The sign on the barrier almost blinked at me in Neon, saying "Come on in!" I pulled back the fence, took a step in, then patted the little penknife in my pocket. I had sharpened it in preparation for the visit, just in case. But I wasn't the least bit sure I could do what Peg did.

I peered down the sloping passageway. "Come on. Come on," the voices I heard seemed to be saying. I patted the penknife again and looked down at my two sound feet. *Decisions, decisions.* I had gone on vacation to get away from decisions. But I made my choice. I pulled the forbidden zone's fence closed, drove back to the hotel, and started to pack my bags.

# Center of Attention

*A self-conscious fellow strolls through a crowd and finds
all eyes are upon him.*

On most days, nobody pays much attention to me except for Doris, my very special wife, who makes sure I get the attention I need but not enough to spoil me. A long time ago, my devoted cat, Cindy, made me the center of her universe. She didn't say much, but she always hung around and tried to participate in my activities. That was about the closest I've come to stage center for any person or critter.

Certainly, when I go to the big city I can count on remaining thoroughly anonymous and unnoticed. And I like it that way. I can go about my business without trying to live up to other people's expectations.

Imagine my surprise yesterday, when practically everyone I passed on San Antonio's River Walk smiled at me, and some even talked to me!

A small boy stopped, pointed at me and shouted, "Look, Mama!"

Embarrassed, she shushed the boy, but then looked at me very carefully and showed an approving grin.

Almost every pedestrian I encountered paid some attention to me, in his own way. A couple closely engaged in conversation paused to give me a long look and two very warm smiles. I could feel the approaching eyeballs track me as I walked. Some pedestrians showed their attention only with their eyes, and averted their glances when they sensed I had noticed their interest.

But most passersby openly stared and turned their heads toward me as they walked by. Some waved at me and grinned. Others spoke to me.

Normally, this amount of attention would have set me to worrying about what was wrong with me. *Did a low flying pigeon soil my cap? Was my fly unzipped?* But I marched ahead with supreme confidence, for I knew I had something very special going for me this day. I smiled back at the people and acknowledged their interest.

Diners at the sidewalk cafés stopped chewing, their forks immobilized, as their heads turned to flash me appreciative glances. I was the focal point of a wave of heads turning as I progressed up restaurant row. My onboard radar picked up those eyeballs as they followed me.

As I crossed a foot bridge over the river, a park ranger paused to chat with me amiably. "I see you've been to Monte Wade's," he said. Not only do they pay attention to me, but they know where I've been!

This was confirmed when I stopped at a river-side café for coffee. A police woman approached me and I started feeling defensive until she said, "You must've visited Monte Wade's. They have some nice stuff and you picked a good one."

Refreshed, I hoisted my treasure and resumed my long walk to the parking lot. It was really an armful and just a little bit heavy. I carried it as if it were a big doll or maybe even a small child. I knew it was prominently positioned for all to see. The public display of what I had chosen and bought no longer troubled me. I just basked in all the admiration. A glow of euphoria warmed my spirits and boosted my feelings of self-worth, fed by this unexpected public adulation. *Maybe I should consider entering politics!* I thought.

Shortly before the parking lot, I came upon an elderly Japanese couple who abandoned their traditional Asian reserve to stop, stare, and even smile. Amazed, I returned their smile and greeted them with a good ol' Texas "Howdy!" This sudden affront shocked them back into their normal, restrained demeanor.

Now I'm home and I pause to admire my fine steel-feathered friend, perched in a sea of gerbera daisies and phlox. He's a graceful heron almost two feet tall, his head skewed backward as if looking for danger. He's neither blue nor white. Instead, he's molting to the orange rust of a very special steel.

*You surely look good wading among our flowers,* I think in admiration, *but I might just pick you up and march downtown with you the next time I want to get high on public attention!*

# A Seedy and Nutty Story

*If at first you don't succeed, get that reward any way you can!*

We lived many years in New Jersey and amused ourselves watching the antics of squirrels. Winter in northern New Jersey is very cold and the ground is usually frozen, and often covered with snow. Our feathered friends appreciated the stuff we put out for them, as did their furry and hoofed colleagues.

After a snowfall, I would shovel about a ten-foot diameter area around the bird feeder and sprinkle seed liberally on the cleared ground. Often, this area was festooned with feasting doves. And, yes, a squirrel was often perched atop the feeder after getting past the baffle. But he helped replenish the area below as he scratched stuff from the feeder.

I gave up on the baffle after deer kept knocking it off. They came at night, nuzzling at the feeder to spill out its seeds.

I am convinced squirrels are puzzle freaks. They seem to relish in overcoming whatever hurdles creative humans put in their path to the bird feeder.

In search of a new approach, I bought a couple of plastic feeders mounted on five-foot aluminum rods a quarter-inch in diameter. These were touted to resist the most nimble squirrel. After I pushed the rods into the ground, the feeders were almost four feet off the ground. *That oughta be a tough climb*, I thought.

It didn't take long for the squirrels to modify their climbing technique and adapt to the hard, thin rod.

Frustrated, Doris and I brainstormed the situation. Finally, we had a eureka moment: *Let's grease the rod.*

"Okay, I bet *this* will stump them," I said to Doris after soaking a rag with 10W30 oil and smearing the rods.

And it did. From our living room observation deck we howled with laughter as the squirrels tried to grasp those slippery rods. They got about halfway up the rod before gravity canceled out the oil-weakened force of friction. Time after time, those squirrels tried and slid ignominiously to the ground. They retreated a few feet away and watched in frustration as the birds fed without interruption. If there could be a look of puzzlement on squirrels' faces, these guys had it! Obviously, the direct approach wouldn't work.

We could almost see the "tick-tick-tick" process going on in the squirrels' small brains, as they figuratively scratched their heads. Then, one bright fellow turned and walked away from the feeder. We thought he was giving up. Wrong. He had the solution!

He turned and ran full tilt toward the feeder, took a flying leap at the rod, but didn't try to grab it. Instead, he simply kicked at the rod with his hind legs to deflect his forward momentum upward; his trajectory came within grasp of the feeder. He munched away with immense satisfaction. Soon, his buddies began emulating his newly evolved technique.

My new feeders weren't squirrel-proof, with or without oil. But at least the added feeders distributed the squirrels and enhanced the feeding success of the birds.

Most birds tolerate squirrels and just patiently wait their turn. But crows can outfox the fluffy-tailed critters. I often put out last-year's pecans from our Hallettsville trees, figuring the pecans might distract the squirrels from the bird feeders. Pecans are unknown in this northern clime, and the squirrels loved them. The crows also showed a high interest, but the squirrels chased them away.

A squirrel would run off with a nut, rotate it and nibble at it as if depositing a scent, and bury it in the yard. The crow keenly watched from his safe perch in the tree and waited for the squirrel to head back to the pecan pile. Seizing the opportunity, he swooped down to uncover the nut and steal it. Shells flew from the tree as the crow cracked the pecan with his powerful beak and devoured the sweet nut. He cawed, as if having the last laugh.

Anyone who feeds birds has to deal with the problem of storing birdseed. Squirrels gnawed away the corner of our New Jersey garage door, shredded the plastic storage container, and made a mess of our seed inventory.

Doris often says about squirrels, "I don't understand how such an obviously smart animal is content to live in a tree nest. Why doesn't he build a house?"

# Staff of Life

*What fuels the boy's growth might lead to the man's decline.*

Good bread, especially homemade or bakery bread, has always been one of my favorite foods. We often just take bread for granted, as something that's on the shelf, in the cupboard, or waiting to be thawed out from the freezer. It's a commodity we get from the supermarket.

Mom never baked bread at home, so I grew up on store-bought sliced bread. When we visited Aunt Lelia's farm, my mouth watered at the enticing aroma of fresh-baked bread. Often, the bread was still warm and soft; so soft, in fact, it was difficult to slice with a bread knife. I smeared it with fresh-churned butter and Aunt Lelia's homemade jam. I crammed it in, slice after slice, until Mom in her embarrassment made me stop.

Ordinary, sliced bread fueled my teenage growth spurt, during which I ate prodigious quantities of toast for breakfast. My consumption peaked at thirteen slices, as limited by the broiler capacity of our oven. Toast tastes best when the bread is buttered first and then grilled in the broiler, and I still do it this way. No toaster for me! In fact, my sister-in-law vowed to get me a toaster for Christmas and I begged her not to.

When we moved to a small company town in Normandy, France, I didn't realize, until we settled into a routine life in this charming French town, that our appreciation for bread was about to change!

Each town—even the smallest village—had at least one *boulangerie* (bakery). We tried most of their wonderful breads, but our favorite was the ordinary *baguette*, the long, slim light-brown bread with the chewy crust. One calls this

"French bread" in America.

We bought *croissants* for special occasions. I had never tasted *croissants* so rich in butter and with such thin, flaky layers!

We loved another specialty item, *brioche*, which was a light, yellowish sweetened bread with a very thin crust. This bread was absolutely scrumptious. We lathered bakery-warm slices with butter and red-currant jam. *Brioche* was available only on Sunday mornings, and you had to get to the bakery early to find it. We placed a standing order for a loaf, and we dispatched our eight-year old son to fetch it while we prepared the coffee. Years later, on return visits to the village, we tipped the local hotel manager to procure a *brioche*.

The oil refinery where I worked was close enough to town that I could come home for lunch. Our two sons attended French schools near our apartment and they also came home for lunch, which was usually based on a fresh baguette. We combined the bread with butter, honey, peanut butter, and a delicious assortment of flavorful pates from a local *charcuterie* (deli).

Around eleven o'clock each morning, a red-cheeked Norman worker, dressed in traditional blue, would deliver a baguette to our apartment door and prop it up on the hallway floor—unwrapped. Yes, the delivery people carried several unwrapped baguettes under their arms!

One time, our older son, Fred, said, "Dad, it looks like a mouse tail is sticking out of the bread!"

"Nah, that's probably just a piece of burned crust."

Sure enough, Fred was right. I broke open the baguette and saw a whole, well-baked mouse! Before living in France, I might well have gagged at this. Instead, I calmly cut away the portion containing the unfortunate critter and tossed it in the garbage. We ate the rest of the bread. Previously, we had eaten snails, all sorts of raw sea creatures, rabbits, and hallucinogenic mushrooms—a mere trace of a mouse couldn't be that bad!

We also learned a few things concerning bread manners in France: (1) there are no bread plates; just place your bread slice on the tablecloth; (2) you can break off a bite-sized chunk of bread with your fingers to reduce dental challenges; (3) it's perfectly okay to sop any leftover sauce from your plate.

I loved to sink my teeth into the crust of a French baguette. The crust is really flavorful, but it's tough and chewy, and poses a dental hazard. Once, I felt a molar with a big, ancient filling give way. The top half of the tooth was gone! What was I to do, so far from my regular dentist?

Alas, there was nothing else to do but see Mlle. Pulzet, the only dentist in town. She spoke almost no English, so this was going to be major dental work in French. After a few attempts at explanation, I understood this was to be a root canal followed by a crown. I can still hear her terse commands in French—*ouvrez* (open), *fermez* (close), *mordez* (bite)! Years later, on a business trip to Baton Rouge, a similar scene ensued for the same reason, which demanded a new dentist, but at least he spoke English.

Upon our return from the French assignment, we moved to New Jersey and resumed our usual life with store-bought sliced, whole wheat bread. We tried a few specialty breads, but these were disappointing, given our experience with French bread. For me, bread is a necessary part of eating, and I soon learned to enjoy the available store-bought bread. But I cut back to a more reasonable adult serving of three slices of toast for breakfast.

After retiring, we moved back to Hallettsville, where we discovered there were still bakeries. We treated ourselves to lunches with still-warm, just-sliced bread. We loved the European-style taste of Czech bread. But we found we couldn't use this bread on a daily basis, because it was too tempting to overindulge.

For most of my life, I've enjoyed huge amounts of bread, but this consumption ultimately came back to bite me in the gut. After a long siege of weight loss and illness of the GI tract, I discovered I had celiac disease. The immune system of some people generates antibodies against gluten, the protein in wheat, barley, and rye. This antibody also attacks and damages the small intestine. Alas, no more wheat bread for me!

It hasn't been easy, but after many disasters involving ingredients and methods, I can now bake a decent loaf of gluten-free bread. I mainly use commercial

GF bread mixes. I even found a recipe for gluten-free brioche on the Internet. This resembled brioche, but it wasn't worth the effort.

Fresh, home-baked gluten-free bread is delicious, but once frozen and thawed, it tends to break and crumble. Gluten helps goods baked from wheat flour hold together. I am a naturally sloppy eater, and the tendency of gluten-free bread to make crumbs just opens me up to more kidding from my wife.

In defense of gluten-free bread, however, I can say it makes great toast. That said, I am still unfulfilled. My heart, soul, and stomach still yearn for the now-proscribed wheat bread!

# The Crumbs of Life

*As one ages, he becomes more mindful of his mortality, and continually seeks assurance that things are going okay.*

"Look at all those crumbs surrounding your plate," Doris teasingly pointed out. "There are even crumbs on the floor! How can you manage to miss your plate so much? Should you eat from a serving platter?

"Do you see any crumbs around my plate?" she continued, "And the floor around my chair is clean. You've been making a mess at the table for years; haven't you had enough practice to get it right?"

I always fall back on our standing joke, "I know I can't be perfect, as you obviously are!"

Is it a crime to be a messy eater? In the fork's trajectory between plate and mouth, something often falls off, bounces from my shirt, rolls across my legs, and plops onto the floor. When I eat toast with jelly, the crumbs from my gluten-free bread fall all over the place. Occasionally, the toast snaps when grasped between my thumb and fingers, and a piece of toast falls onto my lap or the floor—jelly side down, of course.

When we choose to eat lunch on the porch, ants happily gather around my feet to feast on the crumbs I inadvertently send their way.

We often take salad, dessert, and coffee in the den, where we can enjoy the last part of our meal while watching the evening news. A rocking chair might not be the ideal seat for eating, but it does allow me to disperse cookie crumbs over a wider area—the table, my lap, the rocking chair, and a larger expanse of floor.

Doris' kidding has sensitized me enough that I occasionally sweep up the crumbs, without prodding from the fastidious eater.

I end such good-hearted ribbing by pointing out, "These crumbs don't materialize by themselves out of the ether; they appear because I keep chomping away—alive and hungry. When the crumbs no longer fall around my place at the table, it won't mean that I've finally learned to eat neatly!"

# Acknowledgments

For their many helpful comments on the drafts of these stories, I would like to thank my wife, Doris, and the members of three local writing groups: Hallettsville Writing Group 1 (circa 2000), headed by Darryl Phelps; Sweet Home Writing Group (circa 2015), captained by Tamara Hartl; and Hallettsville Writing Group 2 (circa 2016), chaired by Beverly Charles.

# About the Author

Bob Zumwalt was born in Hallettsville, Texas and grew up in that small South Central Texas town. He earned degrees in chemical engineering from Texas A&M (B.S.) and the University of Delaware (Ph.D.).

The author in his garage office hideaway.

Bob worked two years as a process design engineer for a large chemical company, served two years as a lieutenant in the US Army, and spent the remainder of his professional career as a specialist and consultant in mathematical modeling and process control for a large international oil company. His career — rich with interesting experiences, travel, and people — inspired many of his stories.

In his spare time Bob enjoys listening to music, reading, writing, tennis, running and walking, and caring for rescued kitty cats. He and his wife Doris live in the old family home in Hallettsville — built by his grandfather in 1893. The couple have two grown-up sons.